HUBBY

A HERE IN LILLYVALE NOVEL

JENNY BUNTING

For my editor, Sarah. What a journey this has been. You've made me a better writer.

I hope I did our short king proud.

ALSO BY JENNY BUNTING

Here in Lillyvale

Here (Zoey and Jonathan)

Hustle (Taylor and Malcolm)

Home (Addison and Kirk)

Hubby (n.) a humorous or affectionate way of referring to a person's husband

— *FROM THE OXFORD LANGUAGES*

DEAR READER

It's me. Your favorite.

It was always meant to be like this, wasn't it? Me, talking to you. Looking back on all my accomplishments.

I got all my friends laid so hard.

There was Jonathan and my darling handful of an ex, Zoey. I made that shit happen.

There was that annoyingly perfect specimen of a man, Malcolm, who wrangled one of the dearest people to me, Taylor Drew. I orchestrated romance for those two, and now they're as happy as a goldendoodle who found a dog park mud puddle.

And let us not forget, Addison, a woman I consider a sister, and her love, Kirk. They are the most responsible, level-headed people I've ever met, so you know that was tough for me to get them to even *touch* each other.

All three were challenges in their own ways, but I did it. Now, they're all happily inserting appendages into orifices and screaming my name during climax.

Well, probably not, but I like to think they are.

However, this isn't about them.

This is about me.

Me and the woman I'm madly in love with. The woman I would take a bullet for, the woman I would jump in front of a bus to save.

This woman who is so beautiful, so razor-sharp clever, that her love for me gives hope to short guys like me across America and beyond.

You have to act like a king to get a true American queen.

This is the story of how I found her and made her mine.

It's also time to come clean, since you've been here since the beginning. Or, if you're popping in for the first time, hello. Funny you're starting here, but I don't judge. I'm honored, actually.

So sit back, grab a delicious Coors Light, and marvel in my strong pick-up game. No one but she and I know the full story.

We have a secret we'll only share with you—we got married, and no one knows about it.

You want to know how the fuck that happened?

Keep reading, all will be explained.

XOXO,

Dan

1

CAROLINE AND BRADY'S ENGAGEMENT PARTY

"Oh my fuck, that is a lot of pink," Makenna muttered to herself as she entered the party space. The room was mostly full, faces a sliding scale of familiarity among the red and pink décor. Every surface held a picture of her brother, Brady, and his fiancée, Caroline, in a frame, looking staged but happy.

Makenna hated this kind of shit.

She was happy that her sensible brother found a woman to marry. It was good that at least one Brady sibling would go the traditional route, continue the bloodline. Relieve some of the pressure on Makenna.

She felt eyes on her as she stood unattended. It was hard to miss her in suburbia, what with the five-inch heels, copious tattoos, and streaks of unnatural color in her hair. Per her mother's request, her tattooed arm was covered by her favorite suit, a dark, tailored jacket over slim pants, which she'd paired with her shiny Louboutins. While other women wore boring sheath dresses, discussed marriage and weddings, and spoke in high giggly pitches, she stood out in her pantsuit and talked to no one.

She also maybe stood out because she wore no blouse underneath the jacket. Her mother said nothing about covering her surgically altered cleavage, and the hint of purple flowers tattooed under her breasts peeked out from her lapels.

Whoops.

I need a drink.

"You looked dry," said a voice next to her.

She crinkled her brow as she looked at the man handing her a champagne flute. He was short, about five-four and change, and she towered over him in her heels. He probably had an unhealthy level of bravado and lack of self-awareness.

This happened to her all the time.

"As opposed to wet?" She took the champagne flute since she was desperate but longed for whiskey.

Only whiskey could truly get her through this night of performative happiness.

"Wow, sexual innuendos already. Let me limber up," the man said, stretching his arm across his chest. He wore a Hawaiian shirt, tucked into khakis over a soft middle and brown shoes. His hair stuck out every which way and his skin was pale, almost translucent.

He wants to play. Okay.

She loved to toy with overly confident men. It was so satisfying when she brought them to their knees.

"Who are you?" Makenna asked.

He stuck out his hand. "Dan Price. Friend of both the bride and groom. You're Brady's sister, right?"

She shook his hand. "In the flesh. Makenna." She took a sip of champagne and winced.

"Not a champagne person? Me either. Pick your poison."

"Whiskey. Neat."

"On it. Don't move," he said, scurrying off to the bar. Makenna held the champagne as she floated away from her spot. Whatever she was told to do, she did the opposite.

She acknowledged vaguely familiar faces until she caught a glimpse of big hair attached to an enthusiastic voice.

"Zoey," Makenna called out. The woman turned. Her face burst into a smile, and she charged Makenna, wrapping her in a crushing hug.

"I didn't think you would make it!" Zoey exclaimed.

"Mom forced me. Bought my ticket," Makenna said. "Here to celebrate my brother's engagement to your best friend."

"I'm glad you could make it even though I know you hate these things. You look so fierce," Zoey said. "Your boobs look amazing in that."

"Thank you. You look great too." Makenna had always envied the volume of Zoey's hair, and her effortless style. She wore a jumpsuit in black that cut down her chest, showing a hint of cleavage.

"I saw you talking to my ex-boyfriend," Zoey said. "Well, we were never official-official, but he still counts."

"That guy?" Makenna asked, pointing to the short man who chatted with the bartender, gesticulating wildly with his hands. "You dated him? He looks like the kind of guy who would get kidnapped while on vacation."

Zoey shielded her mouth and lowered her voice. "Best sex *I've ever had*."

"Really?" Makenna asked. From looking at him, she assumed he was a power tool in bed. She usually trusted her instincts, and she would've completely dismissed him.

"I don't mind if you're interested," Zoey said.

"I appreciate that." Makenna's lips parted. "Why did you break up?"

"He told me he loved me. But I wasn't feeling it, so I broke up with him."

"Atta girl," Makenna said.

"We had so much fun. I just didn't feel that thing."

Makenna knew why that was. Zoey had never quite gotten over her first love, and everyone knew it.

Speaking of. "So I hear Jonathan is the best man."

"Shut up, shut up, shut up," Zoey said. Zoey was Caroline's maid of honor, and Makenna's brother picked Jonathan, Zoey's ex-boyfriend from high school, to stand beside him. It had *not* ended well between Jonathan and her, so much that Zoey hadn't spoken to him in over ten years.

"Where is he?" Makenna asked.

"He's not coming to the party, like the asshole he is," Zoey said. "*Asshole.*"

"What are you going to do at the wedding?" Makenna asked.

"Avoid him at all costs. My mother still can't stand him. When she goes through her strong man-hating phases, his name *always* comes up."

"How did our mothers become such great friends?"

Zoey shrugged. "Angela is quite the outgoing one."

"No kidding," Makenna said, looking around. "I don't recognize most of these people."

Her mother was somewhere, performing for her friends. *At least one of my children isn't a disappointment*, her mother would say, sipping red wine while her friends congratulated her.

"I'm back. Sorry, I was catching up with the bartender," Dan said, handing Makenna her whiskey.

Dan hugged Zoey, and there was obviously still some friendly affection. Makenna had no idea how she did it. Zoey had dated Makenna's brother Brady a little bit before he started dating Caroline, so two of her exes would be in the wedding with her. One of Zoey's most admirable qualities was forgiveness. If someone crossed Makenna, she cut them out forever.

Well, except for her on-again, off-again, currently on boyfriend, Spencer. Like the eczema on her hand, he always came back when things were dry.

"I understand you've already met Makenna," Zoey said.

"Oh, definitely," he said with a wink.

Zoey's words had intrigued her. How could this guy in front of them be the best sex of her life? She knew Zoey, and it wasn't like Dan was her only lover. There was a decent sample size.

It took a lot to climb to the top of Makenna's dick tier.

"Makenna is a makeup artist in L.A.," Zoey said. "She worked on an Ariana Grande music video."

"Once, as an assistant," she clarified.

"I'll let you two talk," Zoey said, walking away with a look that communicated approval.

"I heard you're going to be the one to marry Brady and Caroline. That's pretty rad," he said. "I've always wanted to be an officiant, but I haven't had my shot. Once it comes though, *I am not throwing away my shot.*"

Makenna gave him a blank look.

"*Hamilton?*" Dan asked. "Really?"

"Haven't seen it."

"You have to. It's innovative. Spectacular," Dan said. He studied her for a moment. "Is this party uncomfortable for you?"

"What?" His question shocked her; she thought she was hiding it well.

"I just sensed that you might be uncomfortable, that's all."

"Actually, this is *very* uncomfortable for me."

"Why?" Dan leaned against the tall table, draped with a pink tablecloth.

Hot tingles covered her chest, and her lips parted. Might as well scare him away now. "I'm the screwup in my perfect family. Brady is the perfect older brother, marrying the perfect woman. and I'm...me."

"I think you're pretty awesome," Dan said.

"You don't know me."

"I want to, Makenna." Something about her name on his lips struck her.

"Just wait. You'll get to know me and you'll hate me," she said with a little laugh, trying to lighten the atmosphere.

"Or love you," he said. He patted her on the arm. "It was a pleasure to meet you."

Then he walked away.

She was shook. A short guy, a man she would never give a second glance to, had unnerved her. He *saw* her. A black cloud always followed her when she came home to Lillyvale, but she had never said it out loud to a stranger so soon after meeting them.

In L.A., reinvention was easy. She could blend in and out of crowds, meet new groups of friends every week. Make new enemies. Lillyvale had always stayed the same—judging her. Her defenses were strong as iron, so she *almost* didn't care, but sometimes a knife found a hole and it bled her.

A man like Dan didn't know women like her would destroy everything they touched.

Makenna knew she would destroy him.

~

"I SAW you talking to Brady's little sister," Kyle, Brady's other groomsman, said. Kyle and Dan were both on the shorter side, and Dan always talked to him for at least twenty minutes every time he saw him.

"She is *magnificent*," Dan said.

"She is so out of your league," Kyle said.

"Hasn't stopped me in the past."

"How do you do it?" Kyle asked. "I wouldn't even know *how* to approach a woman like that. She scares me."

"Confidence," Dan said. "But you don't have to figure it out. You have Evie."

"I do," Kyle said, looking at his wife, who was talking to Caroline. Kyle and Evie were so adorable together that Dan couldn't even. Both children of Chinese immigrants, they met on a blind date Dan set up three years prior.

Now Evie was pregnant, expecting their first child and Dan was so envious, he could scream.

Caroline was touching Evie's baby bump as they laughed and chatted. "I just hope the baby stays in there so I can do the wedding."

"When is she due?"

"July seventh."

"The wedding is the middle of June. You have plenty of time."

"You never know. Evie doesn't think it will be a problem, but the timing makes me nervous. I've already researched hospitals in Tahoe," Kyle said. "You could be my backup. You could probably fit in my suit."

Dan examined Kyle. They both had bodies that could be

described as out-of-shape jockeys. Dan took a sip of his Coors Light. He was going to be groomsman for the thirty-first time in May. Always the groomsman, never the groom.

Katherine Heigl's character from 27 Dresses had nothing on Dan Price.

"You dating anyone?" Kyle asked.

"Nope. I was seeing this woman for a little bit but didn't feel that glimmer. That sparkle."

"Your ex looks good," he said.

Dan looked across the room at Zoey. They'd dated a long time ago, but his heart always hurt a little bit when he saw her. He had fallen in deep love, the kind Taylor Swift only sang about after meeting Joe Alwyn. Then Zoey took his heart and threw it in the dumpster. It was over now, and he'd moved on. They were friends, but he was careful never to hang out with her alone or to let his mind go there.

"Maybe you'll meet someone at this wedding," Kyle said. "Caroline has so many hot, single friends, it's cra—"

"Hi honey," Evie, Kyle's pregnant wife, said, sliding under his arm. "Hi Dan."

Kyle turned the color of strawberries, but his wife didn't shoot daggers at him so Dan assumed she didn't hear Kyle call Caroline's friends hot. Evie barely cleared five feet with small hands and small feet. Dan had no idea how that woman would move once she got to the late stages of her pregnancy.

Dan kissed Evie's hand. "Evie, you look radiant."

She laughed, placing a palm on her husband's chest, looking up at him. "Thank you, Dan."

Dan wished he had a wife who looked at him like Evie looked at Kyle. His mid-thirties were fast approaching, and all his friends his age were married and had a couple kids by now. One of the reasons he started finding younger friends was so they could hang out and drink without worrying that their spouses might be plotting their murder.

He was successful, had a great house, great friends. But something was definitely missing.

Someone to share it with.

Makenna Brady still meandered through the crowd, holding the whiskey he had brought her. Her red-painted lips touched the rim of the glass, and he wished he was that glass.

No, we are done chasing women like that.

Then Makenna caught eyes with him from across the room and held his gaze for a second. He looked behind him, wondering if there was someone else. No one stood behind him.

Makenna lowered her heavily eyelashed eye in a wink, like she was at the end of a Victoria's Secret Fashion Show catwalk.

"I am in so much fucking trouble," Dan muttered to himself.

2

DAY BEFORE CAROLINE AND BRADY'S WEDDING

"Is that your brother?" Makenna's mother Angela asked, lifting her sunglasses.

Makenna smirked to herself. "Sure is."

"So funny that they're here having brunch just like us. I was hoping we could keep Jonathan from Rachel as long as possible. She is going to lose it. Don't say anything," her mom said.

Rachel, Zoey's mom, had driven up with them to carpool to Brady's wedding. She had spent most of the car ride asking Makenna about her tattoos in a malicious way. "I *never* understood why women as pretty as you would ruin their bodies like that," Rachel had said, her eyes darting to Makenna's fake boobs.

Makenna bit her tongue so hard, it bled.

Brady's best man and Zoey's ex Jonathan sat at the table with Dan, filling in for Kyle as a groomsman. His wife went into labor the day before so they subbed Dan in.

Her brother may have texted her asking for the name of this restaurant.

And Makenna may have conveniently omitted that they were going there too.

Brady deserved some drama to his perfect weekend. Jonathan *definitely* needed to know where he stood with everyone, with how he destroyed Zoey's heart.

"Is that your brother's funny friend, Dan?"

"Yep," Makenna answered with a huge grin. Something about Dan being there fluttered her heart a little bit. Especially since she was single as of last night.

"It's a shame that Kyle couldn't make it, but I'm so happy for them. They're going to make wonderful parents," Angela said. "Today is so pretty. I'm excited to try this restaurant. You say so many great things about it."

"I'm going to say hi."

Angela sighed. "Okay, do it now before Rachel notices they're over there."

Makenna stood up and turned to face the restaurant so she could arrange her boobs for maximum effectiveness. She pulled out her phone to check her makeup on her camera app.

She couldn't see the texture of her skin with the lighting. Perfect.

In L.A., Makenna wouldn't look twice at Dan. He had a scraggly uneven beard with longish ash blond hair and a soft belly. He wore a Hawaiian shirt to an engagement party, for god sake. His outfit today wasn't much better, but Makenna didn't care about that now.

Zoey's words had haunted her since the engagement party. *Best sex I've ever had.*

She had recently sought out porn with average-looking actors with a few extra pounds treating gorgeous women like they were all-you-can-eat buffets. The actors' enthusiasm and gratitude made her come hard and often, and her thoughts lately had veered toward Dan.

Rachel passed her, brushing her arm with her hand, and sat down to happily chat with Makenna's parents and their other friends who were already in Tahoe for the wedding.

It was a beautiful day, without a cloud in the sky, and the sun felt warm on her skin.

Makenna watched Jonathan slide down his chair. Clearly he had spotted Rachel and didn't want to deal with his ex's mom.

Time to face the music, *asshole.*

Dan held a mimosa in his hand.

Why am I so attracted to him? Her usual type drank aged whiskey, not champagne with juice.

Brady saw her too and said something to Jonathan and Dan as she sauntered over.

"Hello boys," Makenna said, resting her hands on the back of a chair. "Fancy meeting you here. I meant to text you that we were coming, but Mom told me to stop being on my phone."

"Hi Makenna," Brady said. "Did you, by chance, decide to come here since I texted you this morning about this place?"

"Mom wanted to come here, I swear," she said, pulling out the chair to sit down. Dan's mouth gaped as he looked at her. It was flattering. Her inner hoe was going to come out soon. "I didn't know you were going to bring Jonathan."

Makenna knew. She usually hated lying, but a tiny white lie was effective in these instances. It was her perfect brother, after all. He had it coming. It was always fun to fuck with him. Makenna only got attention from her brother if she was *really, really* annoying.

"He's my best man. You knew that, right?" Brady asked.

"Maybe?" she said, looking to the sky to hide her fib. "Yeah, I knew that. I think I forgot."

Makenna took Dan's champagne flute from his hand. She lifted his slowly, and Dan let out a tiny cry. She made sure to touch her lips to where his lips had touched. Between avenging Zoey through Jonathan, making Dan lose his mind, and toying with her brother, nothing could make today better. Makenna even threw in an insult about Jonathan's ex-wife for good measure. Jonathan had married a woman named Nikki right after he broke up with Zoey. She'd met her once, and Nikki did what most women did to Makenna.

Looked her up and down and said bitchy things.

"Are you still in L.A.?" Dan asked.

Makenna froze. L.A. was a sore spot at the current moment.

"Yeah, but I've been thinking about moving back. L.A. is so expensive. The traffic is terrible. My job would transfer me no problem," Makenna blurted out without thinking.

Where did that come from?

"Let me take you out. When you get back in town," Dan said eagerly.

"Dude, I'm right here," Brady said, opening his hands. His brow crinkled. Nothing made Makenna happier than seeing her brother distressed.

Seeing Jonathan squirm was pretty fun, too. Even though this awkwardness didn't make up for half of the heartbreak he'd caused Zoey all those years ago.

Maybe it would be good for Rachel to confront Jonathan now, before the wedding.

She was just doing a service, really.

"It's been a while since you've seen Zoey's mom, right,

Jonathan? Might as well get it out of the way. Let me call her over. Rachel, over here!"

Rachel, Zoey's mom, walked over, and it was just as awesome and amazing as she thought it would be. Makenna crossed her arms and sat back, watching. She wished she had popcorn.

Makenna watched Dan dazzle Rachel and diffuse the situation, and she squeezed her legs as she watched. Jonathan glared a death wish at her, and she cackled inwardly with glee. He never deserved Zoey Benton. Not even close.

"Aren't you eating with us, Makenna?" Dan asked.

Makenna paused. She ached to stay with them, instead of her parents and their friends. Dan walked away at the engagement party, and so could she.

"You wish. Duty calls."

She stood up, pulling down her frayed jean shorts, and walked back to her parents' table. A tiny smile crossed her lips since she knew if she looked back, Dan's eyes would be glued to her ass. She grabbed the plastic menu and opened its front flap.

"That was so awkward," Rachel said, rejoining the group. She arranged her bangs in exasperation and took a long sip of the ice water in front of her.

"I'm sorry my daughter caused a run-in," Makenna's mom said. Her stare could cut glass. "She has a tendency to do things like this."

"It's fine. Makenna meant no harm," Rachel said. "I have no idea why your son stayed friends with Jonathan. He was mean and terrible and..."

"Exactly," Makenna agreed, pulling out her phone to unlock it. Thinking about all the notifications she had to clear on Instagram could give her hives. Sponsors might be trying to get in contact with her...

"Please don't use your phone at the brunch table. It's rude," Makenna's mom said. Makenna turned her phone over and crossed her arms.

Fuck, this weekend was going to be torture.

"Have you prepared the ceremony?" her mom asked. Somehow, Brady and Caroline still wanted her to officiate their ceremony. Makenna wanted to do a good job so she had practiced with her best friend, Sierra.

"Many, many times," Makenna said. She tapped her temple with her finger. "It's all up here."

"I just don't want you to be unprepared."

"I'm sure you'll do great," Rachel said, covering Makenna's hand with hers.

"Our Makenna is also doing the hair and makeup," her mother said.

"Your daughter is very talented," Rachel said.

Makenna closed her eyes so she could pretend her mom had been the one saying those words about her.

"She is," Angela said. "At least with the makeup. She buys enough of it."

Makenna grumbled at her mother's comment. She always thought Makenna was on her phone. Growing her Instagram into a viable revenue stream took work and *lots* of time on her phone. She wasn't there yet, but she knew she had what it took.

She snuck one last glance at Dan. He sat back, sipping his mimosa and checking his phone.

"Don't even think about it," her mother said in her ear.

"What?"

"Him," Angela said. "Dan Price."

"What about him?"

"I know you broke up with Spencer yesterday, but it doesn't mean you go back to your old ways."

"Or stay on brand?" Makenna said. "I enjoy sex, mother."

Her mother closed her eyes, like she was making a silent prayer. "You are my daughter, and I love you. I'm just asking for no more drama this wedding weekend."

"Okay, got it," Makenna said. She looked at Dan again, and their gaze caught.

Without thinking, she winked at him. He blushed like the scrumptious dollface he was.

Rules were made to be broken.

3

LATER THAT DAY

Dan tilted his head, looking up to the trees at the vacation rental. He felt a sneeze coming on.

Nature was constantly trying to kill him. Patios were nice only if you didn't have allergies.

The seats were mildly uncomfortable, but Dan could put his feet up. Anytime he could drink a Coors Light and relax, he was happy. Even if it was out in itchy nature.

The vacation rental Caroline and Brady had booked for most of the bridal party was huge and spacious. It was also a thinly veiled ploy to get Jonathan and Zoey to finally talk.

"How do you feel, bro? About getting married?"

"Great," Brady said, rotating his beer on the patio table. "I'm just hoping nothing goes wrong tomorrow."

"Seriously," he said. "Zoey and Jonathan, huh?"

"Yeah, Caroline's plan seems to be working, though," Brady said. "When you dated her, did you ever feel like Jonathan was the elephant in the room?"

Dan took a drink. "Sometimes? She never wanted to talk about him, though. Now that I've seen them together, I get it."

Zoey and Jonathan together was bittersweet. On one hand, he wanted his friend to be happy. On the other hand, she'd never looked at him that way, and it still hurt a bit.

"Are you over her?" Brady asked.

Dan paused. "I hope so."

"So, when do you think you'll settle down? When are you going to get married?"

"Ah, I don't know. The business is doing really well, and that's the only girlfriend I can handle right now," Dan said. "I've dated here and there, but no one special. No one like your sister."

"Shut the fuck up."

"I was only joking," Dan said. *Well, kinda.* After their brief interaction at the engagement party and then at brunch, there was something there. Dan lived for drama, and Makenna bringing over Rachel to confront Jonathan made him that much more intrigued.

If a woman didn't scare him a little bit, he wasn't interested.

"My sister is not ready for anything serious," Brady said. "And she wouldn't go for you anyway."

"I feel a wager coming on."

"Don't even try with her. I mean it," Brady said, then changed the subject. "Derek was such a dick last night."

"Seriously," Dan said, taking another swig of beer. The other bridesmaid, Addison, was engaged to the biggest asshole. They had been over for a thank-you barbecue at the vacation rental. Dan had offered to drive Addison and Derek back to the hotel after she got drunk and puked on Zoey, who had to hose her down to clean her up. Derek's low-key jabs disguised as teasing toward Addison made Dan grip the steering wheel so hard, his knuckles went white. He eventually threatened to make Derek walk back to the hotel, and that shut him up.

"He keeps getting worse. I just pray for everyone's sake that he doesn't ruin our wedding tomorrow. Him, and Aunt Lisa. Jesus." Brady rubbed his head.

"You really don't think your sister would be into me?"

Brady rolled his eyes. "Usually, she's into these douchey, brooding types. You're too happy for her. It's probably for the best. She breaks things."

Dan shrugged one shoulder and took a pull from his Coors Light. "Maybe I want to be broken. Who knows, maybe there's candy inside."

"You're too much," Brady said. He stood up and rubbed his forehead again. "I need to take a nap."

"I'll go take a walk," Dan said, following Brady inside. He threw away his beer can and whistled as he closed the rental's door and locked it. He breathed in and out—the air smelled so fresh and clean.

Then he sneezed.

"Today is a great day," Dan said, although his eyes watered.

Dan walked in the direction of the lake, passing other vacationers and waving hello to them as they passed. The sun was shining, and his friend was getting married.

Maybe he and nature could come to a peaceful understanding.

Then he sneezed three times in a row, making such a loud noise that a family walking by stared at him.

His thoughts drifted to Makenna, and his dick hardened.

It was a shame that her brother said she was off-limits.

He had felt vibes with her at brunch. Sexy, strong vibes that confirmed everything he had felt at the engagement party. A huge danger sign hung over her head. Women like that were a challenge Dan liked taking on, even though the woman usually used his good dick and eventually moved on and fell in love with someone else.

He reached the lake and searched for a bench or a rock to sit on. This weekend was for Brady and Caroline's wedding, but he needed a damn vacation. His business had eaten up all of his time. Tiana, his lovely assistant, had promised a work-free weekend for him, and she delivered.

After this blissful weekend, he planned to give her a raise.

This time away had already been just what he needed. He went for a run, he read a book, he got to day-drink and relax.

The only thing missing was some good sex. Too bad he couldn't make Makenna scream.

Dan walked to a picnic area shaded by evergreen trees and caught a flash of dark hair streaked with pink.

He stopped in his tracks. *Oh shit.*

This *had* to be destiny.

He *happened* to be on a walk, and she *happened* to be there.

"Fancy meeting you here," Dan said, walking over to her. Makenna looked up from her phone, and her face lit up.

"Hey, how are you?" Makenna asked, standing up. Even with flats on, she looked down at him. She had been a little cold at brunch, but now she smiled and hugged him. Makenna gestured for the bench, and Dan obliged, facing her with his hands folded on the table.

"What are you doing here?"

"My mom became a phone Nazi," Makenna said, holding up her phone. "What are you doing here?"

"Your brother can't hang. He's weak," Dan told her. "He needed to take a nap."

"He had Fireball last night, didn't he?"

"You know him so well," Dan said. "I try to stay away from that garbage, so guess who slept like the angels kissed my eyelids?"

Makenna squinted one eye and cradled her chin on her hand. "You, of course."

Should I flirt or keep it cool? Oh, what the hell.

"The lake is gorgeous today. But not as a pretty as you."

Makenna laughed. "You're smooth."

"Like ten-dollar peanut butter," Dan said.

"Okay, okay." Makenna grinned. They watched a few college-age students playing beach volleyball. A strapping, tanned bro jumped to set the ball, completely missed it, and face-planted directly into the sand.

Makenna and Dan both burst into laughter.

"Oh, so you're a piece of trash, just like me," Makenna said.

"I hope he's okay and all. But it's just so funny." The guy's buddies helped him up, and he smiled, pushing them off.

"I love people-watching," Makenna said. "I could sit here for hours. Lake Tahoe is my favorite place in the world."

"I only started coming here when I moved, but it's great."

"Where are you from?"

"L.A.. North Hollywood, actually."

"No shit, really? I live in Silver Lake. Were you born there?"

Dan nodded. "Born and raised."

"Is your family still there?"

Dan shook his head. "They moved to Lillyvale eight years ago. I was the last one to leave."

"Why didn't you say anything at brunch earlier? Or at the engagement party? When I was talking about L.A?"

"I was mesmerized by your beauty," Dan said matter-offactly. "And telling people you *used* to live in L.A. doesn't make you cool."

"I hear that," Makenna said. She paused and looked at Dan. "This is so random, but can you take a picture of me in front of the lake? For Instagram?"

"I would love to," Dan said. She handed him her phone, and Makenna posed, as Dan snapped picture after picture of her. When she stopped and walked toward him, he furiously typed his number into her contacts. Makenna's smile looked hesitant.

"You have my phone number now," he said, handing it back to her.

Makenna flipped through the photos. "These are actually really good."

Dan moved closer to her. He smelled her perfume, pears and flowers. "You're so fucking gorgeous, it was easy."

Laughter hung on her lips. "Thank you. I think you're pretty cute yourself."

"I know, right?" Dan held his chin in his hand. "I could be a model."

"Definitely. With that beard? I think they call that lumbrosexual," Makenna said. "All you need is some flannel and a big axe."

"Oh, I have a big axe," Dan said, wiggling his eyebrows. "I feel so much better now that we've cleared the air. I'm attracted to you. You're attracted to me."

"I didn't admit that," Makenna said. "Even if I was, I don't think anything can happen."

"Brady warned me about you, told me not to try anything with you."

"What did my perfect brother say?"

Dan shrugged. "He thinks you would break me in half. I disagree."

"I *am* taller than you," she said.

"I might be short, but let's circle back to the fact I have a big axe." Dan gave her a wink. "I don't look like much, but I will ruin you for subsequent gentleman callers."

Makenna covered her face with her hand, giggles floating through her fingers.

She was laughing.

I got her.

"So, that's why we can't start anything. It would be all over for you the second we start," he said, leaning his elbows onto the picnic table.

"Oh, really?" she said.

"Definitely," he said. "You'd fall in love with me, marry me..."

"That's rather presumptuous of you. I didn't even admit I'm attracted to you," Makenna said. "Where did you get all this confidence?"

"My mom thinks I'm God's gift."

"So, you're a mama's boy."

"I do love my mama," he said. "I saw some interesting body language when you talked to your mama. Everything okay there?"

Makenna laughed again. "I need some whiskey before we talk about my mother."

"Fair enough," Dan said, looking around. "Do you want to create backstories for all these strangers?"

"Absolutely," Makenna replied, rubbing her hands together.

"Them," Dan said, pointing to a middle-aged couple. "Into bondage."

"Totally," Makenna agreed. "The husband loves nipple clamps."

"Wife, totally into handcuffs. She's watched *Gerald's Game* five times and gets off on it."

Makenna had to cover her mouth, she was laughing so hard. "You are so sick."

"Don't worry about it, but I have handcuffs in my luggage."

Makenna crinkled her brow. "Why?"

"I said don't worry about it," Dan said. "But I could use them on you."

"You're not worried about what Brady said about me?" Makenna asked, leaning her elbows on the table. "That I could destroy you?"

Dan leaned in, right next to her ear. "Not if I destroy you first."

"You are such a flirt."

"And I'm obsessed with you," Dan admitted.

"Is it these?" Makenna asked, touching her breasts seductively, making Dan's dick harder than it already was.

"They are wonderful. And I definitely want to stick my face in them. With permission, of course."

"I appreciate that," Makenna replied.

"However, there's something here," Dan said, leaning forward. He brought his hand toward Makenna and then to him. "Do you feel this? This connection?"

"Maybe," she said coyly.

He was *definitely* in trouble.

She could break his heart into a million pieces.

And he was handing her his sledgehammer.

∼

MAKENNA'S CHEEKS hurt from all the smiling and laughing.

It was the best idea to go on a walk to people-watch and answer her messages.

Dan's joy infected her. Their hug, his body pressed against hers, woke up her lust gremlin. She usually felt this way with emotionally unavailable men who cared more about their watch collection than their girlfriend.

Not a charismatic, unassuming man who looked at her like he wanted to take her clothes off with his teeth.

This guy has "wants a wife, two kids, and a dog" written all over him, and you might need to make sure that jet ski incident last week didn't give you a concussion.

"So, you're thinking about moving back to Lillyvale. Excellent. I can take you out on a date," Dan said.

"Like I said, this can't happen," Makenna said. "And I'm still not sure I want to move."

"Oh, right," Dan said. "We can't be together. I forgot since I'm having so much fun with you."

"I'm having a great time too," she said. "Do you dance?"

"Do I dance?" Dan asked, pressing his hand to his chest with a fake chortle. "Oh, I dance."

"Perfect," Makenna said. "If I can't take you for a spin around the bedroom, I'm going to take you for a spin around the dance floor."

"Dip me like a starlet from the forties," he said, pressing his lips together to kiss the air and winked at her.

"Gladly," she said.

"What does L.A. have for you? I mean, *I'm* not there anymore?"

Makenna paused. The city had held so much promise when she was younger, but reality had grayed and dimmed any optimism. It no longer glimmered with possibilities. She just saw smog, too many people, and struggle.

"I wanted to be a makeup artist for celebrities. Instead I

work at the Eloise Winston makeup counter four days a week."

"My mom likes their perfume," Dan said.

Makenna chuckled. Eloise Winston was a British makeup artist who'd developed a line that had begun with bold lipsticks and a cult-favorite mascara. EW tried constantly to stay relevant, one of the reasons they hired Makenna, with her tattoos and nose ring. But their main customers were women over the age of fifty, who avoided her and usually picked her male coworker who did a better smoky eye than her.

It was supposed to be a temporary job that turned into a five-year gig.

"I work at a mall in the Valley."

"How come you aren't working on a movie set? Zoey mentioned the music video."

Makenna looked down at her hands. "I had a connection, but it only happened once. Everything is so competitive down there."

"Do you really love it? Like, do you feel passion down in your soul?" Dan asked.

Makenna leaned back. No one had questioned it before. They saw the thick makeup she put on every day and assumed it was her life's calling. Her only interest and hobby.

Sometimes she looked at the products at the EW makeup counter, asked herself the big life questions, and was shaken out of thoughts by a customer or a coworker.

Do you really love it?

"I've always been into makeup, ever since high school," Makenna said. "I'm good at it."

Dan nodded. "You just acted like makeup was trigonometry."

"I can say with absolute certainty that I do not love trigonometry," Makenna said. Dan smiled and his hand brushed her arm, right over her bluebird tattoo. His touch left a sizzle, like bacon on a frying pan.

This was bad, very bad.

"I had really bad acne in high school so I started wearing makeup and fell in love. I've never wanted to do anything else. My parents wanted me to go to college for a little bit, but all I wanted was to get tattoos and play with eyeshadow."

"Well, you look great," Dan said. "I'm a fan."

"Thank you," Makenna replied. It felt nice to have her forty-five minutes of makeup application that morning acknowledged. "What do you do?"

"I like to start businesses," Dan answered. "I'm really into real estate right now. Development, investment. Stuff like that."

"How many businesses do you have?"

Dan leaned forward conspiratorially. "All I can say is I'm kind of a big deal in Lillyvale."

"Oh, really?" she said, not believing it at all.

"I have maybe three enemies. The rest of the town loves me," he said. "When you come home and say 'Dan Price,' at least four people will drop, like those adorable fainting goats."

"I *love* fainting goats," Makenna said.

"That's it. We're soulmates."

"Remember, Dan, we can't be together."

"Oooh, right. Let's make this *angsty*."

"I'll be real with you. The flirting has been *great*."

"I agree," Dan said. "So, tell me what's not working."

"I'm not looking for a relationship," Makenna said. "I feel like you're ready to buy a minivan."

"How dare you," Dan said. "However, I wouldn't be opposed to owning one, if my wife and I had a lot of children."

"See?" Makenna said. "It would never work. I have no interest in getting married or commitment or minivans." She shuddered. "But you're ready to propose to me. I can feel it."

Dan leaned back against the table. "Well, shit. What do we do? About this sexual tension?"

"Probably nothing. I'm kind of seeing someone," she admitted. "We had this huge fight so we're technically not together right now, but I might get back together with him if I'm bored."

"Oh," Dan said. "Well, that settles it."

"What?"

"I don't go after other men's women. It's my code."

Makenna squinted one eye. "It's probably for the best. He's six-five, maybe two-fifteen, and takes selfies of his muscles in the gym mirror."

"I don't fuck with guys like that. Sounds like he could launch me like a javelin."

"Probably. You're like a chihuahua. A cute chihuahua."

Dan pondered that comment. "If I agree with you, will you hold me like one? Just as friends?"

"You have to stop flirting with me."

"Only if you stop."

"I'm not doing anything. Flirt switch turned off." Makenna pretended to flick an imaginary light switch.

"Well, it ended before it could even begin. Shame."

Makenna laughed and looked to the sky. "You might be one of the cockiest men I have ever met, and I adore you."

"And you might be one of the sexiest, snarkiest women I have ever met, and I adore you too."

"Friends?" Makenna said, shooting her hand out.

"Friends," Dan said, connecting her hand with his. He tried for a fancy secret handshake, and his thumb overshot and skimmed her skin. The skin on her forearm prickled with his touch. What *was* this? How did it keep happening every time they touched? There was a split second she looked up and caught his gaze. She swallowed slowly, and Dan did too, mirroring her movements.

It was just one weekend. She could keep it in her pants, easily.

But as she sat with Dan and continued to make up stories about strangers on the beach, she wasn't so sure she could.

4

CAROLINE AND BRADY'S REHEARSAL DINNER

Dan stopped when he looked in the mirror at the golf club and rubbed his fingers against his facial hair.

His mustache looked fantastic. The scotch in his hand made him look debonair, and he strolled around like the only cock in a hen house.

His troll had gone perfectly at the rehearsal. He had grown a beard for four months, just to shave it into a seventies porn star mustache to freak Caroline out. Her reaction would be played over and over in his head when he was having a bad day.

He loved Caroline to pieces, but she was wound so goddamn tight. He did promise to shave it for pictures, but it was worth all the time it took.

He got an unexpected bonus when Makenna told him the mustache was "kind of hot" and touched his bicep. No one knew of their flirting at the beach, and he tried to act cool around her while he was slowly losing it inside.

This whole "let's be friends" thing was utter bullshit. He felt like he was the one being trolled.

At the rehearsal, Makenna was a knockout in a navy dress that hugged her curves like the dress was spray-painted onto her. Her heels elevated her to tower over him by a few inches, but he'd never cared about height difference.

It was always the women who cared.

In his downtime before the rehearsal, he had looked up Spencer, Makenna's off-again boyfriend. She was right, he was *massive*. He had also found out he'd played football at a Division II school as a quarterback. Dan was smart enough to know that his own unfounded cockiness couldn't rival former college athlete confidence. Spencer had a neck tattoo and wore stupid hats. Seriously, what the fuck was with all the backward newsboy hats? *Newsies* called, they wanted their look back.

His frustration about this douchebag followed him to the rehearsal dinner.

There were so many reasons why Makenna was off-limits. She was kind of unavailable, even though Spencer was not a worthy opponent. Their basic wants were not compatible; he wanted to find his queen, and Makenna never wanted to get married. She was Brady's little sister, and his friend had already asked him to not pursue her. So he wouldn't.

Unless she started it.

She was just like every woman he had fallen in love with. Slightly hard to catch, mildly aloof, and mysteriously unavailable. If history repeated itself, he would be eating ice cream and not showering for three days straight soon.

He bought Zoey a tequila since she was freaking out about Jonathan and gave her the best advice ever. She was Exhibit A for the case against Dan getting involved with women who would rip his heart out.

Sometimes, he felt like the funny best friend who sat on the sidelines, like in an eighties romcom. He wanted to be the hero, who got the girl.

Makenna appeared like a goddess in the hall of the golf club, an aggressive overhead light creating an artificial halo around her. The brightness of her phone screen bounced off her makeup, causing her to glow.

"Hey you," Dan said, setting the scotch down on a decorative table. Makenna looked up and grinned, flicking an eyebrow up at him.

"Hey yourself," she said. She threw her arm out, and he tucked in next to her for a hug. When she pressed him into her, he smelled the pears and flowers again, heard her breath catch. He avoided pressing his cheek against her breast since he was a gentleman.

"I love these heels," he said, closing his eyes. "I feel like a tycoon who married a woman just after his money."

She pushed him away with a playful shove. "You are way hotter and younger than some gross tycoon. I know. I live in L.A.."

"You warm my heart," he said. He nodded to her phone. "How's the Internet treating you? As vile as ever?"

"Only five DMs from creepy guys. Slow night." She tucked her phone into her clutch. "I see Zoey is having a freak-out."

"Abso-fucking-lutely. She's precious."

"Is she going to fuck Jonathan?"

"Probably. Knowing Zoey. Not slut-shaming at all or anything, though."

"I didn't think you were," she said, taking a sip of her drink. "Women should never be shamed for wanting and asking for sex."

Oh, please ask me. Dan deserved a gold star for not saying that out loud.

Looking back at her, he shoved his hands in his pockets. "How are the festivities for you so far?"

"Oh, you know. Everything's perfect. My perfect brother marrying the perfect woman. I'm obsessed that you grew a beard just to shave it into a mustache. Caroline's reaction was epic."

"It was pretty great, wasn't it?" Dan said. "Too bad you don't want hop on and take a mustache ride."

And the gold star was taken away.

Makenna laughed so hard, she snorted. Both of them spiraled into a fit of giggles at that.

"I didn't expect you to be a snorter."

"I only do it when I'm comfortable."

"Well, come and try me on like a pair of hundred-dollar sweatpants."

"We said no flirting, you know," she reminded him.

"Sorry," Dan said. "It comes naturally with you. I can't help it."

"Well, knock it off," she said with a smirk.

"Fine, I'll leave," he said. Her hand grabbed his forearm, and he flicked his eyebrow at her. "Or you don't want me to leave."

"You're fun to talk to," Makenna said. "Plus, I'm procrastinating about going back to the table. I'm so bored. Aren't rehearsal dinners the absolute worst?"

"One hundred percent agreed. I have a question," he said. "I love Brady, don't get me wrong, but it's rather bold of him to go by one name only. How does that work?"

"He never liked the name Ethan. A kid made fun of him once, and then he started going by Brady. Which is ironic as hell because of that TV show not to be named. So. Many. Jokes."

"Do you think someone will mention it tonight?"

"Abso-fucking-lutely," Makenna said. "*Brady Bunch*. It's an easy, unfunny slam dunk of a joke. It's a gift-wrapped joke to my dad, the king of dad jokes."

"They don't have an elevated sense of humor like us."

"Not at all," Makenna said. "I like you, Dan."

He stopped laughing and moved closer. "Do you now?"

"Um-hum," she said. "I don't like many people. But I like you."

Dan stepped even closer. *This is playing with a forest fire, Dan. Don't do it.*

He noticed her breasts rise and fall. He wanted to trace his tongue down the seam off her neckline, around the curve of her breasts, explore under her dress with his hand.

"I like you too," he said, his voice lowering an octave. He leaned in, and she lowered her ear. His lips were inches from her skin, so close, and he could smell her perfume dotted behind her ears.

"Do you talk dirty, Mr. Price?" Makenna asked. "Out of curiosity."

"I thought I wasn't supposed to flirt with you. But I can, with the best of them, if you want me to," he said. He leaned in further and noticed Makenna's body tense with his proximity. Her magenta streak of hair tickled his nose.

"Say something right now," Makenna said. "Let me be a proper judge. For science."

Well, she asked.

He leaned in further, noticing goosebumps forming on her chest, and lowered his voice. "If we weren't 'just friends,' I would make your pussy quake so hard, you'd forget every orgasm before me. Every one because of your hand, every one that useless Spencer gave you. You'll only remember my tongue on you and in you, and how it made you feel."

Makenna's lips parted with a tiny squeak. *Mission accomplished.*

"I'm going to walk away now. Try not to look at my ass," Dan said as he spun around.

You are not going to look back. Cool guys don't look back.

He looked back.

Makenna stood there, one of her toned legs peeking out from the slit in her dress, breathing in and out deeply between her red lips.

Dan's erection enhanced his swagger, although his dick was getting him in all sorts of trouble.

Oɴ, holy hell.

She did not expect that from Dan.

She swallowed again. She could feel a light sweat breaking out on her forehead line. It had been a long time since a man's words caused her to lose all composure.

Her inner hoe was supposed to be on her best behavior this weekend.

Instead that thirsty bitch wanted to stick her tongue down Dan's throat.

It *would* make this terrible weekend bearable. A quaking pussy sounded like a great reward for keeping her mouth shut and being cordial with Brady and Caroline. She deserved a mind-blowing orgasm.

Her footsteps were wobbly as she turned back to the rehearsal dinner, holding her dress as she walked down the stairs to the sunken dining area. Dan's eyes stayed on her as her hand skimmed the bannister.

Don't fall. They don't need another thing to point out as a flaw.

She took her seat next to her mother, who looked her up and down as she sipped her glass of wine.

"What have you been up to? On your phone?" she asked. "The food arrived and is probably cold. You were gone for so long."

Makenna took a bite of the mashed potatoes. Mom was right, but she didn't need to know that.

"They're fine," Makenna said.

"Will you look at Zoey?" Makenna's mom said, pointing to Zoey at the top of the stairs. She outstretched her arms like she was the only peppy cheerleader on a squad.

"I think she's drunk. Really drunk," Makenna said. "I'm worried about her and stairs."

Dan stood up and clapped, looking back while his hands came together. Makenna covered her mouth, to hide the giggles. No one else seemed amused, especially Caroline.

This night kept getting better.

Zoey walked down the stairs and joined the rest of the bridal party, occupying the opposite side of their banquet table. Makenna longed to be in their section.

"Lisa is texting me again," Caroline's mother Judy said, stabbing the phone like she was mad at it. "She still wants to come."

Please show up and make this really interesting.

"Oh my God," Caroline said under her breath.

Please come. Aunt Lisa, I'm counting on you.

"She's more than welcome," Angela offered.

Judy and Caroline said a simultaneous no.

Makenna wondered if she was going to end up like Lisa —invited out of pity to family functions, serially single, and everyone holding their breath in case she made a scene or created drama to keep it interesting. The "Vodka Aunt" trope from Christmas romcoms.

She was well on her way to *that* destiny.

"We're all going out afterwards, if you would like to join us," Caroline said to Makenna.

Is this a pity invite? Makenna wanted to ask, but she didn't let herself say it out loud. She could resist a man's advances and keep things to herself. Maybe she was maturing.

"That would be great," she said. "Thank you for inviting me, Caroline."

"It's no problem," she said sweetly. "Dan will be there."

Makenna brought the cloth napkin to her lips to cover as she coughed.

"You find him interesting, don't you? I think he's into you."

"I'm not interested," she said. The lie flowed out of her. "He's too short for me."

"Okay..." Caroline said, looking doubtful.

Makenna squirmed, the lie sitting like a ton of bricks. Dan intrigued her more than a limited edition Dior red lipstick, but no one needed to know. Caroline and Makenna weren't exactly close.

Ever since Caroline had entered their lives and became a permanent fixture in their family, Makenna noticed her mother doing things with Caroline she would only do with a daughter. They went shopping together, crafted together, went to book club together. Makenna didn't read or craft, but she could definitely go shopping. If she had the money.

The only topic of conversation her mother brought up was Makenna's imperfections.

Makenna followed Caroline on social media like a sadist

and felt the sting every time she saw Caroline post about her mom.

Best future MIL ever. So blessed!

I am so thankful for the woman who birthed the love of my life! Happy Mother's Day!

This woman has taught me so much about life. Love you.

Makenna wore too much black, liked metal music, enjoyed a cigar once and a while. She much preferred hanging out one-on-one, getting to know people and what made them tick. Caroline was a social butterfly wherever she went and had tons of friends. In L.A., most people were fake, and Makenna only had one real friend. Bluntness and honesty were two things Makenna held dear, and many people, Makenna found, could not handle it and didn't take the time to get to know her beyond her outspokenness.

Even her own mother didn't know her. When her mother saw her, all she saw was speeding tickets, debt, and mistakes. Her mother seemed to connect with Caroline more, which always felt like a twist of a knife to the gut.

"The club will be fun," Caroline said. "I just hope Derek can keep it together. I still can't understand what Addison sees in him."

They both looked at Derek, Addison's fiancé. His hands gesticulated wildly, and when he draped his arm around Addison, she flinched. Makenna recognized that look. Addison didn't know how to get out, how to say "enough was enough."

There was more going on there, Makenna just didn't know what.

"Let's not talk about Addison," Makenna said, taking a sip of her whiskey.

"Okay," Caroline said, laughing nervously. "Derek really is the worst, though, right?"

Makenna shook her head. "I have dated some assholes, and he barely scratches the surface. Trust me."

Makenna continued to choke down the tasteless chicken and chew the cold broccoli. Her mother leaned in again when she caught Makenna staring at Dan.

"I know what you're doing," her mom said.

"What?" Makenna asked nonchalantly.

"You're flirting with him," she said, nodding her head toward Dan.

"We don't know each other well," she said, rolling her tongue over her teeth.

"I know that look in your eye, Makenna. Please don't go after him."

"Why, Mother?"

"He's shorter than you, for one. He's probably eye level with those." Her mother pointed to her chest. Makenna had had to sit through an uncomfortable, passive-aggressive phone conversation with her parents when she spent her college savings on a pair of boobs and a deposit on an L.A. apartment instead of finishing college.

"You two would look odd together, that's all. He's also older than you, by a lot."

Don't give in. Don't say it.

"He's not the oldest I've dated, Mom."

Her mother blushed and scoffed. "Do I want to know the age of the oldest man you've dated?"

Makenna smirked. "Fifty-two."

"Makenna," she said with a huff.

Dan still looked over, and Makenna bit her lip.

"You just toy with the nice ones. I have no idea why. Like that precious boy from high school. Poor Holden. Or those other two? The ones who proposed? Seriously, Makenna."

She rolled her eyes. Mom had to bring up Holden, the

lovable goof she fell for when she was sixteen. They had talked about going away to school together at University of Nevada, Las Vegas, and instead Makenna took a job at a makeup counter and signed up for classes at Sacramento State instead. He was still a great friend, one of the only friends she had left from high school.

"Do you suggest I just date assholes, mother? I know you hate that too."

Angela let out a heavy sigh. "You're going to do what you want to do, but please don't cause a scene at your brother's wedding," her mother said. "You're going to hurt that man's feelings."

Wow. Her mother was worried about a white man's feelings.

Makenna looked at Dan, the now-forbidden man who could flirt his ass off and made her lady parts tighten.

Her mother held up a manicured fingernail. "Don't do it."

Makenna crooked her lip and looked across the room at Dan again. Their gaze locked, and Dan winked.

Put a *don't touch* sign on something, anything, and Makenna would touch it.

Her mother thought someone was wrong for her—and her response was *we'll see how wrong this is*.

She was a single woman, a grown woman.

She could have sex with Dan Price all night long, and no one would have to know.

Challenge accepted.

There was one thing that needed to happen first.

She had had high hopes for many men, but the minute their lips touched, there was no spark. Makenna needed to kiss Dan Price as soon as possible.

5

Dan smirked. Makenna had been looking at him like he was a delicious gazelle on the Savannah and she was the lion.

Their stares could set fires.

He had ordered a limo to take them from the Timberlake Golf Course and Lodge to the Diamond Rough Casino to party at Emeralds, a club inside the casino. Makenna sat down across from him, her legs spread for a half second, long enough to see black panties before she crossed her legs. A smile lingered on her lips.

She knew what she was doing.

His shoe touched her bare ankle, and Makenna's hazel eyes smoldered on him, like *don't you dare.* He jerked his shoulder in a shrug and winked. Makenna's red lips parted as she looked to Zoey, who stumbled into the limo.

Zoey, drunker than he had ever seen her, created a delightful diversion. She chatted with Dan as she glared at Jonathan. It kept Dan honest. Flirting with Makenna was a terrible idea. However, he couldn't help it.

After they checked in at the club, Dan excused himself to go to the bathroom. Walking through the casino, he felt fingernails dig into his skin.

"You come with me," Makenna said.

"Gladly," he replied.

Makenna pulled Dan into the casino, away from the crowd. They passed by the coffee shop, past clouds of smoke from gamblers seated at slot machines. The anticipation was agonizing, as they snaked through crowds, dodging foot traffic and walkers.

He gingerly put his arm around her waist, and she didn't protest as they walked side by side, her arm draped over his shoulders.

"I'm so happy right now," Dan said with a grin.

They walked out of the haze of the casino into the summer night, slightly cooler than when they walked in. The breeze made his eyes squint.

Don't you sneeze, you motherfucker.

Makenna rounded the brick façade of the casino, down an alley toward the receiving dock for trucks delivering goods.

"I'm very intrigued," he said.

"Be quiet," she ordered. Dan's knees almost buckled.

Bossy and beautiful. He loved it.

Makenna turned with her hands on her hips, looking both directions. She kicked off her shoes onto the pavement.

She inched toward him like she was about to run into a freezing cold lake. Dan crossed his arms. This lead-up was entertaining, and he was enjoying every minute.

Then she leaned in and kissed him.

He anticipated a kiss with Makenna would be fun and sexy.

He didn't expect it to be an action movie explosion that could lift a fainting goat to the moon.

His hand rose to the back of her neck, and his tongue entered her mouth at the next pass. Her tongue mirrored his, and the corners of his mouth turned upward. Hers did too as they dove in again, toward each other.

She tasted like smoky bourbon and danger.

Heat invaded his limbs. His hand pressed against her lower back, pulling her toward him. His hand fisted her soft hair as he tasted her, and he knew she could feel his hard length, how she drove him wild.

Kisses like this were why a broody hero held up a boombox blasting love songs outside a window on the off chance the heroine was home.

A tiny moan echoed through her mouth to his, and he slowed the movement. Time stopped. It was only them, in this moment.

When they pulled away, they gasped for breath like they had been underwater. Her hands rested on his shoulders.

"What was that for?" Dan asked. "We're not supposed to be flirting."

"That wasn't flirting. That was kissing," she said, pulling out a small mirror from her purse. She turned from side-to-side, examining her makeup while Dan braced himself against the wall to stay upright.

"Do you want to do it again?" Dan asked, gripping her waist. Makenna wiggled out of his grasp. She slid her feet back into her heels and turned with a teeter. The clack of her shoes on the sidewalk was the final nail through Dan's heart.

"Makenna?"

She turned back. "I had to test it."

"And...?" he said, running up to her.

"It was okay," she said. He saw the slight smirk on her lips.

"I heard a *moan*." He stopped and rested his hands on his head with his elbows out. "I almost died, it was so good."

"You're so dramatic," she said, with a laugh. "If you're a good boy, maybe I'll let you kiss me again."

"Wha—"

She shook her head as she turned back around. That devil woman.

"We should go back in before the bloodhounds zero in," Makenna said, grabbing for the heavy door. Dan snuck in between her and the door and opened it for her.

"I'm still interested in a spin around the dance floor."

"Maybe," Makenna said. "Maybe not."

"Ugh, you are a terrible, insufferable woman and I'm *obsessed* with you."

She threw back her head and laughed again.

He needed this woman naked and underneath him as soon as humanly possible. Or above him—he wasn't picky.

No, that is a bad idea. Look how fucked up you are after one kiss. She's going to annihilate you.

"We should probably stagger our entrances," Makenna said. Dan motioned for her to go ahead, and her body *almost* pressed against his again.

It was good he was forced to avoid her for a second; his cock was hard enough to bang steel.

Dan threw a twenty down at a blackjack table for ten minutes to kill some time. He got a few good hands, enough to fund a couple of drinks, and re-entered the club. The bouncer nodded once after he flashed his wristband.

He took a sip from his left-hand Coors Light, then his right-hand Coors Light.

When he reached the VIP booth, Jonathan sat on the

edge of the couch, his legs bouncing. Makenna was talking to Addison and Taylor, another one of Caroline's friends who came up for the wedding. Brady and Caroline were nowhere to be found.

He slowly walked by them, and Makenna didn't even flinch.

Best kiss of his life, and she barely acknowledged him.

This was not a good idea. Absolutely not.

Was he going straight toward a cliff of sadness? Absolutely.

"Where's Zoey?" Dan asked Jonathan.

"I have no idea. She went into the bathroom twenty minutes ago. Did I do something wrong?"

Dan shrugged. He looked over at Makenna, chatting like nothing happened. The kiss hadn't tilted the axis of her world.

He was a crazed man, desperate for another taste, another chance to be around her.

"Well, I'm going to call it a night," Makenna said, standing up and waving with both hands.

What about the dance? What about another kiss? What the fuck?

His heart sank as she grabbed her purse, like she was actually leaving. Against his better judgment, he stood up. "You owe me a dance."

"Maybe next time," she said, slapping him on the arm.

He watched her slink off like a jungle cat, clutching her purse in her fingernails. The purse might as well be his heart.

You've got to get your head on right, Dan fucking Price. Go home, take a frigid shower, take care of business, and do what you got to do.

He drank his Coors Light. The beer barely dented the

dejection. Dan snuck out while everyone in the wedding party watched Jonathan and Zoey and their drama.

A shower, an empty vacation rental, and one of those stale cookies Caroline bought might be able to comfort him while he figured out what the hell to do about Makenna.

6

CAROLINE AND BRADY'S
WEDDING DAY

The wedding had been stuff frenemies' dreams were made of.

First, it *rained*. Not a sprinkle, but a torrential downpour, making Caroline's hopes of an outdoor ceremony impossible. It had forced the beautifully planned ceremony inside to the ballroom, with a small aisle and guests crammed in tables around them. Aunt Lisa had worn a white, dated dress with a flower crown, which made Makenna laugh. Watching that woman create havoc through the wedding ceremony was beautiful.

Thankfully, her officiating had gone smoothly; she had gotten some laughs, and she only fumbled once. She could hear Dan's laughs to her side, and she looked at him once. His gaze reminded her of the explosive kiss the night before. A kiss she hadn't forgotten. After her duties for the evening had concluded, a giant weight lifted from her as she followed the happy bride and groom down the makeshift aisle.

It all went downhill when Makenna made a tiny comment about Zoey and Jonathan eating each other's faces in public. It launched a spirited discussion of public displays of affection.

Then Dan said to her, "I don't think you've ever been in love before."

Again, he saw something in her she hid. She had cared for others, but she knew she had never loved anyone.

"No, can't say that I have," Makenna said, trying to sound casual.

"Just wait until you fall in love with me, baby. You won't be able to keep your hands off me."

Makenna paused, those words hitting her like a sack of flour. Dan had mildly flirted with her in front of her brother and Jonathan, but this felt overt and forward and...hot.

"Oh Makenna, just fuck him already. Playing all coy with him..." Derek, Addison's fiancé, said loudly, drunk and belligerent.

Before Makenna could say something, Dan jumped in. "Excuse me?"

Derek's eyelids hung low as his words came out slurred. "Makenna, we know you hook up with random guys anyway, so it won't be anything new. This 'will they or won't they' is exhausting."

Dan hopped up like a chivalrous knight and got in Derek's face. "I will lay you out if you don't shut the fuck up."

Oh yeah. I'm going to fuck Dan. Not a single question in my mind. Who cares if it means this prick is right.

While she appreciated and lusted after Dan for his alpha response, she could fight her own battles.

"No, I got this," Makenna said, standing up. Derek wasn't even worth taking off her earrings.

Derek's look of terror made her soul soar.

"Addison, can you please remove your man from this wedding? Before I gouge his eyeball out with my heel?"

Addison said nothing as she pulled him away by the elbow.

There was only one way to act. Unaffected.

Makenna had been slut-shamed before, accused of stealing boyfriends or husbands when it wasn't true, looked down on for dating around in high school and after. No one ever came to her aid, even her own family, so she relied on herself. Took it on the chin.

Seeing Dan stick up for her, like her honor was being challenged, made her want to dishonor him in the bedroom.

"You owe me a dance," he whispered as he pulled her onto the dance floor for the first song. A song started, and he held up one finger, like he was testing the direction of the wind.

"We did this song for dance team," he said.

Makenna's eye narrowed as she watched him launch into a full dance routine. It was so good, she stood back and watched, clapping and cheering. She kissed him softly when he returned to her, his face dripping in sweat.

"What was that for?" he asked.

"For the dancing. For sticking up for me. For everything," she said.

After dancing with Dan, the wedding ebbed and flowed. The absolute highlight was seeing Derek return to the wedding, try to fight Caroline's grandpa, and *lose*. Dan hauled him out the wedding with Brady and Jonathan, and Makenna heard Addison dumped him.

Finally.

Aunt Lisa brought out a limbo pole, and Makenna watched in delight as Dan limboed to victory.

As the wedding wrapped up, Makenna and Taylor were

the only ones left at the bridal party table, although Taylor wasn't technically a bridesmaid. Makenna barely knew Taylor, but she liked her a lot. Taylor owned a successful spin and yoga studio in Lillyvale and took no bullshit, just like Makenna.

"Great wedding," Makenna said sarcastically.

"I know," Taylor said, the bouquet she caught in the bridal toss in front of her. "I fucking hate weddings."

"Me too."

Taylor crossed her arms. "I doubt I'll ever have one. Why the parade? You can go down to the courthouse for a hundred bucks, and boom, it's done."

"I'm not getting married," Makenna said. "I'm destined to be alone. It's why I've turned down two marriage proposals."

"Two? Wow. I can't even get a guy to call me his girl-friend," Taylor bemoaned.

Better than two men delusional that you're the one they want when they don't know how miserable you'll make them eventually.

"I think they liked the idea of marriage more than me." Makenna shrugged. "I hate the idea of marriage. Just chained up, forever. Too many variables."

"Marriage scares me. I want to get married, though. I want kids. I just don't want all *this*."

"Weddings are definitely overrated."

"A hundred percent agree." Taylor took a sip of wine. "You did great up there, by the way."

"Thanks," she said. "If you ever need me to do a cere-mony in a living room, give me a call."

Taylor laughed. They were both quiet for a moment.

"So..." Taylor looked down and back up. "What about you and Dan?"

"Oh no, you too?" Makenna said, sitting back and crossing her arms in front of her.

"There's something there," Taylor said. "I know it when I see it."

"Nothing's there," Makenna replied.

Except a couple amazing kisses that made my toes numb.

"Well, it's a fun idea anyway," Taylor said, tipping her wine glass to get the last drips of her white wine on her tongue. She stood up. "I'm going to get some more wine. Do you want anything?"

Makenna shook her head, and Taylor knocked the table with her fist and left her.

A wave of loneliness came over her. In a room of people she knew well, even family, she felt alone.

That's what happened when you're difficult to like, she guessed.

She breathed in, her nostrils rattling.

"Makenna," a voice whisper-shouted from the direction of the doors. She looked back. Dan stood at the entrance, his face peeking from behind the door. Makenna took the last swig of whiskey and stood up, gaining footing on her heels, trying not to twist her ankle.

Dan pulled her around the door into the lobby, holding one of her hands delicately.

"Hey you," she said.

"Hey yourself," Dan said, leaning against the wall. He had ditched the jacket, and only wore the vest that barely fit him and the too-short pants. He still looked scrumptious.

"I saw you kill at limbo," Makenna said.

"Yeah, I started going to Taylor's yoga studio. I've gotten *very* flexible," Dan said, wiggling his eyebrows. "How's the wedding been for you?"

"It's been wild. I wish there was better whiskey here."

Makenna's smile broke, and she play-punched his stomach. "Thank you so much again for sticking up for me with Derek. You know I could've handle it on my own, though."

"I knew you could handle it. I just don't think a gentleman should talk to a lady like that," Dan said.

"I'm not a lady," Makenna said.

"To be honest, I'm not a gentleman," Dan replied.

Makenna flicked a manicured eyebrow. "Oh?"

"Are you sure you're not with that guy in L.A.?" Dan asked.

"Positive." Her phone held twenty-three notifications from Spencer, all unread.

Dan nodded once. "I got kicked out of the vacation rental so Jonathan and Zoey could bone. I'm babysitting Derek now in his room if you want to swing by. I think Addison is staying in Taylor's room." His fingertips settled on her waist. "I promise it doesn't have to be anything more than tonight. I just want one night to worship you like you deserve. It'll get it out of our systems."

His words and touch sent flames through her core, and a gasp came involuntarily. She wanted to, but it always started like this. Fun, until it was serious.

She wanted to so bad, though.

"I don't really want an audience."

"Derek's completely passed out. It's fine."

Makenna pondered for a moment. She could decline. She could walk away and drink loads of water and get a good night's sleep.

Or she could do something her body said yes to even while her brain said *hell no*.

"If we do this, it's a one-time thing," she said.

"Done."

"I mean it. We get it out of our systems, and no one knows we did it. I don't want to deal with all the questions."

"Also done," Dan replied.

Makenna looked around, and then brushed her lips against his. When she pulled back, she whispered. "Come to my room instead. Two twenty."

Dan tilted his head. "Two twenty, got it. I'll be there at ten."

"Great," Makenna said. "I look forward to it."

Dan looked either way and pulled her close again and kissed her, his lips hard against hers.

The worst decisions always felt like the best.

"I hope Brady doesn't kill me, but I would die a happy man even if he did."

"He doesn't have to know," Makenna said, kissing him again to breathlessness.

When they pulled apart, both gasping for air, Dan whispered, "It'll be best if we keep this secret."

"Thank you," she said, biting her bottom lip. If they were alone, her dress would've fallen off her body at this point. Instead she swallowed hard.

"One hour," he said, dropping his hands and walking away. She could still feel his handprints on her.

This was a terrible idea. She couldn't wait.

Makenna deliberately didn't leave the party at ten. Even though she had promised to meet Dan then, she needed to maintain the upper hand. She wanted him waiting, panting for her.

And people said she had no self-control.

Makenna sipped a new terrible whiskey. And waited. And waited.

She talked to Addison, who had just broken up with Derek. Addison apologized profusely for Derek's behavior, and Makenna shooed it off. It wasn't Addison's fault her now-ex was a jackass. She had to cross her legs when she thought about her planned tryst with Derek's guard. She imagined him in his cute vest, the way his ass looked in those pants.

To pass the time, she took shots of cheap tequila with Aunt Lisa, who she was obsessed with. She finally had a decent buzz going, her arms all loose and her head dreamy and happy.

The party wound down, with his brother and Caroline holding each other, the last ones on the dance floor.

Brady was so in love with Caroline.

Makenna's cold heart usually kept to a strict no-feelings zone. However, seeing her brother hold his new wife, even after the heinous wedding they had, made even her heart flutter.

At least long-lasting love would happen for one of the Brady siblings.

Makenna checked her watch. It was now an acceptable time to eat Dan for dessert.

She tucked her phone into her clutch and passed by her parents' table.

"I'm going to hit the sack," Makenna said, pointing with her thumb in the general direction of the rooms.

Actually, Mom, I'm going to get dicked down hard by a groomsman. The one you said not to pursue. Aren't you proud of me?

"Okay, honey. We have brunch at eight a.m. tomorrow. Please don't be late," her mother said.

Makenna waved to Brady and Caroline, who thanked her from across the room.

I'm about to go fuck your groomsman, goodnight!

She passed by a mirror on the way out, checking her lipstick and fixing her dress over her tits.

Let's go test out this man to see what he's made of.

Every step up the stairs was delicious, expectation building for this encounter. Two flights of stairs, and she reached her floor. She pinched the card key out of her wallet as she scanned the gangway, the hallways bordering an atrium so she could see from the lobby to the skylights.

When she reached her room, he wasn't there.

A cold sweat covered her.

Did he decide he didn't want to? Well, fuck. Her plan didn't work.

Her hair fell in her face as she stuck the card key into the door.

"Hey," a man's voice said, coming from an alleyway. "You're late."

A small smile tucked away on her lips. She looked down and back up, parting her lips, pretending to look innocent and demure.

"I lost track of time," Makenna said with a sly smile.

His pupils smoldered to embers instead of igniting with amusement.

This fun-loving man had turned into all business, and Makenna's pussy dripped with the anticipation.

Dan leaned against the wall and rubbed his hands together. "I guess there are ways you can make it up to me."

"What is that?" Makenna asked.

"Let me in, and I'll show you."

Makenna arched an eyebrow and turned the lever to open her dark hotel room. Dan followed her in. He hadn't even touched her yet, and her body was already begging for it.

"Strip," he ordered.

She turned with a smirk on her face. *Oh, we have an alpha on our hands here. Okay.*

Makenna could take charge or take the lead, depending the man. Intrigue morphed into aching desire as she bent to undo her heels.

"Those stay on," he told her.

Fuck yeah they do.

Instead, she expertly unzipped the back of her red dress, slowly pulling it away from her skin. She wore no underwear, since the dress plunged down to her ribcage and satin was unforgiving with panty lines.

She stood naked in front of him and watched as his breath hitched. She tilted her chin up.

If he didn't touch her soon, she was going to die.

"Oh my God, M, you're stunning," he said. There was the glimmer of the Dan she knew before, the eager Golden Retriever of a man, desperate for praise. Now, this new Dan, with his hungry gaze and blunt direction, surprised her and created a level of desire she always aspired to with a sexual partner.

She wanted to appear confident, like she made men beg and kneel on the regular. However, her breath betrayed how aroused she was. Dan held all the power.

He grabbed her neck and brought her to him, their mouths crashing into each other's. This kiss pleaded, hungered, proved insatiable. It grew in its need as they sucked and licked. She bit his bottom lip again.

"Come here," he growled as he pulled her to the bed. She bounced on the mattress, her legs draped over the side. He covered her body with his, kissing her again, his hands creating a flurry of sensation all over her. He snaked down her body to kneel beside the bed, positioning himself between her open knees.

His hands pressed into her inner thighs, and her body shook. His finger traced her slit and she almost sat up.

He didn't waste any time; he dove toward her clit, and Makenna's head rolled back.

Makenna had received terrible to amazing oral sex. But this, this trumped every previous experience. Dan's tongue swirled and sucked and lapped with precision. It usually took men several tries to figure out her wants and desires, and only with incessant coaching and prodding and feedback.

Not Dan.

He knew her body already. He knew when to squeeze her thigh, when to palm her breast or play with her nipple.

Their bodies communicated without words, only action and breath and tremors.

She was already so close, and Dan stood up, kissing up to her neck.

"I want you to sit on my face," Dan whispered into her ear. "Ride my mouth like you're going to ride my dick later."

His words almost made her come right then.

Dan laid down, and Makenna shivered as she straddled him, lowering onto his tongue with a gasp. She stayed motionless, letting the torturous pleasure cascade over her. Dan squeezed her ass and smacked it as she found her rhythm. His tongue licked her clit as she hovered over him, his hands on her breasts. He pinched her nipple and Makenna fell over the edge.

Into the strongest, most intense orgasm she had ever had.

It lasted for intense moments, radiating through her limbs and her hair and her toes.

"Holy shit," Makenna said as she swung a leg off of him. "Holy *shit*." She sat against the headboard, pushing her hair out of her face. "Where the fuck did you learn that?"

"I strive for excellence, baby," he said, wiping his mouth. Goofy Dan was back.

She took his lips with hers, taking a reprieve to rip open his shirt, buttons landing on the comforter. The pants came off, and the condom was rolled on.

Thunder serenaded their encounter, and Makenna rode him to another intense orgasm, probably stronger than the first. Rain mirrored their cries, incessant and unapologetic.

Makenna usually monitored her moans or cries in the bedroom. But she let herself let go with Dan, a guttural moan as her pussy pulsed for the third time, Dan's cock inside of her. When he came, he grabbed her hand and interlaced her fingers with his.

The intimacy pricked her eyes with tears.

When they were done, Makenna fell off of him, leaning back against the headboard.

"Oh my fuck," Makenna said. "I haven't smoked since high school, but I need a cigarette."

"You are sensational," Dan said. He laid his head on her stomach, as she played with his sweaty hair. "What a way to end a wedding weekend."

"That sex was..." Her words trailed off.

"I always aim to make women speechless," he said with a laugh, brushing his lips over hers.

Makenna wrapped herself in a short, silk robe as Dan dressed.

She wanted him to stay the night.

No. This was just a casual, one-time thing. It was no one's business that she just had three life-changing orgasms and that Dan was the best lover she had ever had. Goddamn, Zoey was right. He was way better than the sloppy sex she had had all over Europe, the men with motorcycles and chest hair. He even bested Lorenzo, the passionate lover who had worshipped her body for forty-eight hours straight in his flat on the outskirts of Florence.

Dan opened the door, his jacket over his shoulder. He turned back and cupped her cheek with his hand, his thumb brushing against her jawline.

"I know we said this was a one-time thing," he said. "However..."

Makenna softened against the door. "I'll miss you. More than you know."

"You have my number," he said. He looked into the hall, the hotel quiet except for the punishing rain on the skyline. There were faint noises of the cleaning crew mopping the entrance, dirty from the rain and footprints.

"Goodbye, Dan," she said. He kissed her passionately one last time, and she almost pulled him in for another round.

However, this was a one-time thing.

It would never work.

He wanted forever with someone, and Makenna was destined to be alone. No one really loved her when they got to know her, once the shiny veneer dulled and they saw her ugly inside.

It was easier this way to let him leave now.

"Give me a call if you're ever in Lillyvale," he said, pressing his forehead to hers.

"Of course," she said.

She thought he would kiss her again, but he turned quickly and strode away. Makenna closed the door and leaned against it.

She thought sex with Dan would scratch that itch.

She thought it would be over after tonight.

Her mind raced with thoughts of Dan so much that she couldn't sleep, and when she turned her head, she could smell him on her pillow. The memories of their night together followed her to brunch the next day, her thoughts scattered and unfocused, even while her mother was talking to her.

Sitting across from Brady, knowing the type of warning he'd given Dan, and that Dan did it anyway, made her smirk to herself. The weekend had turned out much better than she expected.

The only thing that sucked were the memories of Dan that followed her back to L.A..

7

FIVE MONTHS LATER

"I can't believe Spencer did that. Actually, scratch that. Not surprised. At all. Spencer is wet, hot garbage," Sierra said over the phone. Her best friend always shot it to her straight, grumbling every time she had to hang out with Spencer and her. There were even texts that came through from her while they were hanging out: *Why are you with him?*

When Makenna got back to L.A. after the wedding, Spencer had groveled, and Makenna reluctantly started seeing him again. It was part habit, part mask for the turmoil of her heart.

This whole time she thought she would be the one to destroy Dan, but in a strange twist, Dan had destroyed her.

The loneliness hit harder, the nights alone colder now that she had met him.

So, she took Spencer back to fill the nights, fill her bed with a warm body. Spencer always had an expiration date on him, which was exactly what she wanted. It kept her from self-sabotage, since there were many times she composed a text to Dan, almost called him just to hear his voice. Since she had Spencer, she didn't. She might be a lot of things, but she wasn't a cheater.

But it seemed Spencer was. When she found out he was seeing multiple other women behind her back, she ended it on the spot forever.

"Don't call me ever again," she had said with fake anger. In the recesses of her mind, she was relieved.

Sierra was on a month-long work trip in Asia, but she always took Makenna's calls, no matter what time it was. Makenna talked to her as she hovered next to the huge metal sculpture of a rabbit in the middle of arrivals at Sacramento International Airport, delaying calling an Uber to go home to Lillyvale.

"I think you should text that guy you told me about. The one from the wedding," Sierra said. "What was his name again?"

"Dan."

"Dan. He seems like a way better option. The stuff you told me...girl, I would've called him already. Waxed that pussy, bought new lingerie. Broke into his house and laid naked on his bed, waiting for him to come home..."

Since Sierra had no connection to Lillyvale, she knew all the details. The kiss, the amazing sex, some of his dirty talk. She had gotten up and stood in front of the freezer to cool off when Makenna had told her everything.

"Dan would be Adrian all over again."

"I'm still *baffled* how you found the only male model in L.A. who wanted to get married and have babies. Oh, and I totally forgot about Craig too. Makenna, you were such an asshole."

"I know," Makenna said.

"But I get it," Sierra said. "Once you say he's like Adrian, I get it."

Makenna's phone beeped. "My phone is about to die. I'll text you once I get a charge."

"I still think you should text him, though. Go back on that dick. Then, text me once you've done it." Sierra hung up.

Makenna ordered an Uber and walked to the pickup point. Once in the back of a Nissan Altima, she scrolled her contacts and found his name. Dan Price. Six percent battery on her phone, and she spent it contemplating a bad decision.

She bit her lip and opened a new message screen. This was a terrible idea, a slippery slope. One day she was casually having fun with Adrian, then he knelt down on one knee. There was a moment she thought she could be happy with Adrian, or with Craig, who also proposed after a whirlwind few months together.

If they would've really *known* her, they wouldn't have done it.

It's why she always said no.

Makenna loved nice men, but she knew they needed nice, agreeable women. Not her. It was always for the best to cut it off at the knees. Or just date assholes. They were easier to leave.

The devastation Adrian and Craig expressed after she broke it off, broke *them*, flashed in her mind when she gave into self-loathing. Adrian's hurt still gnawed at her, the guilt at letting what they had turn into something serious, and she had let it go on far too long.

Knowing all of this, her thumbs still flew over her phone buttons. Playing chicken with her conscience was always a good time.

Makenna: I'm back in town for the holidays. Do you want to get together?

She tilted her head back and forth as she deliberated. A low battery notification pulled her out of her indecision, and in one moment, she hit send.

Then her phone screen went black.

"Ugh!" Makenna grunted, and the Uber driver looked into the rearview mirror.

"Everything okay?"

"Fine," Makenna said. "Do you have a charger?"

"Nope, sorry."

Makenna sat back with a huff. L.A. Ubers had spoiled her with bottled water and copious chargers.

The Uber dropped her off, and she stared at her childhood home.

Home for the holidays to spend with parents who judged her, who didn't know what to say to her unless it was a criticism.

Makenna entered her parents' home without announcement, dropping her bag in her room, still decorated with her teenage obsessions. She found her charger among her clothes and plugged it into the wall to juice up her phone. She stared at it, waiting for the charge to breathe life into the screen again. Nothing happened so Makenna walked away.

A watched phone never dings.

After pulling on a pair of joggers, Makenna went downstairs to find her mother baking.

"Hi Mom," Makenna said.

"Hi honey, how was your flight?"

"Fine."

"Your father could've picked you up, you know."

"And miss the opportunity to compare L.A. Uber drivers to Sacramento Uber drivers? Not a chance."

"I don't trust those things. They'll know you're going on vacation, and then they rob you."

Makenna rolled her eyes. Angela was always worried about her house being robbed when all the neighbors loved her, were incredibly nosy, and watched her house like it would do tricks.

"So, we're going to the Rhodeses' house for Thanksgiving?"

"That's the plan."

"Don't you think it's weird that we're going over to Caroline's parents' house and Caroline and Brady aren't even going to be there?" Makenna asked, plucking a carrot from the charcuterie board and snapping it with her teeth.

"It will be a lovely time," her mother said, pulling a pie out of the oven with her cat oven mitts. "This holiday is about family, and they're our family now. We're going to share grandchildren someday, and I want to be great friends with Judy."

Angela made friends easily. One conversation, and she was your Facebook friend and eventually knew everything about you. Sent greeting cards for no reason. When Angela had dinner parties, friends poured into her house, bringing gifts and stayed for hours, even though she was a terrible cook. But getting close to Makenna was like running a gauntlet; the only person to get there in recent memory was Sierra, who had beat down her defenses.

She always knew she was a hard person to love.

"Where are Caroline and Brady again for this blessed holiday?"

"They're visiting Zoey and Jonathan in Phoenix."

Jonathan and Zoey had successfully rekindled their romance at her brother's wedding, and Zoey had moved to

Phoenix to be where Jonathan moved to from Lillyvale. She followed them on social media, but didn't see their posts most of the time due to following a little over a thousand people. Once in a while, she saw a cute photo of them and smiled.

"Ah," Makenna said. "How are the two lovebirds doing?"

Her mother turned conspiratorially. "Supposedly, Jonathan is going to propose to Zoey on Saturday. Another wedding! Hopefully I'll be invited. I love weddings." Her mother pursed her lips, a typical Angela Brady move. "Are you seeing anyone, honey?"

Makenna took another bite of a carrot. Her mom hated Spencer and usually passive-aggressively sighed when Makenna mentioned him. She *loved* Adrian and when it ended, she blamed Makenna.

It was her fault, though.

"Nope. Absolutely single."

Her mother breathed out in relief. "It's probably for the best. You don't do relationships well, honey."

Makenna rolled her glossed lips and looked down.

Her mother's comment could fill a whole hour with the therapist she loved but couldn't afford anymore.

I need to get out of here.

"I think I might see a friend tonight since tomorrow is the family togetherness. It's not Holden. Is that okay?"

"You have a friend to see besides Holden? Oh, that's wonderful," her mother said with a smile. "Be back by ten. Your father and I can't sleep if you're out late."

Makenna bit her tongue. She was twenty-six-years-old, not sixteen. After the debauchery and havoc she made of her teenage years, she swallowed any snarky comments and nodded once. "Ten at the very latest."

"Have fun," her mother said, kissing her on the forehead. "I'm so glad you've got a friend here. Usually you're just on your phone, but seeing someone is just great."

Makenna smiled tightly. "I'm trying to build my Instagram, Mom."

"Can you make money from that?"

"Yes," Makenna said.

"I would love to stop sending you money if you are."

Makenna bit her lip. Her following wasn't big enough yet, although she had about twenty-five thousand. She refused to buy followers or engagement, so it was slow-going. No real sponsorships yet, just free product to feature.

"I should go get ready," Makenna said, changing the subject. "The pie looks amazing."

"Thank you! I think I did a great job," Angela said, leaning against the counter and admiring her work.

She wasn't certain Dan would want to hang out, but she grinned from ear-to-ear when she saw a text from him.

Dan: Definitely. I'll pick you up at 7.

DAN PULLED UP TO THE BRADYS' house, his fingers drumming against the steering wheel.

"You are Dan fucking Price. Stop acting like a silly goose," he told himself in the mirror. Makenna told him to text when he got there, so he pulled out his phone and sent a heart emoji.

Should he be outside his car to greet her or stay in the car?

Nope, any true eighties romcom hero would be outside his car, looking suave as fuck.

Dan leaned against the car, adjusting his body, crossing his arms.

Perfect.

Seconds later, Makenna exploded out of her house. Even with her hair piled on top of her head, a big puffer jacket over leggings and Uggs, she was still the sexiest woman he had ever seen.

"Hi," she said. They bobbed toward each other and ended in an awkward hug.

There was that perfume again, flowers and pears.

"It's so good to see you," he said, kissing her on the cheek. He wanted to kiss her for real, but he had seen Spencer appear on Makenna's Instagram again and had to assume they were seeing each other.

Why am I doing this to myself?

"Thank you for texting me back," Makenna said. "It's good to see you too. How have you been?"

"Great, now that I get to see you," Dan replied, walking around to the driver's side. "I have an idea."

"Oh?" Makenna asked.

Dan sat down, and Makenna slid in next to him. His whole car would smell like her, and he wasn't sure if it was a good or bad thing.

"Trampoline," he said.

"What?" she asked. "Like in a backyard or..."

"No, there's this trampoline park in Roseville. I got us in."

"Okay," she said. "I'm surprised they're open the day before Thanksgiving."

"They're not. I may have pulled some strings."

"You're a big deal in Roseville too?"

"Maybe," Dan said. "I figured if we can't fuck, we can bounce in other ways."

Makenna's hand landed on his on the center console.

He pulled his hand away.

"Sorry," Makenna said.

"It's not a big deal," he replied, smiling toward her.

He was already pushing his limits texting another man's girlfriend when he heard she was in town. Being so close to her might make him forget she was with someone else.

He pulled into a shopping center and parked in front of the trampoline park, then pulled out his phone. After a few quick jabs at the keys, the storefront illuminated.

"Let's bounce," he said. Makenna laughed at the pun.

Chuck, Dan's protégé, opened the glass door.

"Thanks, Chucky," Dan said to the tall, slender guy with glasses and clusters of acne on his cheeks.

"No problem, Dan. Anything for you."

"Chuck, this is my friend, Makenna."

Chuck shook her hand in awe like he had never touched a woman.

"Makenna, excuse us. I have some business to settle with Chuck."

"No problem," she said, shucking her coat and pushing up the sleeves of a huge cream sweater.

Dan pulled Chuck to the side.

"Chuck, we talked about this. You have to get used to being around women. This sweaty, nervous act has *got to go*."

"I'm sorry, Dan, I just clam up around women who look...well..."

Dan huffed out a breath. "We'll talk about it in your next coaching session."

Chuck nodded once. "If you can teach me how you"— Chuck pointed to Dan—"get a woman like that"—he motioned to Makenna—"I will do whatever you tell me to."

"She's not mine," Dan said.

"Still, I can't even get women to talk to me at the supermarket."

"We're going to have to circle back on why you're talking to women in the supermarket," Dan said, walking back to Makenna.

Her sweater slid off her shoulder, and Dan wanted to bite his fist.

As they followed Chuck into the main area, Dan kept himself a few feet from Makenna, so he didn't accidentally brush her hand and go into a silent panic like he was in a Jane Austen novel.

Chuck turned on all the lights to show a massive room, accented in green and yellow squares, with black trampolines on the side.

"Oh my God," Makenna said, looking around.

"Right?"

Her mouth hung open. "All this, for me?"

"Of course," he said. "We're friends, right?"

Makenna's face softened. *Is she bummed?*

Makenna crouched down to pull off her boots, and Dan kicked off his sneakers.

"One hour," Chuck said, then disappeared.

Makenna looked back and then at Dan. "What did you talk to him about?"

"Chuck is one of my clients," Dan said. "I'm kicking around a new business idea. Dating coaching, possibly a matchmaking service."

"Interesting."

"I'll race you," Dan said, running toward the trampoline area. He jumped broadly, bounding between the sections of trampoline. He looked back to see Makenna jumping cautiously, her socked feet barely elevating.

"Come on, Makenna. Feel the jump!"

"I'm scared!" she yelled. She stood on one of the multicolored borders of the black trampoline squares. "I broke my arm once doing stupid shit on a trampoline."

"Don't be scared!" Dan yelled. "You're with me!"

He jumped back toward her, contemplating offering his hands. There was enough distraction with the jumping that he wouldn't dwell on her touch and let it drive him nuts.

He stretched his arms out to her, and she braced on them, feeling the bounce under her feet. She let out a squeak and slipped, taking him down with her.

Somehow, his body landed on hers.

"Are you okay?" he asked, pressing his body into hers. He *should* roll off. Her hands were on his ass. *His ass.*

"I'm great," Makenna said, looking up at him. The way tiny wisps of hair escaped her bun, her light freckles across her nose. Her hazel eyes.

"Your hands are on my ass," he said, propping himself up to look at her.

"Oh, they are?" she said innocently. Hands were not moved.

God, she was beautiful. He knew her kind, though. She was a cat who played with a terrified mouse before she killed it.

Tempting all of his self-control, he took a finger and brushed a hair away from her forehead.

You're playing with fire around dynamite, you dumbass.

Although he wanted to stay there forever, Dan forced himself to wriggle out of her embrace, and stood up. He offered his hand to pull her up.

His pants felt uncomfortably tight from the hard-on he'd developed, so he bounced from square to square, even doing a back flip to claps from Makenna.

"So, if you're opening a dating service, are *you* dating anyone?" she asked.

"Single and ready to mingle, baby," Dan said. "Though I'm going through a bit of a rough patch. Lots of dates going nowhere."

The truth was, no woman had made him feel as remotely as alive as he had when he was with Makenna.

"Shame," she said with a smile.

"What's with the smile?"

"Nothing," Makenna said. "I'm just happy."

"What about you?"

"Single, now."

"I saw your Instagram with that guy. Spencer?"

"Oh, we broke up again. This time for good."

Dan knew the type. Makenna was in a dance with a guy Dan's polar opposite. Never able to stay away, always circling back.

"Why did you break up?"

Makenna bent her knees to start a bounce, holding her arms out. "He was seeing other women. It's fine if we're not serious, but I want to be the only woman a guy is sleeping with."

"That sucks," Dan said. "You want me to go down to L.A. and get my ass kicked defending your honor?"

"No, that's okay," Makenna said with a laugh. "It's probably for the best it ended. I don't know if L.A. is for me anymore."

"I remember you said that," Dan said. "I got to that point as well."

"Everything is so fucked up down there. It's lonely."

"It's settled, then. Move back here."

Makenna shook her head. "I don't know."

"Lillyvale is going to be way better. I promise you. I'm revitalizing Central Lillyvale and filling it with more restaurants and nightlife..."

"I'll think about it," Makenna said. "My best friend is in L.A.."

"You don't have any friends left around here?"

Makenna shook her head. "I hang out with Holden, my ex, a little bit, but we're just friends. If he has a girlfriend, we can't hang out. His girlfriends hate me."

"What about Caroline?" Dan asked. "Her friends are really nice. You should get to know them."

"Maybe. But Caroline and I are so different."

"I get it," Dan said. "Okay, I'll be your friend, then. You'll have one more when you come back to Lillyvale."

Makenna laughed and shook her head. "Right." She bounced away, gaining her confidence. Dan followed her.

"You don't think we can be friends?"

"Men and women can't be friends if they've seen each other naked. You know too much."

"I'm still friends with Zoey, and we saw each other naked. A lot. Also, what about Holden?"

"I didn't have sex with him," Makenna said. "I know, it's shocking."

"His loss," Dan said with a wink.

"It was kind of a mutual decision. It's the only good decision I've ever made about men," she said. "Except for you, of course."

"Of course," Dan said. "Did you get the 'men and women can't be friends' from *When Harry Met Sally?*"

"I haven't seen that one. I just know from personal experience."

Dan gasped. "What?"

"Yeah," Makenna said. "I'm not really into old movies."

Dan collapsed onto the trampoline, lying across multiple squares of black mesh. Even with his eyes closed, he knew Makenna was standing over him.

"What's wrong?"

"I'm a corpse, is all. You called a movie younger than me old."

"I didn't mean it like that!"

"That hurts. You are missing *so many* good movies because they're 'old.'" Dan made air quotes with his fingers.

"Maybe we can watch some of them this weekend," she said. "As friends. Maybe I can turn over a new leaf. Be a changed person."

"Uh huh," Dan said, standing up, bouncing away. "I know us. You would have me naked before the first pinch point."

"That's a valid concern," she said. She held her hands up. "I will be on my best behavior. Promise."

"Uh-huh," he said. He didn't hear her moving or following him. When he turned back, he saw her still standing there. He leaped back, bounding from one trampoline to another back to her.

"I thought this was going to be a horrific weekend," Makenna said. "You've made it better."

"I'm glad," Dan replied. "I'm always here if you need me."

"I appreciate that," Makenna said, opening her arms for a hug.

"Are you doing this so you can touch my ass again?"

"Nope," Makenna said. "I just want a friendly hug."

Dan walked into her arms, squeezing her into his embrace. Her arms felt right around him, but he knew it was a fantasy. On-and-off relationships took some time to fizzle, and she had just broken up with Spencer. Zoey had dated Jonathan eons before Dan met her, and he had still hovered over their entire relationship like an annoying ghost.

If Dan slept with Makenna again, he would slide into the

role of a delicious piece of ass, a part he knew too well. *And* Brady would be pissed.

So their night together would remain perfect in his mind, and their relationship wouldn't have time to get messy.

So, they bounced like children until they were sweaty and sticky. Afterward, Dan pulled through the Taco Bell drive-thru, and they devoured tacos as they laughed and told stories. When he dropped her off at her parents', she looked back once and paused, about to say something. Then, she walked into the house, and Dan's heart began to hurt.

8

THANKSGIVING

"I t's science," Harry Rhodes yelled, with a slap of the table.

Makenna just sat back and sipped her wine. She honestly thought going to Caroline's parents' house this Thanksgiving would be boring and awkward. It delivered on the awkward, but in the absolute best way.

Caroline's aunt Lisa, who had worn white and started the limbo contest at Brady's wedding, had come to Thanksgiving after a supposed end to her long feud with Caroline's mother, Judy. But it seemed Lisa was working on rekindling the feud, since she brought a guy named Chet who swore up and down that the earth was flat.

Watching Caroline's dad Harry wither into a ranting, crazed lunatic was a Thanksgiving miracle.

"Earth's gravity is an illusion. The government has you all fooled," Chet insisted, scooping mashed potatoes into his mouth.

Staring her sister Judy, Caroline's mother, down, Lisa rubbed Chet's back. "He's just really passionate. You can't fault him for feeling strongly about something."

"His beliefs are horseshit!" Harry yelled, his face growing a pissed shade of purple.

"Now, calm down Harry," Judy said, clenching his arm in her hands. "No need to break a blood vessel."

Makenna turned to see her parents quietly eating, not engaging. Her mother, who usually interjected herself into every conversation, reacted by grumbling and continually refilling her wine glass.

Caroline usually hosted Thanksgiving, and her food was delicious. She clearly didn't get her cooking skills from her mother. Makenna had barely touched her plate. The vegetables were slimy, the bird dry. The only edible things were the salad and the rolls.

Caroline's little brother Brandon sat across from her. He was a tiny, lean dude, who was about Dan's height and could meet her rolled eyes and raise her with pantomimed mocking.

A kindred spirit—someone as petty as she was.

"Harry, all I am saying is..." Chet said, as he continued to gesticulate with his hands, presenting points that were absolutely false and plucked straight from a Facebook conspiracy theory group. The points continued to anger Harry, and Makenna choked back laughter when Harry's voice cracked with anger.

As they continued to argue, Brandon pulled out his phone, robbing Makenna of a partner in this dinner.

She wondered what Dan was doing.

"Excuse me," Makenna said, grabbing her phone and heading in the direction of the bathroom. She closed the door and sat on the closed toilet, pulling up a text message screen.

She paused, looking at Dan's name. Texting him was the wrong thing to do.

Makenna closed her phone, her cheeks warming with heat. Just the memory of being so close to Dan the night before at the trampoline park sent shivers through her limbs. She'd almost kissed him, when they tumbled down together and his body pressed to hers. His touch had burned into her skin, tattooing her just like the art on her body.

It was just an insane sexual connection, nothing more.

Before she could talk herself out of it, she typed:

Makenna: This dinner turned crazy. Aunt Lisa brought this guy who thinks the earth is flat.

The three dots appeared instantly.

Dan: Want me to rescue you? I'm almost done at my mom's house.

She paused. *Don't do it. Don't do it...*

Makenna: Please.

Dan: Be right there. Text me the address.

To kill time, Makenna opened the medicine cabinet but didn't find anything interesting. She washed her hands a full thirty seconds although she hadn't used the bathroom. She found some old Bath and Body Works lotion in a decorative straw basket so she squirted some in her hand and rubbed it in between her fingers, really working the liquid into her skin.

When she walked back out to the dinner table, everyone was silent, quietly eating. Brandon looked up with the face of a hostage victim.

"Everyone is so quiet," Makenna said cheerfully, secretly hoping to start shit again.

Chet ripped a roll in half and jammed the bread into his mouth, chewing with an intense stare at Harry.

Makenna pushed the green bean casserole around her

plate, the vegetable soggy from too much soup mix. Her stomach growled.

Might as well drink more wine while she waited for Dan.

The arguing started up again. Brandon massaged his temples. Makenna kept checking her phone, and her mother glared at her every time she picked it up.

When her phone buzzed, it felt like a life raft to a Titanic victim.

Dan with a heart emoji to save her.

"So, I'm going to go," Makenna said, standing up and walking to the chair by the door that held her purse next to her hung up coat.

"Makenna, we are in the middle of dinner," her mother said tightly, with a fake smile plastered on.

She pulled her coat on. "And it's been a pleasure. I just don't subject myself to false theories fueled by rage posts on Facebook. I'm going to remove myself as a form of self-care."

Her mother, dumbfounded, watched her as Makenna opened the front door. The cold air bit at her cheeks, and there he was, his car idling on the curb.

"My prince," she said, sliding into the passenger seat.

"Was it really bad in there?"

"The fucking worst," she said.

"I need to know everything. Every word said, every scoff Harry Rhodes gave. Where did do you want to go?"

"Anywhere but here."

"I have no idea what's open." Dan paused and said, "Do you want to head back to my..."

"Yes," Makenna blurted out.

"Back to the Price Palace, then," he said, pulling away from the curb. Makenna regaled him with a replay of the night. At stoplights, she mimicked Harry Rhodes's expressions.

"Wow," he said. "Your Thanksgiving was a lot more entertaining than mine."

Makenna eyed the leftovers stacked on the center console. The car filled with the faint smell of Thanksgiving —turkey, definitely some stuffing. Her mouth watered, and her stomach rumbled.

"Was that you?" Dan asked incredulously.

"Empty stomach sounds," Makenna said. "The food was terrible."

"You are in luck, since my momma is the best cook in Lillyvale. She sent me home with leftovers."

"I don't want to take your leftovers, Dan."

"Nonsense," Dan said. "You're hungry, and I have delicious leftovers."

"Thank you," Makenna said.

"Anything for you."

They drove south to central Lillyvale, turning on a few side streets to a modest two-story house painted white with blue shudders and a blue door. The lawn was well-manicured and the bushes neatly trimmed. If Makenna had to guess, the house was about twenty years old.

"Your house is really nice. Do you live here by yourself?"

Dan nodded. "I got a good deal on it. But it's too big for just me. I'm thinking about getting a dog."

"You should," Makenna said. "Although dogs scare me."

"Oh, that's good to know," Dan said. "I thought you were perfect."

Dan pulled into his garage. It was clean and surprisingly empty of the usual boxes of crap she saw in people's open garages in Lillyvale.

"This way," Dan said, leading her into his dark house.

When he flipped a switch, warm light illuminated a homey living room with worn cognac leather couches. Makenna's body shivered from the night air so Dan hustled to the couch and grabbed an afghan, wrapping her in it. "The women at the old folks' home like to knit me blankets. I have probably fifty of these."

She wrapped it around her. It smelled faintly of old people, but it was warm and cozy.

"Do you want food now?"

"Sure," Makenna said.

"I'll fix you a plate," Dan said. Makenna wrapped the blanket around her as she walked to a series of three photo collages on the wall. The rest of the walls were barren, except for a glowing Coors Light sign by the fireplace.

One collage held four photos. In the first, two taller men flanked Dan, one older, one younger, with the same ash blond hair and goofy grins. In the second, Dan was hugging a plump woman about his height, their faces squeezed into smiles. Dan standing straight next to a man Makenna could only assume was his father. Another of a little boy with the man from one of the photos, the child's arms around the man's neck.

Dan reappeared with a plate of food and a tumbler glass full of amber liquid.

"I figured you should have some good whiskey for listening to that idiot."

"Thanks, Dan," she said, taking the glass and nodding toward the wall. "Is that your family?"

"Yep," Dan said. "The whole fam damily."

"Two brothers?"

"Correct. One older, one significantly younger." Dan walked over to the coffee table, and placed her plate down, next to a napkin and silverware. He pulled a Coors Light beer can out of his jacket and cracked it open with a hiss.

"Middle child," Makenna said. "It explains so much."

"Oh yeah," Dan said. "But my little brother didn't come along until I was in high school, so I was the youngest for most of my childhood."

"Who's the little boy?"

"My brother Sam's kid. Elijah."

"Oh, Uncle Dan," Makenna said. She dropped to her knees in front of the food on the coffee table.

"I have a kitchen table if you prefer," Dan said. "I barely use it."

"No, this is perfect. Thank you." Her stomach rumbled at the sight of delicious Thanksgiving leftovers. She decided to try the mashed potatoes first. The creamy, buttery taste hit her mouth, and her eyes bulged.

"I told you. Ma is the best."

"What's her name?"

"Joyce."

"And your dad?" Makenna asked.

Dan paused. "Matt."

Makenna took a sip of her drink. "Wow. This is really good." She swirled the liquid and looked at it.

"Oh good. That bottle was a gift. Maybe you've heard of it."

Dan disappeared again as Makenna took a bite of the turkey. It melted in her mouth, and her eyes rolled with pleasure. When Dan presented her with the bottle, Makenna shrieked.

"You have got to be shitting me," Makenna said, holding the bottle.

"What, is Pappy Van Winkle popular or something?"

Makenna let out a sound. Holding this exclusive and

elusive bourbon in her hands felt like a dream. "How the fuck did you get this? It's hard to get *and* expensive."

"One of the bars I invest in got a shipment and gave me a bottle. It's been sitting in my cabinet for a little bit."

"You've had a Pappy Van Winkle this whole time?"

Dan nodded and held up his Coors Light. "I drink only these, really. I've tried it, and it's pretty good. I'm just off of the hard stuff now."

"Well, I can drink it. All of it."

"I would love you to," he said. "Come drink it whenever you want."

Makenna took a bite of the stuffing and fell back onto the couch. "This food is so *good*."

Dan sat forward. "I'm glad you're enjoying it."

Makenna placed her fork next to her plate. "Seriously. You've made my Thanksgiving weekend. Thank you."

She rose to her feet. His kindness toward her, the memory of their one night together, made her want to do very bad things to him.

She rifled his hair first, Dan's eyes looking up at her. Her hand cupped his cheek, and his eyes stayed on her.

"Don't do it," he said, his hand fisting a handful of her top.

"What if I want to?" Makenna asked. "Do you want to?"

He was quiet for a moment, so quiet she pulled her hand away. "Yes."

Makenna lowered her head down to kiss him.

She tasted the cold beer on his lips. Her tongue breached his lips and licked his. His hand pressed into her back, and he lifted from the couch to kiss her, threading his hands through her hair.

This was a fire she couldn't ignore. This connection was real and raw.

"Bedroom?" Makenna asked through gasps of breath.

Dan set his beer can down on the coffee table and stood up. He led her up the stairs, down a darkened hallway to the bedroom. A soft glow covered the bed, a neatly-made queen with a black headboard and matching nightstands.

The kissing was a detonated bomb, creating havoc and frenzy within their limbs and Makenna's heart. His hands covered her body, roaming to touch every square inch of her.

She pushed him onto the bed, and she straddled him, pulling his shirt off first, then hers. His hands cupped her breasts through her black lace bra, and she moaned.

"My God, M," he said, sitting up to kiss her flesh. "I prayed this would happen again. Still, I don't know if this is a good idea."

"Do you want to stop?" she asked, pulling away.

Dan shook his head. "No."

Her lips touched his again, and she lost herself in his arms.

There was no way she could be just friends or stay away from him now. She wanted him too much.

He removed her bra, and then her jeans. She stripped him of his pants, and then his underwear. When they faced each other naked, he looked at her, and it scared her.

He saw her, and he understood her.

He found a condom and sheathed himself. She laughed as he turned her over onto all-fours, lining himself up with her entrance. When his cock entered her from behind, she cried out. His movements were slow at first, and then quick. His fingers reached around to massage her clit, driving her to divine pleasure, as she moaned as loudly as she wanted. He pulled her up so his chest was against her back, his hand squeezing her breast gently. His breath against her skin, his kisses on her shoulder sent her over the edge. When her pussy pulsed around his cock and he cried out soon after, they collapsed into a pile on the bed.

They laid there for a while without words, Makenna's head on Dan's bare chest, as he played with her hair.

Her stomach rumbled.

"I'll be right back," he said, kissing her on the nose.

He returned with the Thanksgiving leftovers, warm from another reheat, and her glass fuller than she'd left it. She ate naked in bed, while his head laid on her thighs. Filling herself with good sex and good food made for a hell of a night.

Once she finished, she put the plate on the nightstand and laid down, still naked. She closed her eyes, letting the satisfaction overtake her.

Maybe she could handle a move back to Lillyvale. Maybe Dan was a good reason to move home. Even if it ended, feeling like this would be worth it.

Dan moved so he was looking in her eyes. "What are we doing here, M?" he asked seriously.

"I don't know."

Dan's fingers traced her skin. "Tonight was amazing, but we can't keep doing this like this, you know."

Makenna stabbed her elbow into the bed so she could sit up and look at Dan. Dan looked off to the side, not in Makenna's direction. His jaw was clenched, and she could see moisture at the corner of his eyes.

"Why not?"

"You appreciate honesty, right?"

"Right," Makenna said.

Dan's far-off look scared her.

"If we keep going, I'm going to fall in love with you. I can already feel myself starting. And when I love, I love hard. If there is any chance you might break my heart, any little chance you're unsure, it's best we end this. Now. For my sake."

Coldness ran through her veins.

For a moment, she saw a glimpse of them together. Really together. There was a possibility she could fall too, for the first time in her life.

Then, she remembered Adrian, holding his grandma's engagement ring out along with his heart. How she talked about marriage with Craig in broad strokes of "one day," and then the next week, he took her to the beach and dropped down on one knee.

How she broke up with Holden in a very public and very embarrassing display when he said he loved her and she said thanks.

All of those relationships where she thought she was in control swirled away from her, where every guy felt something bigger than she did. And then she broke them, because that's what she did.

Better break them then, before it was too late.

Those men just loved the idea of her. They saw the fake boobs and the tattoos and didn't peel back the layers. A strong woman was just a wild horse to break to them, but she would never be broken.

Her previous lovers hadn't listened to her and fell in love anyway.

Makenna had to respect Dan for believing her.

She dressed without a word. When she looked over at Dan, his nostrils were flared and his eyes glassy as he watched her. She slid her boots on and slapped her thighs.

"I won't tell anyone about this," Dan said. "I'll order an Uber for you to get home."

"Thank you. It's probably for the best," Makenna said, sitting up.

Her heart beat so fast in her chest as she walked down the stairs and found her purse. Dan followed her, his eyes on the ground. Dan's phone pinged with the notification from the app that her car was arriving.

Her hand settled on the doorknob. "I wish things were different."

He said nothing as she opened the door and left his house, fighting back tears as she approached the sedan waiting for her on the street.

9

CHRISTMAS

"Honey!" Joyce, Dan's mom, said when she opened the door to Dan. Dan laid a small peck on his mother's cheek as he shuffled in with arms full of presents.

"Uncle Dan!" Elijah said, running over. "Are those for me?"

"Some of them are," Dan said, walking over to the tree. He knelt down, and pulled them out, one by one to place them under the tree. A train chugged around the presents, and the lights twinkled, but sadness still tugged at Dan.

He had heard Makenna was in town, and it was taking everything in him not to reach out to her.

Their time together was beautiful, but it was over. It had to be.

It still fucking hurt, though.

"Elijah, are you bugging Uncle Dan?" Sam, Dan's older brother, said. Sam was the taller, more distinguished brother. While Dan looked like an overgrown frat boy, Sam wore button-down shirts as casual wear and listened to NPR.

"No," the little boy said, walking over to the couch and climbing onto the cushions.

"Dan, I have eggnog," he said, holding up a plastic moose mug, a present to their mother years ago. The family was obsessed with *National Lampoon's Christmas Vacation*.

"No thanks," Dan said.

"You seem sad, Dan. Is everything okay?"

"Everything is fine."

"You know what you need? Eggnog." Sam handed Dan a mug identical to his.

Dan took one sip. "There is so much alcohol in this." Dan sipped it again. Usually, his Coors Light was enough, but he needed a stiffer drink than a beer that also doubled as hydration.

Nick, Dan's little brother, appeared from the hall, his nose buried in his phone. As he passed, Dan got a glimpse of what was on Nick's phone and froze.

Was he looking at Makenna's Instagram?

"Nick. Nick. Nicky," Dan said, trying to get his attention, putting him in a headlock. Nick turned his head, and Dan saw an AirPod sticking out from his ear. His brother finally reacted when he pulled one out.

"Hi," the teen said, annoyed.

"All my boys together," Joyce said. "This makes me happy."

They all gave tight-lipped smiles, unsure how to react. Last Christmas, they had gone to their dad's in a small town in the middle-of-nowhere Nevada, where they sat and watched TV and sometimes shot a gun at a tin can. They all agreed after that that Christmases in the future always would happen at Mom's house.

"What are you looking at, Nicky?" Sam asked. Sam was thirty-seven, almost nineteen years older than Nick, who was a senior in high school. He was in college when Nick was born, so they were never very close. It wasn't a secret that Nick was an oops baby who became a save-the-marriage baby.

Nick held up his phone. "Possibly the hottest woman I have *ever* seen."

Dan glanced away quickly. That was undeniably Makenna. In a black, barely-there bikini, thigh-deep in water. Tattoos inked her body, art he remembered tracing with his tongue.

"Yeah, she's pretty good-looking," Sam said.

Dan contemplated telling his brothers that he had slept with that woman in the Instagram, but it would serve no purpose, so he kept his mouth shut.

"I mean, I don't think either of you could ever get that caliber of woman," Nick said. "What does one have to do to get a woman like that?"

Being my own fucking charming self, baby brother.

It still hurt his heart to see a picture of her. They hadn't texted each other since Thanksgiving. He claimed he was going to fall in love with her if they continued to hang out. As time had passed, he became acutely aware that he probably already had. He had gotten a beer recently with Brady, and his heart had dropped when his friend had mentioned his sister.

His friendship with Brady had happened because of Zoey, an ex who reminded him why he couldn't continue with Makenna. It also reminded him of how fragile his relationship with Brady was.

Joyce sat down on the couch next to Dan. "Is next year finally going to be the year I get a daughter?"

"Oh my God, are you pregnant?" Dan asked, slapping his cheeks.

"No, silly. A daughter-in-law. Or a serious girlfriend at least."

Sam covered Elijah's ears. "Mom. Please."

"I just think you two aren't getting any younger and need to settle down. That's all."

"I want to meet someone. It's just hard with..." Sam said, motioning to the unassuming child.

"I want to meet someone too, but..." *My heart belongs somewhere it shouldn't be.*

"There's a perfect woman for both of you out there. I just know it," Joyce said.

"This is the perfect woman for me," Nick said, showing another post, this one of Makenna, smiling, wearing blue light-blocking glasses she was promoting, her hair up into two pigtails like a schoolgirl.

Me too, Nick. Me too.

His phone buzzed, and Dan looked at it in confusion.

The woman in the Instagram was calling him.

CAROLINE AND BRADY sat on the couch opposite Makenna, arms wrapped around each other, the glow of the tree shining on their happy faces. Makenna's boyfriend for the night was bourbon. He was turning out to be perfect.

He didn't complain. He didn't talk back. If she finished him, there were no consequences but a potential headache in the morning.

She needed it after having to sit through Caroline opening present after present for a baby that didn't exist yet.

"Oh my God, this is *so* sweet," Caroline said, pulling out a baby outfit, a sleeper with baby ducks on it. Makenna rolled her eyes. Caroline had been married for six months and was obsessed with getting pregnant and having babies.

Makenna couldn't even keep a cactus alive.

"It's never too early to start collecting items," Angela said, her voice dripping with anxious excitement. Makenna rubbed her lips together, anything to keep from screaming.

"Makenna, how is the boyfriend doing?" Caroline asked, refolding the unisex sleeper back into the box, recovering it with the box's top.

"Which one?" she asked after a hearty sip.

"Spencer, I think?"

"Oh, we broke up before Thanksgiving. He was seeing a lot of women," Makenna said. "It's fine since we weren't together-together. It's fine. Everything is fine."

"Did you get your roommate situation figured out?"

Makenna shook her head. The cute blue house covered by trees, built into a mountain, that she'd lived in for years was slipping from her grasp. Makenna knew her roommates, a married couple, hadn't been paying their share of the exorbitant rent. The husband, Kent, was a struggling screenwriter, while the wife had lost her job and was having trouble finding a new one. Every time Makenna came home from work, they were on the couch, surrounded by wine bottles and false promises.

It has always been tense between the three of them, since Kent always leered at her when she came out of the one bathroom in the house in a towel after a shower. She made sure to dress in the bathroom if he was home and she installed a deadbolt on her door.

"I might need to stay at my friend's apartment soon," Makenna said.

"Is that your friend, the travel blogger?"

"Sierra," Makenna said. "She's the best."

"She sounds like your Zoey," Caroline said. She was trying to relate, but Makenna prickled with irritation at the conversation.

"Excuse me," Makenna said, standing up.

Makenna found her favorite place in the house, the hard liquor cart. She poured a good three fingers and snatched another ice cube from the freezer.

Her mother always forgot how easy it was to hear whispered conversations in this house. They were always about her so she knew to listen.

"Is everything okay? With her?" Caroline asked.

"L.A.'s not working. She's running out of money, I know it. I think it's only a matter of time before she's back home."

"That boyfriend was terrible. I'm relieved, actually."

"She didn't seem that into him, anyway. I just want her to be happy, you know. She's so tough. I..."

She heard rustling of clothing, and she knew Caroline was comforting her own mother about her. A hug that should be going to Makenna.

Makenna's chin quivered as she drained her glass and filled it again, the liquid scalding her throat and warming her belly. A grimace usually kept any tears at bay, so she took a deep exhale and a deep inhale.

You are strong. Nothing can get to you.

She hated to admit it, but her mother was right. Her credit card balances kept climbing, her savings disappearing. Her hours at the Eloise Winston counter had dwindled considerably, and the freelance jobs were as sparse as the grass on the hills. Her parents' help wasn't enough to shovel out the utter shit show she had created for herself.

The air felt thick and too warm around her. Deep breaths weren't cutting it so Makenna walked to the closet where her coat hung, grabbed her phone, and headed outside. She pulled on her coat, but the frigid air nipped her skin. The backyard backed up to a nature path, and she watched the air rustle the trees.

How the fuck did my life get this way?

She sniffled and wiped her dripping nose with her coat sleeve. It was times like this she missed cigarettes, since now would be a perfect time to light one and feel her whole body relax.

She pulled out her phone and unlocked it, her thumb hovering over one contact's name.

She remembered the peak of pleasure, then the crash.

If we keep going, I'm going to fall in love with you.

Dan Price. Her heart twisted in knots at her mother, L.A., Caroline's fake pity. How she was incapable of falling in love. How she never let herself get there. If she got there, they might realize who she truly was and leave.

She punched his name.

"Hi Makenna," he said after two rings.

She breathed in, and her nose rattled with the cold. "Hey Dan. Merry Christmas."

"Merry Christmas. Are you in L.A. or Lillyvale?"

"Lillyvale," Makenna said. "Brady and Caroline are over, and I..."

The words couldn't come.

I'm worried that my life will always be a catastrophe.

Maybe you're the only one who can fix this.

Maybe I'm scared to death of us, but I want to try.

"What do you want, M?" he asked quietly.

"I don't know," Makenna said with a sniffle. "I just wanted to hear your voice and maybe..."

Dan breathed out over the phone.

"Listen, I'm with my family right now and I really can't talk..."

"I get that," she said, her heart sinking. Everything was floating away, everything was falling around them.

"Merry Christmas, Makenna," Dan said. She closed her eyes hearing her full name. Just once, she would love him to call her M again.

"Merry Christmas, Dan."

"Take care." Then the phone line went dead.

Hearing that made her crouch down, balancing on her heels, tears dripping onto the concrete.

A text message dinged through. She smiled, thinking it was Dan, changing his mind. She thirsted for his breadcrumbs, any message that she hadn't fucked this up forever.

Instead, it was the sweetest woman she had ever met. A woman who felt so bad about her ex-boyfriend Derek slut-shaming her that she sent apology flowers and apology texts. Addison had shown her kindness that she didn't feel like she deserved.

Addison: Merry Christmas Makenna! I hope you're doing okay. :heart emoji:

Her fingers typed without any thought.

Makenna: I'm not.

A moment later, her phone rang.

"Hi," Addison's voice said through the phone. "I got your text."

All the floodgates open, and Makenna sobbed, gulping on tears.

"What's wrong?" Addison asked.

"I feel so, so lonely."

"Oh Makenna," Addison said. "You're not alone. I'm here. I'm always here."

"I'm keeping you from your Christmas," Makenna said, wiping her tears with her sleeve. "I'll go..."

"No," she said. "You're my friend."

"You barely know me."

"Still, you're my friend. I care about you."

That made Makenna cry harder.

When the call naturally ended, Makenna thanked her and slipped the phone in her back pocket. Addison made her promise to call once she got home to L.A. when they both had more time to talk. She wiped away the tears and went back inside.

WHEN SHE RETURNED HOME to L.A., she found a large Notice to Vacate from the sheriff's department. Her roommates were nowhere to be found. She closed the door to her small room and collapsed onto her bed. Even with being paid the week before, she had less than a hundred dollars in her bank account. She had stopped looking at her credit card statements, peeling back the corner of the paper statement for the minimum balance due.

She found she was scheduled for only twenty hours at the Eloise Winston counter, not enough to sustain any kind of living situation in L.A., not by a long shot. She could barely afford her third of the rent.

She considered calling Sierra, but she was in Germany for work, touring Berlin for her blog and Instagram. It was the middle of the night there, and she didn't want to wake her even though she knew Sierra would answer, no matter the time.

It was a lot of work being her only friend.

Makenna opened the Recents log on her phone.

Addison had been so kind on Christmas, listening to her cry. It was afternoon, in the middle of her winter break from teaching. Addison did say she wanted her to call. Without thinking, she clicked on her name.

"Hi Makenna," she said brightly after two rings. "How are you? Did you make it to L.A. okay?"

"Yes," she said, sniffing and wiping her face. "I'm sorry I called you, I..."

"It's no problem. Really. I wanted you to call," she said. "How are you doing? Are you feeling better?"

A tear fell, and Makenna wiped it away. "I don't know what to do."

"Well, let's talk it out and figure it out. I'm happy to help."

"Everything is so fucked. Sorry," she said quickly. Addison didn't curse, so she always felt guilty saying certain words around her.

"It's okay. What's so messed up?"

"I'm going to get evicted. I have no money. Christmas was a disaster. I'm alone."

The line went quiet, and Makenna asked, "Hello?"

"Sorry," Addison said. "I was just listening."

"What should I do? I don't know what to do."

Makenna heard her breathe over the phone. "I think you should come home."

Move home to Lillyvale, like a failure? Her family would treat her more like a sob story, gossiping behind her back. The only person who made Lillyvale at least a little bit appealing wanted nothing to do with her. He had dismissed her, even though she understood why he had.

He had to protect himself from hurting, too.

"I have no friends, no job there... I don't know, I..." Makenna said. She looked around her room in the house that would no longer be hers in ninety days.

"I think home has the answer," Addison said. "Lillyvale has always grounded me. When I was in college and so lost, I came home and everything made sense."

Home has the answer.

"Wow," Makenna said. "Just wow."

"You don't have to move home right away," Addison said. "Think about it. Also, you do have friends in Lillyvale. Like I told you at Christmas, *I'm* your friend."

This was the only good thing that could move her to tears.

Kindness.

"Are you okay?" Addison asked.

Heaviness lifted, and Makenna laughed through the tears. "I'm okay."

10

TWO MONTHS LATER

S o much had happened since Christmas.

To everyone but Dan, that was.

To forget about things—well, one thing, or one woman—Dan had thrown himself headfirst into business ventures and started the pursuit of something he had always wanted.

A six-pack.

He had started attending yoga and spin at his friend Taylor's fitness studio, Cycle Yoga Love, and then another fitness studio had opened next door. The owner Malcolm Grant was everything Dan was not—beefy, tall, red-headed, shy. Malcolm's fitness programming focused on weights and barbells, so Dan signed up to finally put some muscle on his frame. To avoid the pain in his own heart, he focused on lifting and the intense hate-flirtation going on between Taylor and Malcolm.

If he couldn't have the love affair he dreamed about, he would meddle in someone else's.

Hence, the perfect orchestration of the stoking of an

attraction Dan had witnessed one day at yoga between Taylor and Malcolm.

So. Much. Grab-ass.

His schemes had distracted him from looking at Makenna's Instagram, from the utter sadness of a new diet plan with less-than-ideal carb volume, from drinking Coors Light, and watching his guilty pleasure *The Golden Girls* all the way through for the millionth time.

Sitting in the backseat of Brady's car, Dan rubbed his hands together. His dastardly plan was coming to fruition tonight. Brady had volunteered to drive to the restaurant, which was excellent, since it allowed time for Dan to coordinate his magnum opus.

It was Taylor's birthday, and Dan had gotten her a big, beefy, ginger present.

Dan smiled. Malcolm had just confirmed his estimated time of arrival, slightly after everyone else was set to arrive, for peak dramatic effect.

"This is going to be epic," Dan whispered.

"What is going to be epic?" Caroline asked.

"Nothing," Dan said, his voice a touch too high.

"You're up to something."

"No, I'm not," Dan said, covering his mouth to hide a laugh. "I'm completely innocent of anything that's about to happen tonight."

"Is this about Taylor and the gym owner?"

"Maybe," Dan said.

"Dan. You devil."

"What? Sometimes people need a little push. A little matchmaking." Caroline gave him a significant look.

"Caroline," Brady said warningly. Dan was riveted by the sternness of Brady's voice. He rarely stood up to Caroline.

Everyone knew that Caroline was the alpha in their relationship.

"What's going on?" Dan asked.

Caroline ran her fingers through her sunset-colored hair. Dan couldn't see her expression from the backseat but saw a faint curl of her lips.

"My sister is going to be there," Brady said. He looked in the rearview mirror, and Dan swallowed a lump in his throat. It was easy to pretend that Makenna wasn't related to his friend and compartmentalize. They didn't look alike at all and acted completely differently. Brady had strong does-taxes-three-months-early energy, while Makenna came into his life like a naked Miley Cyrus on a wrecking ball.

"Oh, Makenna. Cool," Dan said, trying to sound chill.

"I'm glad you toned down your slobbering over my sister," Brady said. "I had enough friends growing up that tried to get to her through me, and it's refreshing you're not one of them."

"Yeah, I wouldn't do that to you," Dan said, squirming in his seat. The night they'd spent together after Brady's wedding flashed through his brain, and he crossed his legs. Then Thanksgiving. The lies flowed out of him like melted butter at a crab feed. "I will *never* touch your sister."

Again.

"I'm so relieved," Brady said.

"You should be," Dan said, chuckling.

Shut up. Shut up. Shut up. You're digging yourself a bigger hole.

Brady, Caroline, and Dan were first to the restaurant, seated at the largest table in the corner.

"Are you nervous?" Caroline asked, as she reviewed the menu. "You look clammy."

"No, I'm fine. I'm just excited for Taylor's face when

Malcolm waltzes in. I told him to come twenty minutes late for maximum effect."

"Be quiet, here she comes."

Taylor and her sister, Ellie, had arrived. Ellie had been Dan's intern last summer, and he hired her occasionally if he had extra administrative work to do. He had thought about including her in his new project, Happily Lillyvale After, a matchmaking idea to expand his dating coaching side business. He hugged Ellie and kissed Taylor on the cheek. They sat down, and his goddess stood there.

Makenna Brady.

She had picked a black dress with tiny straps he wanted to tear off her. Her perfume hit his nostrils, and it took him back. To the wedding. To the trampoline park. To Thanksgiving, when she was in his arms for the last time.

Dan marveled at his self-control as he slid back into the booth after giving her a quick and friendly kiss on the cheek.

"Why are you acting weird?" Taylor asked him.

"Why should I be weird? I'm not acting weird."

Dammit, his cover *might be* blown. He looked at Brady. But he didn't seem to suspect a thing.

The group chatted as Addison and Kirk arrived. They were next on his list to matchmake. They had been friends since childhood, holding Skype book clubs and being adorable and shit. Too bad that Kirk lived in New York and had a girlfriend there. It would be a slam dunk to get them together if he lived here and was single.

The anticipation of Malcolm showing up to surprise Taylor kept his mind off the incredibly sexy woman he had tried to forget, sitting mere feet from him.

"Is he coming?" Addison asked, and she was immediately shushed. Dan had taken a yoga class with her the other day and let his plan slip. Dan nodded covertly, and Addison clapped her hands in excitement.

"What's going on?" Taylor asked, alarm etched on her face.

He might die tonight. Between avoiding a hard-on around Makenna so Brady wouldn't notice and Taylor killing him for inviting Malcolm, well, he obviously had a death wish.

"We got you a birthday present," Dan said. "A tall, redheaded present."

"No," Taylor said. She shook her head so violently, Dan worried about whiplash. "You *did not* invite Malcolm."

Dan nodded, since his evil genius plan was about to be set in motion. Taylor dropped to the table in a blonde heap.

"You said you wanted birthday sex," Makenna said. Her eyes flicked toward him, just for a moment, and Dan's pants grew even tighter. Her look acknowledged their scorching night of fucking at the wedding, and the tender lovemaking at the Price Palace.

No, I will not make this a trifecta of fucking.

Malcolm, Taylor's hunky love interest, walked toward the table with a swagger Dan could appreciate, and Taylor immediately began dressing him down, setting boundaries.

He laughed on the inside. Taylor's resolve had crumbled once already; he was sure it would come crashing down again.

Not like with him and Makenna.

He had to protect his doughy, sensitive heart.

Oh, and he'd promised Brady he would not touch his sister, but she was a grown adult woman, and an overprotective brother was nice, but outdated as fuck. Dan usually adhered to a strong bro code, but this woman was making him break all of his rules.

Like how he really wanted to kiss her, even though he swore he wouldn't.

Malcolm said hello to Addison and Kirk and they chatted, and then the group started asking Malcolm about his gym, the reason Taylor first hated him.

"It's nice to finally meet you. How's your business going?" Brady asked Malcolm.

Don't interrupt. Don't...

"It's going great is what it is," Dan said nervously. "I now go three times a week and I have muscle for the first time in my life. Makenna, feel this bicep. *Feel it.*"

Makenna touched his bicep, giving his muscle a good squeeze.

Just like her pussy did with his dick in Lake Tahoe.

"What's absolutely hilarious is Malcolm's fan club," Dan said, laughing as he pulled his arm away from Makenna's touch.

"You have a fan club?" Makenna asked.

Malcolm's pale skin blushed, looking down.

"I've told them to leave so many times. They brought a quiche and mimosa bar a couple days ago," Taylor said, rolling her eyes.

"I asked for none of it," Malcolm said, blushing red, his lips pressed together, looking at Taylor like a donut he couldn't eat.

Oh, they were definitely going to bang.

Makenna's pinkie was getting way too close to his thigh, testing his willpower. Which, he realized, he had none when it came to her.

Oh, they might definitely bang too.

He focused on Brady across the table. Dan could justify the two times he had slept with Brady's little sister, since it was technically over. If it stayed in the past as a secret, Brady didn't have to know. However, all Makenna had to do was nibble on his ear, and all his convictions about bro code would crumble like a dry chocolate chip cookie.

Makenna leaned in and whispered with Taylor, pulling her hand away.

Dan breathed a sigh of relief. All eyes were on Makenna and him, so he needed to deflect, deflect, deflect.

Plus, he really wanted to eat that curry the server just put down in the middle.

"Maylor, focus," Dan yelled, too loud to be natural. "Pass the curry."

"Maylor?" Taylor asked as she passed the platter to Makenna. Her hand deliberately brushed against his, causing a whole police-interrogation-room sweat to spring up on his forehead.

"Maylor, your couple name," Dan said. "It's cute, right?"

Not my best work, but smile!

Malcolm and Taylor acted coy, denying their attraction and insisting they hated each other. Whatever.

"I do recommend hate-fucking. It can be quite therapeutic," slipped out of Dan's mouth, just as Makenna squeezed his thigh. He shot a look at Makenna.

You're going to blow our cover, he tried to communicate with his eyes. She pulled her hand away, but their gaze held. The whole table noticed.

"So, Brady, how about those Kings?" Dan asked about Sacramento's basketball team that he knew his friend was obsessed with. Malcolm happily joined in, and Caroline switched spots with him so Malcolm and Brady could talk sports directly, instead of over Caroline. That barely switched the focus, since Dan noticed Caroline pointing between Makenna and him.

In a perfect world, they would be sitting here as a

couple. Brady would welcome him as a potential brother-in-law with open arms, Dan could date Makenna without a guarantee of a decimated heart, and he would be close to his version of happily ever after.

Instead, he was in a torture chamber, disguised as a semi-decent Thai restaurant.

Taylor and Malcolm replaced him in the backseat of Brady's car, so Addison waved him over.

If he went in Brady's car, he was the smallest so he would definitely be in the middle of the backseat. Between Taylor and Malcolm. If he went in Addison's car, Ellie was the tiniest, so she could be stuck in the middle.

Where will I be more comfortable? Sitting between Taylor and Malcolm being suffocated between sexual tension, or in a car with the source of my own sexual tension?

Like a glutton for punishment, he chose the car transporting Makenna.

He stuck Ellie in between them in the backseat to keep them honest, and Dan pushed Kirk to the front seat because he secretly wanted him and Addison together.

"This is so comfortable. I've never been more comfortable," Ellie said dryly. She scrunched into herself, trying not to touch Makenna or Dan.

"This is perfect," Dan said.

Makenna crossed her arms over her chest. "Never been better."

Deflect, deflect, deflect.

"So, bets on Taylor and Malcolm?" Dan asked.

"Oh, they're definitely going to fuck," Makenna said. "No doubt in my mind."

Makenna looked at Dan, then quickly looked away.

Ellie's head went back and forth, like she was watching a ping-pong match.

"Are you still seeing that music executive, Makenna?" Ellie asked.

"We broke up for good," Makenna said quietly. "Right before Thanksgiving, actually."

"I'm so sorry to hear that," Addison said.

"I haven't seen anyone since him, actually. I'm really, *really* single."

Have mercy.

A big, bright smile crossed Dan's face. Addison caught it in the rearview and smiled to herself, looking back to the road.

"Well, maybe you'll find someone at the club tonight."

I volunteer as tribute. It might as well be the Hunger Games since I'm gonna die.

Makenna laughed. "All I'm looking for is a stiff drink. Nothing else stiff."

"Nice," Ellie said, with a bobbing head.

"That's too bad. You're a wonderful person, Makenna. Truly. You'll find someone new," Addison said.

Don't encourage her, you beautiful angelic woman.

"I don't know," Makenna said. "I think I'm going to give up on dating."

Dan exhaled, and Ellie's head snapped toward him. Her eyes squinted. Ellie held up her pointer finger and a thumb in a circle and took her index finger on the other hand and inserted it in and out of the hole. *Did you do it?* Ellie mouthed to Dan in the darkness of the car.

Dan shook his head violently. He *had* to work on better boundaries with his employees.

"Same, Makenna, same," Ellie said, turning back to her. "When I finally broke up with Camila, I realized I had been devoting so much to my relationships that I'm too drained to work on my side hustles."

"Like what?" Dan asked. Ellie, like him, was full of big ideas and dreams but, unlike him, lacked focus to follow through.

"Something pet-related. I love dogs, and I can't think of a better way to spend my days but covered in puppies."

"I have an idea if you need some extra money," Dan said. "We'll talk."

"Thanks, Dan," Ellie said. "You've always taken great care of me."

Makenna shifted in her seat. *Yes, I've taken care of you too. Great care.*

"We're almost there!" Addison said cheerfully, pulling into a parking garage and parking next to Brady's car. Malcolm and Taylor stood feet apart, with awkward, crossed arms.

Makenna slid out first, since Dan's side was too close to an Escalade, then Ellie. Dan stepped out of the car, he tripped—okay, maybe it was on purpose—and looped his arms around Makenna's waist.

What the fuck is wrong with you? he thought to himself.

Makenna didn't flinch, just looked down at him like a peasant.

They may not be destined to be together, but he missed the playfulness they had at the trampoline park. The laughing, the teasing.

"Didn't see you there," Dan said. Makenna swatted at him playfully and pulled him up by the arm. She wore high stilettos so he had to look up at her. A flick of an eyebrow warned him.

The entire group walked to the Luna Ultra Lounge. They waited in line, and only Dan and Ellie were carded.

"Drinks!" Taylor shouted. Malcolm stepped in like the dreamboat he was to get her drink.

Victory. It looked like Taylor and Malcolm were on their way to boning in the near future. Dan accompanied Malcolm to the bar. His buddy, Tom, an old friend from L.A., was bartending so he shook his hand and rattled off the drinks order, gave Malcolm a pep talk, and paid for everything.

It was a drop in the bucket so paying for a bar tab was no big deal.

He took a drink. So what if he and Makenna acted like strangers with only the angst of a passing gaze? Maybe a turn around the room to see if there were any options.

He did a perimeter check, watching drunk people hump. There was a stripper pole on a podium, and sure enough, there was a girl in a short dress, shaking it with her hair flying back and forth. Another woman climbed up, grabbing part of the pole, engaging in some weird dance battle of barely moving to the music with the other woman.

He saw people kissing, including Ellie, who found a woman to make out with right away. Good for her.

When he swung back to the group, he saw Makenna standing on the outskirts, holding her drink. He didn't hear her voice, and he wondered if she was having a good time.

He pulled out his phone. He leaned against the wall by the bathrooms, hidden by a large potted plant.

Fuck it.

MAKENNA BARELY PAID attention to the chatter of the group. She sipped her drink and half-listened, checking behind her for Dan.

He disappeared after he returned with everyone's drinks from the bar. Their fingers had brushed when he handed her a whiskey. The liquor was smooth, coating her mouth in caramel and sliding down with fire.

Then he was gone.

Makenna didn't blame him for checking out his options, milling around the club for a woman who might be a better fit.

It might be for the best she didn't mention she was moving home.

Her phone vibrated in her hand.

Dan: Can we talk?

Her lips pressed together in a smirk.

Makenna: Sure, where are you?

Dan: 11 o'clock.

Makenna turned around, seeing Dan, partially hidden behind a potted plant. She looked back to the group, all engaged in a conversation that didn't include her.

She slinked away, checking to make sure the group's attention stayed on each other.

A group of men passed her and muttered something under their breath, looking her up and down. She was used to it, but it didn't make it feel any less gross.

"We can't talk here," he said, pulling her down the hall as quickly as her heels could scamper.

They found an empty all-genders bathroom, and he looked both directions down the hallway. Makenna turned her head. They couldn't see the group from their vantage point, and there were no witnesses as they ducked into the bathroom.

"What do you want, Dan?" Makenna asked. Her eyes looked everywhere but at him, and her arms crossed under her breasts.

Her hard shell always crumbled around him.

"I want to clear the air," Dan said. "I don't want you to be mad at me or have any resentment."

Makenna stared at the ground.

"I thought you didn't want to talk to me. Ever again."

"It's hard," he said. "I mean, it's hard being around you. Talking to you. Seeing you."

"Taylor asked me to come, and I didn't think it would be a big deal," Makenna said. She shifted from foot to foot, her eyes averted and downcast. "I can leave..."

Makenna walked to the door and placed her hand on the lever. Behind her, Dan said, "I want you here."

She turned around. Dan stood there, his face slack.

"I care about you. I wish I felt nothing, but I would be lying. It's killing me, being this close to you."

Her throat grew thick with the confession. She wanted to run to him, be with him. Her past, her failure stayed beside her. "If we do this, there's a chance I'll ruin it. Us. And then you'll hate me."

"I'm at the point where I don't care," Dan said. "Fuck your brother. No, don't do that, that's gross."

Makenna snorted. Dan walked toward her, his hand shaking as he brought it to her cheek. His thumb felt the heat of her skin. She leaned into his touch.

"My brother won't do anything. You should be more worried about me and what I'll do to you. I've hurt people before, and I don't want to hurt you, but I might. I tend to do that. I may destroy you."

"I feel like you already have," Dan said. "I can't stop thinking about you. If I don't give this a shot, I'm going to spend the rest of my life regretting it."

Makenna jutted her bottom lip, looking up at the ceiling. "I'm scared," she admitted.

"Don't be," Dan said. "It's me. Only us. Nothing else matters."

"Only us," Makenna repeated.

"Yes," Dan said. "Forget about what people have told you about yourself, or shit that is ancient history. It doesn't have to be like that again. This is *us*."

Makenna finally looked at him. Her chest heaved.

"I'm ready whenever you are," Dan said.

She took his cheeks in her hands and pulled his lips to hers.

He gripped her neck as he deepened the kiss, his tongue playing with hers, and their lips made the decision for them.

Her body had longed for him since their last time at Thanksgiving. It's why she hadn't dated anyone, why she hadn't re-added the dating apps to her phone. It was the longest she had been celibate, just in case Dan still felt something for her.

"Make sure the door's locked," Makenna said between kisses. Dan separated from her and jiggled the door handle, confirming its security. He took three steps toward her, and their lips were on each other again, hungry and desperate.

He pushed her dress up so it bunched around her waist, revealing a red lace thong that inspired a growl in his throat. She hopped onto the sink, spreading her legs so Dan could fit between them.

His hands went to her hair, her neck down to her breasts as they devoured each other. His kisses trailed hot and ready on her skin. His hand gripped her underwear, so his fingers could tease her. Her panties were soaked, and her body quivered with anticipation.

Makenna ripped her mouth away, a silent cry on her lips. One finger slid into her, then two, his thumb working her clit, spinning her into a state of bliss. She saw colors as she leaned her head against the wall and braced her hand against the mirror.

"I'm going to come, oh my fuck," she whispered, her head tilting back as she came around his fingers. When he pulled them out, he ran his tongue along his pointer finger.

"M, you taste so good."

She kissed him hard, tasting her wetness on his lips.

"Do you have anything?" Makenna asked.

"Absolutely," he said, still kissing her neck, pulling the strap of her dress to the side to reveal one of her breasts, her nipple tight. He took it between his lips, building her up again. He expertly pulled out his wallet with one hand, pinched the condom, and shook it free. His wallet landed on the ground with a thwack. If she wasn't so turned on, she would've been impressed.

"Get that thing on you," she said as she palmed him, his dick rock solid against her hand. He unbuckled his belt and pushed his pants to under his ass, freeing his cock, thick and strained. Her fingers teased him.

"I need to concentrate." Dan ripped the condom open with shaking hands. "These need to go," he said, ripping her underwear from her body and flinging it to the side.

Her body shook.

When he plunged into her, he let out a groan. "Have you been this wet all night long?"

"Ever since I felt your bicep."

Dan laughed out loud into her neck, tickling her enough to make her squirm.

"I've never been able to forget the way this feels with you," she said. She gripped his ass, her long fingernails cutting into his flesh as he drove into her. They fit perfectly, his rhythm playing her like beautiful music. The sensations whirled around her like a cyclone.

"You're going to make me come again. Fuck yes," she said as her mouth opened again into pleasure. She let go, and he followed her a beat later.

He squeezed his arms around her, smelling the crook her neck. She linked her arms around his back.

"Are you okay?"

"I just wanted a hug," Dan said. She kissed his cheek and squeezed him. She always felt right in his arms.

Dan held her until she felt him soften inside of her. He eventually anchored the condom and pulled out, letting out a heavy sigh.

Makenna pulled her strap back onto her shoulder and jumped off the sink, coughing once and approached her red lace underwear on the ground, discarded like an empty drink glass.

"You ripped them." Makenna held them up like they were evidence at a crime scene. She tucked it in the trash. "So you know, I'm not wearing underwear the rest of the night. Just like the first time."

She placed a light kiss on his cheek, and he kissed her hair, her hands settling on his shoulders. His kisses still tickled.

"We need to stagger again. You go first," Dan instructed. She opened the door and looked back. She kissed her hand and blew it toward him. He pretended like it was an imaginary butterfly to catch.

"How are you going to get home?" Addison asked with a worried look on her face.

Makenna shook her head and touched her friend's arm. "I'll be fine. Please don't worry about me."

"Okay," Addison said, a smile creeping on her face as the

guilt went away. "I'll take Kirk home, then. Ellie, do you need a ride?"

"Yes, please," Ellie said. "My sister left with the meathead."

"He has a name."

"I know. Meathead," Ellie said. "He gets the pleasure of me calling him by his name when I know for certain he is not a douchebag."

"That's fair," Makenna said.

Taylor and Malcolm had left together under mysterious circumstances, and the party had slowly dispersed after that. After having sex in the bathroom, Makenna and Dan texted each other and came to a consensus.

Dan: How does a night of my tongue between your legs sound?

Makenna: Perfect. Should I stay the night?

Dan: Absolutely.

Makenna texted her mother not to wait up, lying that she was staying at Addison's to avoid drinking and driving. Her mother had given her a yellow thumbs-up emoji in response.

Makenna: Mom is covered.

Dan: Rendezvous out back in 10.

Her breath hitched thinking about a complete night of nothing but that sexy man over her, on top of her, inside her. They kept distance until they knew the last group had gone. Caroline and Brady had left a half-hour prior.

They met around the block down by a block of homes on G Street.

Dan seized her mouth in his, locking her into a kiss she felt through her limbs and down to her toes.

"I can't wait to get you back to the Price Palace," Dan said. Makenna laughed.

After a high-end Uber took them back to Dan's place, he pulled her by the hand into his foyer, his body on hers before the door closed.

Afterward, her dress hung off her, while Dan had no shirt on and pants halfway down his ankles. They were sprawled on the tile of the laundry room.

"What's going to happen now, M?" Dan asked, kissing her dark hair.

"I'm moving back to Lillyvale."

"Oh, fuck yes," he said, kissing her with the news.

"I'll be home in a couple weeks to move some of my stuff. I have a freelance job I have to be in L.A. for, but…"

"I could take you to dinner in a couple weeks. Please," he said, nuzzling against her neck, tickling her into giggles. Her mind could not process his words and his touch at once.

"That sounds nice," Makenna said. He cupped her between her legs, and she gasped, biting his shoulder.

"I know a place in Auburn. We would be far enough away that there wouldn't be a chance of a run-in. And we can figure this out without everyone watching…"

Makenna pulled away and looked at him. He ceased his hand, looking into her eyes.

"It can be just us. No one has to know yet," Dan said.

She kissed him hard. He knew what she needed before she could even verbalize it.

11

TWO WEEKS LATER

Makenna's suitcases were half-emptied, clothes strewn all over her childhood bedroom. Her makeup covered the white bureau, as she nervously applied a second coat of blush to her cheeks.

She had no idea how she fit all this shit in her small room in Silver Lake.

She dropped her brush, and bright pink powder poofed like a smoke cloud.

"Shit!" A vibrant pink smudge clung to the white yarn. Why did her mother redo the bedrooms with white carpet after she moved out? Makenna spilled coffee at least once a week and was guilty of drinking it while she did her makeup.

Where did Mom put the stain remover? She flinched when she heard her mother walk down the hall as she searched the laundry room. She spent fifteen minutes trying to remove a highly pigmented Eloise Winston blush with less than stellar results. Her efforts finally faded it to a pale pink that she had to squint to see.

Good enough.

Dan insisted on taking her to the restaurant he told her about in Auburn, and she was freaking out. Dates usually didn't make her this nervous. Some dates felt as exciting as getting the mail.

This date, though, turned her into a thirteen-year-old again, going to meet her crush on the track because he passed her a note in class.

She sprayed her perfume and grabbed her impossibly tiny purse. She checked her hair, which she had washed for the first time in a week and styled with every trick she knew. She carefully picked out a black crop top with a magenta A-line skirt and high heels.

Maybe he would ask her to keep them on again.

Dan's car was idling at the curb when she left her house. She sat in the passenger seat, and he took her in a long kiss. They had texted constantly since she went back to L.A., but kissing him again soothed all her anxieties.

"I'm so ready to take you to one of the best-kept secrets in Placer County. Are you ready?" Dan asked, grabbing her hand on the console.

"Yep." It was just them. No pressure yet to be together in a group, no stress to label what they were. It was heavenly.

He drove twenty minutes up the freeway, holding her hand the entire time, his thumb rubbing her skin. He pulled off the freeway into Old Town Auburn by the county courthouse. They turned in a labyrinth of streets and hidden pockets. After several turns and one cursing-filled U-turn, Dan pulled into a non-descript brown strip mall.

"This is it?" Makenna asked. She stepped out to look at a row of stores with dated signs. Large pine trees and redwoods stretched to the sky, and the night had dimmed to a faint purple-pink.

"Trust me," he said, standing next to her with an arm around her waist.

He took her hand. It was warm and comforting, just like him. They approached a small restaurant, stuffed between a darkened bar and a cleaners.

The partially shattered sign read "La Scarola Family Italian."

"Are you serious, Dan?"

"As serious as a pandemic," Dan said, opening the heavy door so she could go first. "They have the best Italian food I've ever tasted. Everyone we know likes that shitty Tuscan Grove, and that's not real Italian food. But this place is legit."

There was no lobby, just a sign that said "Please Be Seated (Seat Yourself)." They weaved in between chairs to a table near the soda and busser station, the only one left. The lightening caused a sepia sheen over the unassuming square tables, adorned with a small vase of flowers. The vibe was happy, and Makenna relaxed her shoulders.

She slid into the booth side of the table and took off her coat. Dan beelining for the chair instead of the booth side of a table was somehow wildly romantic.

A friendly server appeared, took their drink orders, and disappeared.

"So," Makenna said. "We're here."

Dan crossed his arms in front of him and leaned onto the table. "I'm going to cut to the chase. I want to be with you when you move back."

"Me too," she said without a thought. She paused, pressing her palms into the table. "I want to date quietly for a bit, though. Without pressure. In the past, if there's too much pressure, I feel trapped and then I want to bolt."

"I don't want you to feel trapped," Dan said, arranging

the cloth napkin over his lap. "Everyone is so nosy about us. It's none of their goddamn business."

Makenna let out a sigh. "Exactly."

Dan nodded. "They've been relentless. I got mad at them the other day when they would not let up on you and me. Whatever goes on between us is *our* own business."

Makenna took a deep breath. "We can tell everyone when we know what this is. Who knows, this could fizzle out in weeks."

"Doubt it, but okay," he said. "What about your brother?"

"Don't worry about him."

"This will be the most secret, delicious love affair," Dan said. "I'm into it."

"Good." Her limbs loosened, every bit of nervousness washing away.

"I have to ask. Are you clean?" Dan asked.

Makenna nodded. She had gotten tested right after Spencer admitted he had cheated. "I got tested in December. I haven't been with anyone but you since then."

"Same. Clean as a whistle," he said. "Are you on the pill?"

"I can be," Makenna said. "I'll make an appointment for this week."

"I want to feel you all around my cock, bare. Are you okay with that?" His voice was dark gravel.

"Absolutely," she said. The heat rose from between her legs, flushing her already artificially painted cheeks. "I've never done it without one before."

"Get ready." Dan's smile faded, and he shook his head. "It feels amazing for me, and I have ways to make it feel good for you."

"I can't wait to find out."

The food arrived, and her mouth watered at the spaghetti and meatballs she ordered. In L.A., women together at brunch always waited to see who ordered what to one-up each other on who was healthier. They would freak if they saw her eating noodles dripping with oil and cheese. But she felt comfortable eating carbs with Dan.

She spun the noodles around her fork and put the first bite in her mouth. Her eyes widened in the flavor explosion on her tongue and her face numbed, it was so good.

This one bite of spaghetti had given her more pleasure than some of her sexual partners.

"Fun fact: you also make that same face when you climax," Dan said, taking a bite of his pollo scarpariello.

"You're right, so much better than Tuscan Grove," Makenna said, taking another big bite and rolling her eyes back in her head. "God, this is almost as good as your big dick inside of me."

"Hi Dan," a woman said with a small child trailing behind.

Oh my God. Her mouth again, getting her in trouble.

Well, start 'em young, then.

Dan coughed into his napkin. "Makenna, this is my good friend Emily Finch and her daughter, Olive." He laughed nervously.

"Pleasure to meet you," Makenna said, first shaking Emily's hand and then the little girl's.

Emily was pretty in a girl-next-door way, with straight brown hair woven in a braid over her shoulder and expressive green eyes. If she had to guess, Emily was only wearing mascara, which made Makenna jealous of her porcelain skin and perfect pink cheeks. Her daughter was her mini-me, clinging to her side. Makenna was like that when she was her age, quiet and reserved. The little girl studied her.

"Dan, we never see you around anymore. What are you doing here?" Emily said with a genuine smile. Her eyes were focused on Dan, but they flicked to Makenna.

"As you know, this is my favorite restaurant," Dan said. "My good friend Makenna is moving back to Lillyvale, and she's never been here before."

"Well, you should bring her to the brewery," Emily said.

"I like your tattoos," Olive, the little girl, blurted out, touching the spot on her right arm to where Makenna's half sleeve was. Makenna turned her arm to show the little girl.

"Wow," she said with a smile.

Maybe kids didn't hate Makenna. This little girl was adorable, and Makenna rarely thought kids were cute.

She had had a storied history with kids. She babysat exactly once, and it ended with her charge jumping from a chair and breaking her arm while Makenna was chasing her naked toddler brother. She was blacklisted from babysitting in the neighborhood after that.

"We should go up there," Dan responded to Emily's earlier question. Dan looked at Makenna. "Emily and her family own a brewery that I invested in, up 49 in Goldheart. It's a cool spot. We can go up there sometime."

"Woody Finch Brewery," Emily said. "My brother Cameron and him are like the same person."

"Except Cameron is a foot taller than me and way better-looking. Like male-model-in-underwear good-looking."

"You're good-looking, Dan," Makenna said.

"Not like that Finch fu—" Dan stopped himself in time, even though Olive wasn't paying attention—"guy!"

Emily laughed and rolled her eyes. "I'll tell Cameron."

"Mommy," Olive said, swinging her mother's hand, "I want a tattoo like hers."

"When you graduate college," Emily said, wrapping her

arm around her daughter. "It was so nice to see you, Dan. And nice to meet you..."

"Makenna," she supplied.

Emily closed her eyes, then nodded once. "I won't forget it now." Emily paused and looked straight at Makenna. "He's a good one. Grab him and never let him go."

"Mommy, I'm hungry," Olive said.

"Okay, we'll let you enjoy your meal," Emily said. She leaned down and hugged Dan. The little girl threw her body on Dan's in a hug. The hugs looked like he had spent quality time with them before. Once Emily and Olive had left the table, Dan readjusted his napkin in his lap.

Makenna's throat closed. Something panicky set over. Her old friend jealousy was back. She saw no ring on Emily's finger, and her hug looked familiar and personal.

Makenna leaned forward and lowered her voice. "Have you *slept* with her?"

"God, no," Dan said with a grumbled, nervous laugh. "Emily has *three* overprotective brothers. Makes your brother look like a newborn puppy. All three are bigger than me and would beat my ass. Brady would not kick my ass. They already have it out for Olive's dad, wherever he is."

Dan took another bite and swallowed. "The jackass told Emily he was in love with her, got her pregnant, and then he skipped town. He hasn't been back, hasn't called her. It sucks because Emily and Olive are the sweetest. Whip-smart and funny too."

Makenna paused and leaned over the table again. "Why are you so nervous?"

He fumbled with his fork. "Oh," Dan said, taking another sip of his Coors Light. "She's kind of really good friends with Caroline. Like, really good friends."

"Was she at the wedding? I don't remember her."

"She wasn't," Dan said. "Caroline invited the Finches, but they declined. Have no idea why."

"So..."

Dan dabbed his forehead with his napkin.

"I love Emily, and her heart is in the right place. However, she has a huge mouth. So, I wouldn't be surprised if she's texting Caroline like...right...now."

"Fuck," Makenna said.

"Fuck is right," Dan said. "The only thing is I don't think Emily knows anything about the speculation about us."

"What do we do?"

The server strolled by, and Dan ordered another beer and Makenna switched from wine to whiskey. Her desire to keep this secret and stress-free was slipping from her fingers.

"I did call you my good friend, which is true." Dan took his ice water and gulped it down. "It's so hot in here."

"We just need to lie our asses off then."

"Absolutely," he said. "Deny, deny, deny."

"Damn, I'll need to resist the urge to squeeze your ass on the way out of this restaurant."

"I love it when you get a little fistful of Dan ass, but not in front of Emily and Olive."

"No telling if she has a camera for these very instances to report back to Caroline. I really wonder how many people are on her payroll for all the gossip my sister-in-law collects."

"We try to start something, and we already got caught. We're terrible."

"What an auspicious start to our love affair."

"Did you say love?"

Makenna held up a finger. "Don't. That puts pressure on it."

"No pressure," Dan said. His eyebrows lifted with another sip of his Coors Light. "You did say love, though." He grinned.

"Don't get excited." She lifted her tumbler to her lips, and her lips curved upward as she took a sip of her whiskey. "Even if it isn't love, we can make love all night long."

Dan looked off to the side. Makenna studied him as he tilted his beer back.

No, he can't be in love with me. No way.

To avoid panic, Makenna decided to ignore it completely.

12

ONE MONTH LATER

"Makenna, I need to you to come down right now," Angela Brady told her daughter through her closed door. "Brady and Caroline have been here fifteen minutes."

"Coming," she said, standing up from her cross-legged position, wiping the makeup residue off her black leggings. She wound a scrunchie around her hair in a floppy topknot, and she picked a longer tank top from her dresser to pull on over her bra.

She had spent the last two hours cleaning her makeup kit and organizing, making a list of absolute necessities to replenish her kit. She had a wedding scheduled for the following Saturday, and she had just run out of the shade of foundation she had matched with the bride's spray tan.

She slowly entered a reminder on her phone, anything to avoid one extra minute with her brother and his wife.

Somehow, she had successfully avoided a family dinner with them for an entire month. She always took the Sunday evening shift at the Eloise Winston counter one town over, switching with anyone to make that shift happen. Her parents didn't question it since they had some idea of the debt pile she was under. The counter had inventory this Sunday night, and no matter how much she begged, it was only supervisors who worked.

She clomped down the stairs to see Caroline under her brother's arm, wearing a summery sundress and nude flats, a matching green Gucci purse slung over her shoulder.

She felt a pang of envy, since she used to own a blue Gucci shoulder bag too but had to sell it to a sixteen-year-old in Calabasas to pay part of her credit card off.

God, she missed that bag.

"So good to see you!" Caroline said, taking her in for a fake hug. Makenna hugged her brother as well. Caroline gave her a once-over. "You look so good."

Makenna grabbed her sloppy bun. "Thanks, but you don't mean it."

"I just meant you look like you're glowing. What skincare are you using?"

"Just some samples," she said. Makenna used to swear by Drunk Elephant, but when she ran out, she was working through all the samples she had collected from Sephora orders she'd made that she didn't need.

"Drinks?" Makenna asked. She already wanted to run away from this.

"I'll take a beer," Brady said. Makenna scampered off before Caroline could answer. She could only handle her brother and his wife in short bursts.

They kept Brady's favorite beer in the fridge in the garage. When she opened the fridge, she saw a collection of Coors Light, at the back, a stash left over from a party. Dan insisted on sneaking in the house once via ladder, almost breaking his neck. Dan had all the love languages, but acts of service always got him. When she handed him a Coors Light that night, he almost cried.

She used to think Coors Light had no flavor, but she was missing Dan, and a Coors Light sounded refreshing. She grabbed one for herself.

She popped Brady's beer open against the kitchen island like a pro and rejoined them in the living room.

"Thanks, Makenna," Brady said, taking the beer. "You're drinking Coors Light?"

"Yeah, it just sounded good," Makenna said, sitting down on the couch. Caroline looked at her like she was a monster. Shit.

"Drink, Caroline?"

"No, thank you," she said, smiling. "We're in the two-week wait."

Makenna shrugged and sipped her beer.

"I'm trying to be perfect," Caroline said. "No booze after I ovulate."

Makenna nodded. *I have literally nothing to add.*

"It's been great. I'm sleeping better than ever," Caroline said. She stood up and walked into the kitchen.

Brady leaned in. "I have never seen you drink a beer. Like ever."

"People change. I moved home," Makenna said.

"It's almost as if..." Brady trailed off. He shook his head and took a sip of his beer.

Almost like I'm sleeping with Dan Price? Makenna didn't ask for elaboration, didn't add to the conversation.

Caroline walked back to the couch with a glass of water in her hand. Caroline and Brady sat side by side, glued together like the picture of codependency.

"Did you hear?" Caroline asked. "Taylor and Malcolm stopped seeing each other."

This is sad that the only way we can relate is talking about someone we both know behind her back.

Makenna had started supplementing her weight routine with a class here or there at Taylor's studio, Cycle Yoga Love in exchange for a few social media posts. In L.A., she had loved SoulCycle, usually going with Sierra and getting brunch after. When she wasn't posting for Instagram, she picked a bike in the back, wore baggy clothes, and rode fast, draining all her energy. When Taylor taught, she always made a point to talk to Makenna, if only for a few moments.

"That's too bad," Makenna said. She took another pull of her beer.

"She kept it casual, and I think she's in denial with what it is," Caroline said. "I just hope they come to their senses. Taylor and Malcolm are meant to be together."

"Sure."

I don't like where this conversation is going.

"So, Makenna, it's been almost a month. How have you enjoyed being home?" her brother asked.

"It's been swell," she said sarcastically. "I haven't buried Mom's body in the backyard, so I consider it a success so far."

Brady's laugh broke the tension, and Makenna laughed too. His laugh had always made her burst out in hysterics. Brady knew Makenna almost didn't survive high school because she and their mother butted heads so often.

"So," Caroline said. "How is the Roseville mall counter to the one in Canoga Park?"

She is trying to sound interested. Don't jump down her throat. Don't get mad. Don't say something...

"It's fine. More people have heard of EW up here so it's busier, which I like," Makenna said. "I booked a wedding next weekend in Newcastle."

"That's great," Brady said.

"You did a beautiful job on my makeup for my wedding," Caroline said. "I'm glad you're finding freelance work up here."

"Thank you," Makenna replied. *Maybe I'm the shithead for keeping Dan a secret.* Caroline was being so nice that this was downright pleasant.

Their mother rounded the corner with a wood slab covered with meats, cheeses, olives, and some M&Ms in a tiny dish. Makenna eyed it, since she really shouldn't be eating cured meats because they made her bloat, but she loved charcuterie as much as facials.

"Oh good, I'm starving," Caroline said, pinching a piece of salami and cheese, and placed it delicately on a cracker. "Look, olives."

Makenna smiled as she remembered the adorable girl she met who had complimented her tattoos. The first kid in a long time she didn't scare or make cry. Makenna took another sip of her beer.

"Speaking of olives, I heard you met my friend, Emily."

Oh fuck.

"Oh?"

"In Auburn, at La Scarola."

She remembered Dan's words. *Deny, deny, deny.*

"I don't know what you're talking about."

"Her daughter, *Olive*, will not shut up about 'that lady's pretty tattoos.'" Caroline looked like she was a fighter being held back in an MMA match. "You were there with *Dan Price.*"

Makenna pressed her lips together. *I'm not saying a goddamn thing.*

"Don't deny it. Emily is not a liar." Caroline pointed an accusatory finger, her tone riling the hoodrat trash side of

Makenna's brain. The side that pulled hair in girl fights outside the bus stop in middle school. The side who got her suspended three times in high school for talking back to teachers.

The reason Caroline was a better daughter to Angela than Makenna ever was.

Makenna sat forward, shoving a cracker with Brie into her mouth. This conversation made her want to clear this entire spread. Anything to keep her nastiness to herself.

"So what if I was there and met Emily?" Makenna said.

"Dan was there too."

"I'm aware." She slathered another cracker with the gooey cheese and took a bite.

"Why were you in Auburn with Dan, Makenna?"

"That's the only place to get decent Italian around here. With a friend who appreciates good Italian," Makenna said. *A friend who I fucked twice this morning.*

"She said you were acting *cozy.*"

"Honey bun, let up on Makenna," Brady said. "If Makenna said she's just friends with Dan, she's just friends."

Makenna could count on one hand the number of times she had felt bad about lying. This added another finger. Definitely the middle one.

"Thank you, Brady," Makenna said.

Caroline shrugged off that comment. "I don't know why you are denying it when it's perfectly clear that you're dating him. You're dating him. Are you in love with him?"

Makenna's cheeks grew hot. *Don't let the hoodrat come out, don't let it.*

"He is my friend. I'm having a hard time transitioning home from L.A., and he understands since he's from there. We just don't like that shitty Tuscan Grove so we went up the hill to have the best Italian food I have ever had." She was still okay. This hadn't gotten out of control.

"I agree, Tuscan Grove is kinda bad," Brady said.

"Honey bun," Caroline said, giving a look. "You know how I feel about Tuscan Grove."

Brady shrunk in his seat, grabbing a few pieces of pepperoni and tearing each one with his teeth.

Even her own brother wasn't allowed to stick up for her.

"Why won't you believe me?" Makenna asked. The lie flowed a little too easily. "Why the fuck are you so nosy, Caroline?"

Caroline's mouth hung open, then snapped closed, like a pet store fish.

"Dan is a good friend of mine. I want to know if you're going to hurt him," she said. "I wonder if you're leading him on by being friends. If you had sex, then..."

Dan had made Makenna watch *Inside Out* the other day, and Makenna's little anger monster's fire hair encompassed the whole room.

Oh, she wants to play.

Makenna stood up with a tight mouth and a somewhat shaky stance. Her voice came out as a scream. "You have no right to my personal business or who I spend my time with and in what capacity. Dan is a grown-ass man who can make his own decisions. I'm a grown-ass woman. We are friends. That's fucking it. So you need to shut your fucking mouth, Caroline. You are in my house right now."

"This isn't your house. It's your *parents'* house," Caroline shot back, pointing at the table. Tears filled her eyes. "A house your parents are letting you stay while you get your life together."

Makenna should go outside to cool off. Should.

"You're so high and mighty with your Gucci bag and

Tory Burch sandals. Wasn't it just last year you begged me to do your wedding for free since you were so broke when you switched jobs? Didn't Brady support you?"

"That's low, Makenna," Brady said. "You both need to calm down."

"Don't tell me to calm down, *Ethan*." When she called him by his given first name, she was asking for a fight.

"That's it," Brady said, standing up, walking to Makenna. "You need to come outside with me, right now."

"Why?" Makenna asked.

"Come on," Brady said, reaching out for her arm. Makenna ripped it away and walked to the sliding glass door.

Once the door was closed, Makenna walked to the other side of the pool and sat down on a lounge chair. The pool was still covered, but not for long. Her parents' pool was the best part of this house.

"Why were you like that in there?"

"Your wife is so fucking nosy."

"Yeah," Brady agreed, surprising her. "It's not her best trait."

"Are you scared of her?" Makenna asked. "Does she keep your balls in her Gucci?"

Brady rubbed his bald head. "I can neither confirm nor deny. You were really harsh in there. What's going on?"

"She put me down for being home, getting my life together," Makenna said, crossing her arms. "I have one friend in Lillyvale, and she acts like I'm out to destroy him."

Although I worry about doing that very thing every day.

"I'm glad you have a friend," Brady said, sitting down next to her. "I know it's not the easiest for you." His hand came to her knee in a brotherly pat.

"Dan is just a friend," Makenna insisted. *He may be my best friend besides Sierra.*

"I just hope Lillyvale will be good for you. Maybe it'll help steer you to the life you're meant to have."

She rolled her eyes. "You sound like an inspirational poster."

"It doesn't make it any less true. I just really want you to succeed."

"Thank you, Brady." She patted him on his knee in return.

"Please don't call me Ethan ever again, though." Brady wrapped his arm around her and pushed her hair away. He kissed her temple and squeezed her. "No more fighting today."

"Promise," Makenna said. "As long as she doesn't start shit again."

Brady pressed into the lounge chair to stand up. He walked a few feet and turned around. "When you say friends, you mean completely platonic? Since Taylor and Malcolm were supposedly 'special friends' or some shit like that. I mean, none of my friends who were girls ever wanted to sleep with me."

Makenna bit her lip. She could come clean, admit that her screaming match with Caroline was for nothing. That she was, in fact, sleeping with Dan Price multiple times a week, sometimes multiple times in a night.

Her brother, who rarely had her back when they were teenagers, believed her. Believed that she'd turned a corner, that her honesty was still intact. That she wasn't a liar.

If she admitted to lying to her brother, he would think she was back to her old ways. They had *just* had a moment, a rare one, where he didn't look at her like his wild, uncontrollable sister.

"Just friends," Makenna said.

"Good," Brady said. "I just hope Caroline hasn't started sobbing. This 'trying to have a baby' thing is wearing her down."

He walked off, and Makenna walked the perimeter of the pool. She leaned against the shed, out of view from the sliding glass doors, and pulled out her phone.

Her thumbs flew over the keys and then deleted. She tried again and deleted.

She eventually sent the message.

Makenna: I just lied to my brother and yelled at Caroline.

He responded immediately.

Dan: How did that go?

Makenna: Not well.

Dan: Tell me everything. Come over tomorrow?

Makenna: Absolutely.

13

FIVE MONTHS LATER

"I t's the third Thursday of the month," Dan said, pulling up the app. "You know what that means."

"Cheat day!" Makenna cheered from the couch.

"Exactly," he said. "What do you want on the pizza?"

"You." Makenna lifted an eyebrow.

"Tempting, but no. We will not be spreading pizza sauce all over my body like last month," Dan said. "That was an expensive doctor's bill."

Makenna snorted. "I'm sorry, baby."

Baby. His heart warmed when she called him that. It slipped out once six weeks ago, and now it stuck. Dan still called her M, but calling her "baby" just fit better now.

"Should I get the breadsticks or the dessert pizza? Or both?"

"It's your cheat day," Makenna said. "Go wild."

"We can't get both or I will hate myself. I already got Dunkin Donuts this morning. Breadsticks it is," Dan said. "And half Hawaiian and half pepperoni and sausage."

"Delicious," Makenna replied. He knew pineapple on

pizza was controversial, but when she said she liked it, he felt like he found his soulmate.

Dan lifted his shirt, showing her his abs, tracing the crevices he worked and dieted for. "This is about to become a potbelly of delicious calories."

"You look really good, baby," Makenna said. "Seriously. You've lost so much weight. But there is a small part of me who misses soft Dan."

"If you want me to gain those fifteen pounds back, just say the word. More pizza for me," he said. She giggled as he lifted her shirt, knowing what was about to come next. A big, childish raspberry on her stomach, right next to her belly button ring. It always made her lose it.

"You love the six-pack," Dan said. "Admit it. Or I'll do it again."

"I love it. I want to run my tongue up and down it."

"Later. But first, I plan to stuff my piehole with so much pizza, I'm going to sweat profusely," he said, standing up, punching in a few buttons. "Done. It's ordered."

"Perfect," Makenna said. She turned toward him, an arm on the back of the couch. "I love this."

"Me, you love me?" he asked. He waited for her response. She just smiled.

Fuck.

"Hanging out on the couch. Getting takeout. Chillin'. In L.A., it was just go-go-go. I don't know how many parties I went to, how many openings I attended, and they just drained me. I'm realizing nights on the couch with you are my most favorite thing."

"I hear you," he said, jumping over the back of the couch, wrapping an arm around her. "I love hanging out with you too. It's like our own little love bubble."

"Exactly," she said, kissing him quickly. "The sex isn't half-bad, either."

"Hey," Dan said, tickling under her armpit. She squirmed away from his prodding fingers. He pushed her hair away from her face. Lately, she had been coming over to his house with no makeup on, and she was so beautiful without it. Freckles dusted her nose, and her hazel eyes popped without all black to overpower them. When he touched her cheek, he didn't feel the makeup, just the smoothness of her bare skin. Her lips were tinged pinky red with cherry lip gloss that Dan secretly had his own tube of. It tasted like Twizzlers.

They rolled off the couch onto the floor.

"Ow," Dan said with a laugh at the impact of the ground against his skull.

"I'm sorry, baby," she said, laughing, hovering over him, upside down. Her hair hung down around him, the magenta streak in her hair in front. He had learned all the facets of her face, the way her eyes crinkled when she smiled, how she had a small dimple in her left cheek. The scar of a Monroe piercing next to her nostril. How her two front teeth had a tiny gap between them.

The inevitable had happened. He was in love with her.

But he knew from her history and his that it was best to keep *that* to himself.

She kissed him, tracing his beard with her pointer finger. "I don't feel lonely when I'm with you."

His hand reached up to touch her shoulder as she kissed him again, more tender this time.

"Do you feel lonely when you're *not* with me?" Dan asked.

Makenna broke eye contact, looking at the carpet. She nodded.

"I've started hanging out with Addison, but it's sporadic. Sierra is in weird time zones all the time so she's not always awake when I am. And there's Holden too."

Holden, Makenna's ex-boyfriend from high school. A guy Dan shouldn't be jealous of, but he definitely was.

"I need to have a talk with Holden."

"He is completely respectful," Makenna said. "We're buddies, I swear. I don't want to have sex with him. I only want to have sex with you. All the time."

She lowered her head for a peck.

"As long as Holden keeps his hands to himself. If he declares his love for you, run."

"And what about all your female friends, huh? Every day, there's a new girl texting you."

"I can't help it if I've always had more female than male friends," he said. "Ralph the Raccoon for life."

Makenna pulled back her head in a surprise face. "Ralph the Raccoon?"

"I was the mascot at my high school, and I would practice with the cheerleaders. My high school loved me, but guys thought I was too feminine. Little did they know, I was infiltrating."

"You got laid a lot in high school, didn't you?"

"All the time," he said, closing his eyes.

"Me too, but it was a little less celebrated."

"I bet you were wild in high school."

"Too wild." She sat back, combing her hair away from her face. "It's why I just have Holden left. If I didn't steal a boyfriend, I had a falling-out with each friend I had from high school."

"We've all done things we regret. Come here." He sat up on his floor and enveloped her in a hug. She climbed onto his lap, facing him, wrapping her legs around him with her arms. It was moments like this that he didn't mind that they were seeing each other in secret, since these moments were so sweet.

It killed him that she was so lonely, that she didn't have anyone else she could talk to. It honored him that he was her person.

"Do we have enough time?" she asked, reaching between them, grabbing his cock through his lounge pants. He moaned, her hand cupping his junk with confident pressure.

"I don't think so," Dan said. "The pizza...will...be... here...soon."

She pulled her hand out, like she was caught stealing. "Pizza time is sacred."

"I'll take care of your body later. Let's see if I'm strong enough now to pick you up. Hold on." He pressed his hand into the couch cushion to stand up, while Makenna clung to him like a koala. He stood up, one hand under her ass, bracing his other hand for leverage. It was awkward, but he made it.

"I did it," he said, his breath heavy and ragged. She slid down his body to her feet.

"Good job," she said. "Drink?"

"Beer me," Dan said. Makenna walked to his fridge like she lived there, opening the door to retrieve his cheat day drink. She grabbed one for herself, holding two cold cans in her hand.

Her ease around his house made his dick hard. He could imagine her living here full-time, instead of the two or three nights a week she spent. She had her own toothbrush and own drawer, her own towel and washcloth.

He didn't think she could get any sexier, but she started drinking Coors Light with him once in a while.

One night, as a surprise, she wore a Coors Light tank top to bed with nothing else, her nipples hard against the gray fabric.

They clinked cans and took the first sip. He had missed it. Beer wasn't on the new diet.

"There's the beer tear," Makenna said.

"I just missed it so much," he said, cuddling it with fake sobbing and face-scrunching.

Dan's phone buzzed. He usually didn't answer it when Makenna was over. When he saw who was calling, he showed it to her.

"Answer it," she said.

He clicked answer button and putting the phone to his ear. "Hi Dad."

"Hi son," Matt Price said. The connection was terrible; it sounded like his dad was underwater. "How are you doing?"

"Great," he replied. Makenna draped her legs over his lap, leaning back on the couch against his pile of pillows. He rubbed her ankle.

"I wanted to see if you could come out to the farm to hang out this weekend," his dad asked, the phone crackling.

"It's Thursday. It's kind of late notice," Dan said. "I have tickets this weekend."

"To what?"

"A country concert. My company is sponsoring it so I have to go," Dan said. Makenna's brow crinkled at that news.

"Oh, that sounds fun," his dad said, his voice dejected. "Well, maybe another time then."

"Absolutely," he said. "What about next weekend or next month?"

"I'll have to check my calendar," Matt said. He grumbled something and hung up.

Dan pulled the phone away from his ear.

"Did he want you come last minute again?" Makenna asked.

Dan rested his hand on her knee. "I don't hear from him for months, and then he calls me out of nowhere to come visit. He doesn't give me any notice; it's just 'drop everything and come visit me.' I can't remember the last time he came to see us. He didn't suggest another day or time."

Makenna knew the basics—that he barely talked to his dad, but he'd get a random phone call here or there to go out to his farm in the middle of Nevada with no notice.

"That sucks baby. I'm sorry." Makenna paused. "Why did your dad leave?"

"My parents didn't get along. My dad is a lot like me—he's a dreamer, kind of all over the place, and my mom is the logical one. They butted heads a lot. My little brother Nick was an oops baby, and it was the last straw. He left before Nick turned one. I was in high school, and Sam, my big brother, was away at school. My dad is a big topic in therapy."

Makenna froze. "You go to therapy?"

"Every week. Bernice is everything to me. I met her at a chamber mixer. I've been seeing her for two years now."

"Wow, that's great," Makenna said. "I need to go to therapy. I don't have the money, though. I was seeing this fantastic therapist in Silver Lake, but rent became more important."

"You're living with your parents now. You could start up again."

"I guess," Makenna said. "It's just so expensive."

Dan tapped his temple. "It's worth it to keep the noggin in tip-top shape."

"Is Bernice taking new clients?" Makenna asked.

Dan thought about the hours he had spent discussing

her with Bernice. "Oh no. She knows too much. You can't see her."

"You've talked about me in therapy?"

The doorbell rang. *Thank you, Door Dash.*

He opened the door, receiving the pizza and kicking the door closed. Makenna had already pulled out plates and napkins, placing them on the coffee table. She clicked the remote to Hulu and found the show they were currently in the middle of.

His favorite show of all time, *The Golden Girls.*

Much like therapy and Makenna, he kept his love for this show a secret. Spouting random jokes from the show as a teenager created a cheesecake-shaped bullseye on his back.

Dan fed his feelings about his conversation with his dad with grease and cheese.

"I love how seriously you take pizza cheat day."

"It's sacred," he said, popping crust into his mouth. He alternated between breadsticks and pizza until his stomach protruded over his new two-sizes-smaller pants.

"I don't think you're ready for this sexiness," he said, rubbing his round stomach with both hands, bending his legs and swaying his hips back and forth like an unenthusiastic stripper.

"I have you beat," she said, pulling up her stomach, turning to the side. Her stomach barely rounded; she had to arch her back to get any kind of belly volume. In a flash, he imagined her pregnant with his baby, growing week by week. Hearing the baby's heartbeat. Giving him a chance to be the kind of dad his own father never was.

Mark that down for next week's therapy session.

Dan walked over and touched his stomach to hers like

they were wearing sumo suits. "Is this our new mating dance?"

"I think so. There's a ninety-three percent chance you will get laid later because of it," Makenna said. He sat down, and she kissed the top of his head. She cleaned up the plates and greasy napkins, folding the lid back over the pizza box. After she walked to the kitchen, she rinsed the plates and stood them up in the dishwasher.

It honestly felt like she lived here.

Dan didn't mention that Bernice constantly bugged him to say what he wanted to Makenna, that he wanted to go out in public with her, be a real couple. They discussed all of his fears—that she would break up with him, that she would say no.

So, every week, he reported back that he had not said anything to her. That they were still a secret, that they were still unlabeled. It had been this way for five months.

He just remembered how he had said "I love you" to Zoey and then lost her. And Makenna meant more to him than Zoey ever had. Dan couldn't lose her yet.

"Are you coming to the concert with me?" Dan asked.

"Aren't my brother and Caroline going? And Addison and Kirk?" Makenna asked, wiping the counter with a sponge.

"Yes," Dan said. "But they have lawn seats so there isn't a chance we'll run into them. Addison and Kirk have dates so Caroline will be too busy watching them."

Dan had been beta testing his new business venture, Happily Lillyvale After, a matchmaking service, and Addison was one of his participants. Now that Taylor and Malcolm were happily back together and dating, Dan had been deliberately setting her up with guys who weren't quite right. All so her best friend, Kirk, who was staying with

Addison, would come to his senses and realize he was in love with her. He was finally single, having ended his ten-year relationship to some woman in New York.

He had set up dates for Kirk and Addison for the country music festival, Sydney and Curtis. He had told Sydney and Curtis separately that if they didn't hit it off with their dates, they could see if each other would work.

"Where are your seats?" Makenna asked.

"Front row."

Makenna stopped wiping. "Really?"

"Yep. I'm a sponsor. I might've sponsored extra so I could have those seats."

Makenna stopped. "You know I love live music. Even if it's country."

Dan stood up from the couch and walked over. He wrapped his arms around her waist, pressing his cheek to her back. Makenna loved metal, Metallica, Ghost, Tool. His head hurt when he drove with her and it was her chance to pick the music. "I know you usually like screaming singers and drum solos, but please come with me. It will be fun."

She spun around into his arms. "I'll come."

"Really?" Dan asked. She nodded and leaned down, kissing him deeply. The pizza grease still coated their lips. He dipped to pick her up like his cowboy princess. A real date. A chance to hold Makenna in fresh air, around crowds of people. Not tucked away, constantly eating takeout and watching TV at home. He loved it, but he also needed to get out of this house with her.

Dan bounced her in his arms.

"It's time to show you my bucking bronco," he said.

"Oh really?" she said. "Ride me, cowboy."

He kissed her as he headed upstairs with her in his arms.

14

TWO DAYS LATER

Makenna looked around the concert venue, giddy with excitement at the pulse of the crowd. God, she loved live music.

There were so many people everywhere, and her shoulders relaxed. The lawn seats were so far away, on the opposite end of the venue. There was no way she would run into her brother and sister-in-law or Addison and Kirk, unless they came looking for Dan.

All the nervousness she had floated away.

Dan had walked her to the front row, holding her hand the entire time. No one looked at them or paid any mind.

When they reached their seats, he kissed her. "I have to go meet the dates. I'll be right back."

Waiting for a concert alone reminded Makenna of all the shows she used to go to in L.A.. She frequently went by herself, and that was how she'd met a lot of men, including Spencer. She never meant to meet them; she was only there for the music. She usually wore baggy clothing and a hat to shield herself.

Country concerts were a totally different animal.

Sierra loved country concerts and had always demanded they wear revealing attire—short shorts, cowgirl boots, midriff-baring tops. Pulling out those clothes from the bottom of her bureau made her miss her best friend, their nights together in L.A. She was the only person who understood her, truly. Well, until Dan came along.

When she'd arrived to drive with him, Dan looked her up and down in her magenta cowgirl boots and short shorts. "You look like the kind of girl country artists write songs about."

"I guess that's a compliment?"

"Definitely," he said, taking her in his arms and gripping her neck to kiss her.

Six months of dating was a record for Makenna. Spencer had been on-and-off for two years, broken by weeks of not speaking to each other. They never made it more than three months in a stretch before someone screamed and ended it. Adrian proposed at four months as a whirlwind courtship that hadn't gotten completely out of control. Craig got down on one knee at three months.

Dan was the healthiest, longest relationship she had ever had, and it scared her.

"Makenna Brady?"

She turned to see her best-friend-turned-nemesis from high school.

"Piper?" she said, taking her in for a one-armed hug. In high school, Piper had blonde hair just like the rest of her fake friends, but now it was a pale pink color, perfect with the smoothness of her barely made-up face. Makenna had two shades of foundation mixed with two types of concealer to mask the dark circles from all the nights she'd stayed over at Dan's house.

"What are you doing here? I didn't know you were home," Piper said.

"I moved back," Makenna said.

Piper's sympathy face could use some work. "Oh, so L.A. didn't work out?"

"Nope."

"You look great. I see you got tattoos. They're really pretty."

Makenna looked at her covered arm. "Yeah, I've been collecting them."

Piper stood awkwardly, looking around. Her fingers pinned a folded piece of paper.

"Did you see a short guy wearing all black and a cowboy hat?"

Dan? "No, I didn't," Makenna said with creased eyebrows.

"Hey Piper," Dan said, his hands on his hips. "Do you two know each other?"

"Do *you* know each other?" Makenna asked.

"What's going on here?" Piper asked. Her mouth gaped open, looking from Dan to Makenna and back again. "Are you ....? How?"

Fuck secrecy. This bitch needed to know Dan was absolutely not available. "He gives the best cunnilingus in the state," Makenna said.

Dan blushed, and flicked his hand. "Oh, you."

Piper's fair skin burned red. "That's so great. Dan was always an overachiever."

Has this bitch sampled Dan? Don't reach for your earrings, Makenna.

"Yeah, he is," Makenna said. She wrapped her arm around Dan, squeezing his butt. Dan's lips pursed with a smirk.

"Oh, you have the wrong idea. We never..."

"No, never," Dan added. "Do you have that thing, Piper?"

"Yeah," she said, handing the piece of paper. "I was hoping to talk to you privately, Dan, if that's okay." Piper bit her lip and kicked the dirt with her boots.

"Sure," Makenna said, leaning down to kiss Dan passionately. He flinched when Makenna used tongue, his own tongue surprised and frozen. She considered grabbing his cock, but she supposed that would be a little much. She wiped her mouth when she pulled away. "I'll get you a beer."

Annoyance followed Makenna as she climbed the amphitheater stairs to the beer stand. She looked around, balancing on her heels as she waited. If Addison or Caroline appeared, she was fully prepared to reveal herself, her relationship with Dan. Everything.

If their relationship wasn't public knowledge, of course women would be interested in him.

How many women hit on him? Should she be worried?

"Two Coors Lights," she said, handing the vendor her credit card. He handed her the beers in plastic cups. "Thanks."

She walked down the stairs, back to the front row. The stage crew scurried around the stage, doing last-minute sound checks for the first act. Dan took one of the beers and wrapped an arm around her. Makenna looked down, unable to meet his eyes.

What did Piper have to talk to him about? Why was it private?

Worst-case scenarios raced through her head. Makenna felt like a different person being home all these months, being with Dan, like she was coming closer to the person she was meant to be. Forgiving herself. She wasn't the same piece of shit who broke hearts, led guys on just to dump them, sometimes publicly. She no longer slapped people at parties either. Piper had once been the recipient of one of her slaps at a house party off of Baseline in Roseville.

"What did Piper have to talk to you about?" Makenna asked.

"Oh, she just brought me some paperwork." Dan pulled a folded piece of paper from his back pocket. "She wants in on Happily Lillyvale After."

"She's still single?" Makenna remembered that she'd always had a boyfriend, even dating someone seriously senior year, telling everyone she was going to marry him.

"Yep. She was engaged but ended it somewhat recently. Now she's thirsty," Dan said, tucking the piece of paper back into his jeans. "You two were weird."

"Weird," Makenna said with a fake laugh. "No."

"You were all territorial over me, which was so hot." He pulled her to him, pressing his erection to her. If there weren't so many witnesses...

Makenna draped her arms over his shoulders. "I needed her to know that you're my man."

"I'm always yours. However, I need to know why you were about to grab her hair."

Dan leaned his forehead against hers. "Spill."

"She dated Holden right after me," Makenna started. "Remember, this was high school."

"I feel like this story is juicy, and I'm here for it. Do I need popcorn?"

"No," she said. "So, Holden was a virgin and we broke up, and then Piper started seeing Holden behind my back. We were best friends."

"This all sounds very familiar." Caroline had started

seeing Brady after Zoey broke up with him. It was one of the things that always rubbed Makenna the wrong way about Caroline. How she could just follow her vagina without any thought for her friend.

Makenna was all for following one's vagina, but girl code was sacred, stronger than bro code, by leaps and bounds. According to Makenna, female friendship shouldn't survive a boyfriend theft.

"She took Holden's virginity and then dumped him. Publicly."

"The drama," Dan said, sipping his beer.

"So Holden and I hate her with a fiery passion now."

"If we got them in the same place, they would probably fuck again. Guarantee it."

"You don't understand, baby," Makenna said. "He *hates* her. Holden is a big teddy bear, but if you betray him, you're dead to him."

"We'll see about that." Dan lifted his eyebrows and straightened his mouth. "So, someone knows. About us."

Makenna crossed her arms and looked off. Dan snuggled into her, the hat bumping into her shoulder.

"Piper doesn't count," she said.

"When are we going to tell everyone else?" Dan asked.

Makenna ground her boot into the dirt and kicked a rock. "Not right now."

"Why not?"

"Because." *I don't want people telling you how you could do better. How I've done some shit things. How I'm not good enough for you. You'll leave me. Or I'll be scared and leave you.*

Boy, did she need to go back to therapy.

"I'm proud to be with you. I want everyone to know it. All these men are looking at me like I'm a god."

"Good job, man. She's a smoke show," a guy next to Dan said, pounding fists with him.

"See!" Dan said.

"It's not the right time," Makenna said, looking at the stage.

"Look at me, Makenna. Please." She looked at him, her eyes filling up. Sometimes she wondered why a man like Dan would be with her. He had seen her hungry, hormonal, bitchy, cold. He liked her anyway. She had no idea why.

But she knew he was going to come to his senses eventually. She might be pretty on the outside, but her insides were gnarls and thorns, her heart locked in by steel. It came from years of defenses built up to protect herself. Friends left her when they said they wouldn't. Men treated her like nothing, so when she got around a good one, she left them before they could leave her.

Before they realized the kind of person she was.

The reason it was going so well with Dan was because it was in private, away from prying eyes and whispering critiques. No one was pulling Dan aside, telling him how fucked in the head she was, how he should run. Her own brother even told him to when he thought there was some mild interest.

How would they react when it came out they were dating for real?

"Why can't we tell everyone?" Dan asked. His hands were on her arms, looking at her like he wanted to understand everything. "Are you ashamed of me?"

"No, absolutely not," Makenna said. "I promise. We'll tell everyone. I just can't handle it right now."

Dan looked at her, *really* looked at her. Sometimes, the way he saw her scared her. He seemed to understand her better than she ever knew herself.

"I'll give you all the time in the world," he said, bringing her hand to his lips. "So I'm really the best cunnilingus in the state?"

"Absolutely."

15

"Wow, this place is so nice," Addison said, looking around Cork & Barrel, the newest cocktail lounge in Lillyvale. Makenna smiled to herself as she watched her sweet friend take in the décor in awe.

"This is my new favorite spot," Makenna told her. "They have some delicious craft cocktails on the menu and a nice wine list for you."

Addison looked like Makenna told her she'd won a free trip to Disneyland.

Dan encouraged Makenna to call Addison, although she initially expressed hesitation. Addison was Caroline's friend, not hers, even if they went to coffee and hiked together sometimes. And Caroline was currently on Makenna's shit list.

"You can be my spy and figure out why she and Kirk haven't boned yet," Dan had said.

"You don't know they haven't fucked."

"Kirk dropped a liquid creamer in the breakroom and it exploded this week. The jokes about ejaculation write themselves. He is definitely not getting laid. I need him to get laid before he freaks out. Addison and Kirk are made for each other," Dan said. "I know you can do it."

"I'm not sure. She's really busy now with school, and she might not have time."

"Addison is your friend, you know. She would totally get a drink with you."

That was how Makenna got here, with Addison. Addison looked adorable in a dress with sneakers, while Makenna felt out of place in a classy wine bar in pleather leggings and a cropped metal T-shirt. She offered to get the drinks while Addison snagged a table. Since Dan invested in Cork & Barrel, all she had to say at the bar was to put it on Dan's tab.

Makenna had learned long ago that Dan had tabs *everywhere,* and it meant free.

"So you're the girl he keeps going on about," the bartender said with a curious look. He poured a hefty glass of wine for Addison and mixed a perfect old-fashioned for Makenna. He slid the drinks over the bar. "Dan is a lucky man."

I'm the lucky one.

Makenna transported the drinks over to Addison, who immediately asked about her. "How has it been? Living at home?"

"It's been fine, I guess. It's nice not having to worry about rent since I'm staying with my folks. Still, I miss my own space. And not having to deal with Caroline so often. Jesus."

Addison's expression, as usual, was unreadable. Makenna cursed to herself. She shouldn't have brought it up.

Makenna had missed dinner with Brady and Caroline again at her parents' house, taking a last-minute Sunday shift. Caroline had texted her, asking if she was going to see Dan instead. She had also mentioned Dan to Makenna's mom, so she was getting suspicious too.

"You shouldn't be seeing anyone. You should be getting your life in order," her mother told her. "We're letting you live here rent-free. I don't want you to get so wrapped up in a guy that you forget everything. We might not let you stay here if you fall into old patterns."

"I'm not seeing anyone," she had lied.

"I know you don't sleep here every night," her mom said. "I'm not stupid."

Thus was the end of sleepovers at Dan's house.

It became high school all over again. Dan continued to risk bodily injury to climb in her window, since he was a big fan of *Dawson's Creek*. Thank God the neighbors hadn't seen, by some miracle, or they would call the very-bored Lillyvale Police Department. Even that was starting to get iffy.

"We did see you at the concert with Dan," Addison said, taking a sip of wine.

Oh, fucking hell. Act cool. They probably didn't see anything of note.

"You and Caroline?" Makenna asked. Addison nodded.

Fuck, fuck, fuck.

"She's so nosy. Dan and I are *friends*," Makenna said. *If by "friend," you mean I can't stop having sex with him.* "His date bailed on him at the last minute, and he had a free front-row ticket. I'm not a country person, but I went and had a great time. Because we're buddies."

The lie manifested quicker than was comfortable. Addison looked at her with understanding, with belief. It made the pit of her stomach drop.

"Well, we did see you kiss Dan on the cheek," Addison said.

Makenna dropped her head in her hands. She used her one drama class in L.A. to summon nonchalance, indifference.

"So?"

"So, it looks like you're friendly."

You could tell Addison right now. She wouldn't tell anyone.

Then, she remembered Addison was Caroline's cousin, her best friend since birth. They grew up together and played together and did everything together. If someone was lying to Sierra and Makenna found out, she would tell her. Since Caroline definitely talked to Makenna's mother more than Makenna did, it could get back to her family.

Makenna had been kicked out once, she could be kicked out again.

Just admit you kissed him, but play it off, she coached herself.

"Yes. I literally kiss everyone. I'll kiss you right now," she said.

"No, I'm okay. Even though I really like you," Addison said. She took a sip of her wine with hunched shoulders. Her smile didn't return when she set down the glass.

Time to change the subject.

"Let's not talk about Dan and talk about you. You seem down."

Addison told her about a guy who rescheduled, a guy Makenna knew wasn't right for her. "What about Kirk?" she asked.

Addison blushed and her eyelashes fluttered. Makenna knew that look. It was Addison's version of pure animal lust. It was refreshing to see someone so shy about sex when Makenna usually jumped on a dick at the first opportunity she had.

They chatted about sleeping with Kirk, how it wouldn't

devastate their friendship. Makenna tried to be convincing, but Addison was getting in her own way. Maybe it would ruin their friendship, since Makenna knew sex could change everything, Yes, she still liked Instagram posts from guys she had slept with, but she wasn't buddy-buddy with them.

Makenna constantly wondered how her life would've been different if she hadn't slept with Dan at her brother's wedding. Probably still miserable in L.A., dating assholes to avoid breaking nice guys' hearts.

Addison grew in confidence over their chat, eventually sitting up straight and saying, "It's time to start asking for what I want."

"Exactly," Makenna said.

Makenna spotted him before Addison did.

Here we go. Makenna kicked back the rest of her drink as a douchebag approached the table. She knew that look. Addison probably wasn't used to slimy men's advances, but Makenna sure was. This man was up to no good.

"Hello ladies," he said.

"Hi!" Addison said brightly. *Oh, she's so sweet and naïve.*

This guy had HPV written all over him. His eyes leered over Addison, who was completely oblivious.

Showtime.

"Can I help you?" Makenna asked.

The man flinched at Makenna's stern, take-no-shit tone. *I can't wait to see this man crumble.*

"I just saw two hot girls by themselves and thought I would come say hi. Wonder if either of you are in the mood for some fun tonight. At my place."

Makenna rolled her eyes. The brazen, oblivious nature of this advance boiled her blood. But Addison, shockingly, looked more pissed than Makenna.

"Sir, with all due respect, we are women, not girls. With brains and hearts. We are more than just 'hot girls.' How would you feel if someone approached your little sister like that?"

He disappeared completely. Makenna looked at Addison with awe. Usually, men stayed to banter angrily with her, some sick invitation to stay, to argue, to get her to hate-fuck them.

Addison had destroyed that man better than she ever could.

Addison's words also slid into her stomach like decadent ice cream. Sometimes, people only saw her exterior, tough and callous, but forgot that she could be sweet, that she could care. That she had a brain.

"Addison! I'm so impressed. You did better than I could've."

Addison pulled her shoulders back, wiggling her head in satisfaction.

"You don't have to tell Kirk you're in love with him or anything, but maybe tell him point-blank what you want. You know you can do it. Or kiss him and figure it out later."

"Not in love with him," Addison said. "Just sexually attracted to him."

"Yes!" Makenna said, although *bullshit, bullshit, bullshit* ran through her brain. Addison had been in love with Kirk forever, she just didn't want to admit it. Kirk was moving back to New York soon, his time in Lillyvale temporary, and she knew it made it easier for Addison to ignore the feelings, since it would hurt too much if he picked New York.

Makenna's thoughts drifted to Dan, and a calm washed over her. Makenna rarely felt calm; she was always on edge, whether it was about money or job insecurity or housing insecurity. Being in Lillyvale, hanging out with Addison, being with Dan—it was the first time in her life she had felt at peace.

Addison still expressed hesitation on telling Kirk what she really wanted. Makenna couldn't be frustrated with her.

When Addison told her she loved her, it warmed her insides. She said it back without fumbling over her words or questioning whether she did or not. Lately, love had been on her mind. Every time she was with Dan, every time she thought about him.

There was a high probability that Makenna was in love with Dan.

No, she was *definitely* in love with him.

So, Makenna totally got why Addison didn't want to say anything. Fear was a powerful obstacle to happiness. If she never said it, she didn't label it. It didn't make it that much more delicate, breakable.

Makenna didn't trust herself with precious things.

16

LATER THAT DAY

Dan opened the door to find Makenna, looking sexy as hell in a cropped Metallica shirt and leather leggings.

Her hair was in a braid. That meant only one thing.

You can do this, Dan telepathically communicated with his dick.

"I'm so horny. I hope you're ready," she said, charging inside and slamming Dan's front door behind her.

"Good evening to you too," Dan said as she pulled his shirt over his head. Their kisses were feverish as he pulled hers off too, his favorite lace bra of hers cutting across her cleavage. He pulled down one strap and then the other, devouring her breasts.

"No worshipping, just fucking," she said, unhooking her bra.

This kind of sex happened at least once a month, and it always meant Dan would need incredible mental power to last longer than thirty seconds.

When they were naked, Makenna spun around so her

ass was against his cock, which was growing with anticipation. "Fuck me hard."

"Bend over, you greedy woman," he said in her ear, then caught her earlobe between his teeth. She sunk to her knees on his carpet, among the battlefield of their clothes. He pulled out his emergency lube stashed in one of his side tables. He had cleaned three different Target locations out of this warming lube. Bottles were stashed all over the place, since he was never sure where sex would happen. They had hit every surface and room; at last count, there were twenty-three bottles of lube in his house.

He rubbed lube all over his dick and pushed two lubed fingers inside her, causing a laugh from Makenna. He positioned his bare cock at her entrance and eased in, slowly at first. He grabbed her braid and pulled. She moaned in response.

"Oh fuck yes, deeper."

He took her words as an open-ended invitation, sinking his cock deeper in and out of her so hard his hips clapped against her. He rubbed her clit in long, slow strokes, in direct opposition to the quick and dirty thrusting into her pussy. He gripped her braid harder, and Makenna's head pulled back, her panting and cries all the feedback he needed.

Her pussy was so tight around his cock, the sex so hot, he had to do all of his tricks to make himself not blow his load right away.

Lately, Makenna's sex sounds had grown so loud, he worried his neighbors thought he was murdering her. Best-case scenario was jealousy. He tugged at her hair more, pulling with slightly more pressure so she cried out as an orgasm ripped through her. He felt himself come a nanosecond later.

Dan pulled out before he came completely undone, painting her ass and calves with his cum.

He got some on his carpet. Dammit.

Makenna collapsed to the ground with her arms splayed. "Thanks."

"No problem, baby," he said. He disappeared to the bathroom and came back with a warm, damp washcloth so she could clean up.

His legs barely worked as he walked to the kitchen island. "Do you want a drink or..."

"Just water. I had cocktails with Addison already. I'll be back."

She ran off to the bathroom and reappeared, still naked. He would never not be used to this gorgeous woman walking around his house in the nude. Makenna walked out and gathered her clothes.

"So you saw Addison?"

"Yeah, she wants to fuck Kirk. Really bad."

"Interesting," Dan said, pressing a glass to his ice dispenser and filling up a glass with water. "She's usually not the jump-into-bed-right-away kind of person. She's not like us."

Makenna laughed. "Absolutely. I was so horny after talking about sex with Addison, that *that* happened."

"Your hair is also in a braid. That's usually your 'panties on the doorknob.'"

"You're not wrong."

Dan cracked a Coors Light. He showed her one, and she shook her head.

"She's still really hesitant to sleep with him, though," Makenna said. "I don't know what she's waiting for, honestly."

"It's probably Kirk's fault," Dan said. "Maybe I should

say something to him. Get the ball rolling. Both of them are too chicken to talk to each other."

"I love Addison, but she keeps so much inside. They're such a slow burn, I can't take it. Kirk is adorable, and his dick would've been in my mouth day fucking one."

Dan came to a screeching halt. "Do you have a thing for Kirk?"

Makenna shook her head, a rouge tendril falling in her face. "Please. No, I would break him in half. You're the only man I've found who can keep up with me."

"Barely," Dan said. "You exhaust me, woman."

"You like it, baby," Makenna said.

"Fuck yes, I do." He kissed her deeply and then pulled his pants up.

"We have a problem, though. Addison said she saw us at the country concert."

Dan froze. "Did she see anything?"

"Just a kiss on the cheek I gave you. I played it off that it was a friendly kiss, and she's so darling, she believed me," Makenna said. "I'm starting to feel bad."

"Oh?" Dan didn't know what to think. He wanted people to know, but it also felt special, being in their own little love bubble, not coming up for air. Would she run if they were public?

"I hate lying. And I'm lying to everyone."

Dan's voice croaked. "Do you want to stop?"

Makenna breathed in and out. Dan wished he could read her mind.

"I don't know," she said, squirming in the couch. "We've been keeping this a secret for so long, how pissed will people be? My mom told me I shouldn't be with anyone right now."

"They'll be mad," Dan said. "But they'll understand."

Makenna switched the subject abruptly. "Addison is so adorable. It's so obvious that she loves him. I think he loves her too, and they're both just too shy to say something."

I love you, M. I want us to go public.

I'm terrified you'll leave me if we do.

"Kirk is working tomorrow, so maybe I'll say something to him then," Dan said. Kirk had filled in as Dan's temporary finance person at his development company.

Makenna kissed Dan's temple. "They need a good nudge."

I'm so in love with you that it makes it hard to breathe sometimes.

He had blurted out "I love you" to a woman before, and it ended immediately in a breakup. Since then, he had learned to keep strong feelings to himself unless the woman was a guaranteed "I love you" back. It seemed like he only wanted to say it to the ones who kept him at arm's length, who never fully surrendered their heart.

He had talked about this with his therapist constantly.

"What is it about Makenna that you gravitate towards?" Bernice had asked, her pen scribbling on her legal pad.

"I just feel calm. I'm so go-go-go all the time, but with her, I don't have to feel 'on' or have to perform. I love to make her laugh. It's my favorite thing."

"But she wants to keep your relationship a secret."

"Yes, and her brother has told me not to date her. We've gotten mad at our friends for speculating about us. We'll have to admit to gaslighting them for months."

"What do you think will be the best thing to do?"

Dan had stared at a potted plant for five minutes as he thought. He looked up at Bernice. "I don't know. I just know I can't lose her. She's the best thing to ever happen to me. I honestly don't know if I would recover if she leaves me."

Now, he kissed her on the head, and she linked her arms around his shoulders. "I know I want you to myself a little longer," she said.

Her words always melted him to a puddle. Even if it wasn't ideal, even if they had to continue with their secret, at least he had her. Even if his therapist had many legal pads full of notes about him.

DAN WAS about to strangle Kirk.

"I've heard from a reliable source that she wants you. Wants you bad," Dan said.

Kirk looked at Dan like he just told him to swallow a cockroach to keep his job.

"There's no way," Kirk said.

"Way."

He witnessed the realization flow through Kirk as he sat dumbfounded. Kirk might be short-circuiting with this new information. A smile crossed the accountant's mouth, right out of a straight-to-home movie about a serial killer.

"You smiling is very creepy. Knock it off."

Kirk ran a hand over his mouth and rubbed his beard. "I'm sorry. Who did you hear it from?"

"It doesn't matter," Dan said, glossing over his anonymous source and continued to hype Kirk up. Dan's pep talks usually worked, so Dan laid it on thick. Addison loved Kirk, and he loved her. All they had to do was just *talk* to each other. Collide together and be happy.

Do as I say, not as I do.

He knew he needed to talk to Makenna, but he was too chickenshit.

He watched Kirk, being the dweeb he was, make a pros and cons list, weighing his options. The only real barrier for them was geography, which was a hell of a lot easier than imbalanced feelings.

"You are both single. This is your chance. Forget about New York and forget about Lillyvale, and just smoosh your faces together already. Be a motherfucking alpha."

"I'm not an alpha," Kirk shouted. Tiana, Dan's administrative assistant, halted outside the office with a smirk.

Dan left Kirk to mull over the pros and cons. When he got back to his office, he shut the door and closed the blinds.

The couch was his thinking spot. He laid out, his head on the armrest, and looked up at the ceiling.

"I should tell Makenna. See what happens," he said out loud. He thought for a second.

"That is a terrible idea. She might stop seeing me." He paused again. "You can't be fucking scared. You're Dan Fucking Price."

He might be setting himself up to be eviscerated like a victim in a *Saw* movie. Makenna could take his colon out and wear it like a scarf. But dammit, it had been a long time coming.

He was utterly and completely in love with Makenna Brady.

17

"Hi," Makenna said, standing by the picnic benches at Bolder Ridge Park in Rocklin with her arms crossed. It was a rare cool day, and she'd forgotten a jacket. The park overlooked a vista on either side, and the wind whipped up, chilling her skin. Dan approached, wearing a gray bomber jacket, a white button-up, and dark wash jeans, with two coffees.

Lately, they had gone to parks in the area with coffees to hang out. Makenna always made him push her in a swing if there were no children around.

He noticed her shivering and took off his coat to offer to her. It was still warm from his body.

Dan took a sip of his coffee. "How was Zoey's bachelorette party? How drunk did she get?"

Drowsiness tugged at her eyeballs, and she squinted. "I think I'm still hungover."

"Oh baby," he said, sitting down on the bench next to her, wrapping his arm around her.

"Thanks for taking care of me at the club," Makenna said. "I had so much free alcohol. And the flask you got me for my birthday came in *very* handy. Addison even drank some."

"You're welcome," he said, kissing her. "Did the strippers do the balloons?"

Makenna laughed, covering her mouth. Zoey was deathly afraid of balloons, so Dan had special-requested that a dancer attach balloons to him in some way to freak her out. "I got video."

"Perfect," he said with a sad smile.

Gone was the fun, go-lucky Dan she knew, and in his place was a sad guy. He dropped his arm from around her.

Oh God, he was going to break up with her. She could already feel her tears on standby.

"Is something wrong?" she asked, her voice croaking.

"I have something I need to talk to you about. It's been weighing on my mind a lot, actually."

"Okay," Makenna said. She was surprised her speech sounded so normal. Inside, she was freaking out.

She wasn't sure how she could live without him.

He looked at her, his eyes soft. He squeezed her hands three times, and Makenna breathed in and out, staring at him.

A smile crossed Dan's lips.

"I love you."

What?

"Your eyes are bugging out. Are you okay?"

"Fine," Makenna said, standing up and walking around. She put her hands on her hips, pacing along the concrete slab of the picnic area.

"I'm tired of pretending this is only sex for me. It's been incredible, don't get me wrong. I've enjoyed every boob grab, every butt squeeze. Remember that time you took my balls and..."

"I remember," Makenna said. She threaded her hair with her fingers, her brain about to explode. Old Makenna always ran from this moment. "Why?"

"Do you want me to list everything I love about you?" Dan asked. He stood up and walked to the opposite side of the picnic area, next to a charcoal grill.

He splayed his fingers to count. "You're funny and intelligent as fuck. You make me feel so chill, and I *never* have chill. When I see you, I feel like doves swoop around me, unicorns fart rainbows, an otter is hugging a teddy bear. I miss you like crazy when you're not with me, and when you're in my arms, I don't want you to go home. I fucking love you, Makenna Rose Brady."

Makenna almost crumpled to a puddle on the sidewalk.

Dan *loved* her.

In some ways, she already knew.

In the way he held her, the way he delivered lunch to her while she worked at the makeup counter. How he took care of her that time she got food poisoning from some bad seafood. How he always made sure she came first, how he held her and kissed her.

He had even seen the demonic PMS she got and presented her with a heated water bottle and bars of chocolate he kept on standby.

She had tried to fight him, but he always persuaded her to drop her sword.

Of course, he loved her. She just didn't know why.

"We promised this would be casual," Makenna said.

"We did," Dan said. "But my feelings changed. I warned you."

The lightheadedness came back with a vengeance. She sat down on the bench, watching the children on a distant jungle gym, clawing away to burn off energy.

Dan sat down next to her. Conflicting thoughts jumbled in her mind.

"You don't even have to say it back. I just needed to get it out there," Dan said. "I told Kirk earlier today to be an alpha and talk to Addison, and I needed to take my own advice."

Her heart pounded.

"I'm not proposing. Promise," Dan said. "So don't run."

He stood up and wiped his hands on his jeans. He kept his back to her. "I do want to be your boyfriend, though. I want to tell people."

This felt like too much. It felt like her chest would split open with fear and dread.

Her body was telling her *yes, this is the right thing to do*, but her mind said *run*.

It wasn't a matter of whether she loved him. It was if he would always love her.

"This is a lot to process," she said.

"I get it," Dan said. "Take all the time you need. Honestly."

She kissed him without thought, without fear of what could happen. "I need to go."

"Okay," Dan said. "Call me."

She walked away, looking back once.

She opened the door to her car in a brain fog and closed it after her. Her forehead went to the hard rubber of her steering wheel. Catching her breath became impossible since the sobs wracked her body and tears flowed from her eyes like a faucet that couldn't be turned off.

Through the blurriness of her tears, she dialed the number of the person who would know what to say.

"What's up, lady?" Sierra asked when she picked up. When she heard the sob from Makenna, she said. "Oh no."

"He told me he loved me," she said miserably.

"And why are you crying? That's great!"

"I know!" she said with a wail. "I'm so scared."

"Breathe, honey, breathe," Sierra said into the phone, soothing her friend. "Relax, Makenna. It'll be all okay. How did you leave it?"

"I don't know," Makenna said.

"You don't know how it went? Did you break up?"

Makenna found a random food place napkin in the glove compartment and blew her nose with one hand. "I said 'I don't know.'"

"Do you love him?" Sierra asked.

"Yes." Uttering the words started the next wave of tears.

"So what's the problem?"

"Me. I'm the problem," she said. "Everything I touch goes to shit. Every time."

Sierra let out a heavy sigh. "We have been friends for five years. Sometimes, you're a real twat, but I love you. I'm saying this with love—I'm sick of your self-destructive bullshit. Go home, *do not drink*, get a solid eight hours of sleep, and decide in the morning."

"Okay," she said. Her sobs followed her home, to the shower, and to her bed.

She laid awake, watching the shadows on her ceiling from the oak tree outside her window. Around two in the morning, she knew what she needed to do.

18

THE NEXT DAY

Dan breathed out a sigh of relief when he opened the door.

"Hi."

"Hi," Makenna said. "May I come in?"

Dan opened the door wider, and Makenna slinked past him. She turned, playing with one of her rings. Her eyes stared at the carpet.

Dan shoved his hands in his pockets. She still looked at the ground when she began to speak.

"I've never had anyone love me like you love me. I'm not good at relationships or being loved. This might go horribly wrong and be my fault." She looked up with tears in her eyes, and Dan wanted to rush to her, take her in his arms, and never let go.

"All I know is that I love you, Dan. I love you so much."

Dan's heart burst like he was getting the final rose on *The Bachelorette,* like his team had won the Superbowl, like the Golden Girls had found an extra cheesecake in the freezer. He brought his hands to his nose, covering his mouth.

"Are you crying?" Makenna asked. "Oh, baby."

She wrapped him in her arms. She loved him.

A woman he was so scared to lose, he couldn't tell her he loved her for six months. And now she loved him back.

"I'm so happy," he said through tears. He pressed his face to hers as she laughed. Their kisses grew frantic, and clothes went flying. When the woman he loved, who loved him back, was naked in his arms, he reached for the lube stashed in the TV stand. When he eased into her, kissing her, moving into and out of her, her eyes locked his. He looked at her, really looked at her.

He was done looking. He had found her.

Afterwards, they were lying in a heap of blankets and pillows in front of the unlit fireplace. Her head laid on his chest, her fingers playing with his tufts of chest hair. Her phone buzzed. Makenna looked at it longingly.

Dan reached for it on the coffee table and handed it to her. Makenna read the message, and scoffed, rolling her eyes.

"What does it say?"

"I'm absolutely livid right now. It's my mom," Makenna said. She held the phone in front of her to read the message. "Makenna, my friend saw you at a park with a short man and you looked upset. Caroline thinks it's Dan. Is there something you want to tell us?"

Makenna rubbed her face with her hands. "I am so tired of people getting in my business. *Especially* Caroline."

"You know, we could tell everyone," Dan suggested. He watched Makenna for a reaction.

Makenna's face grew into a look he knew all too well. That beautiful brain of her was concocting a scheme. Her slight chuckle developed into a roar of laughter.

"What's so funny?"

"I just had a thought," Makenna said.

"Tell me."

"What if we fuck with our friends first? What if we throw them off our scent before we tell them?"

Dan paused. While scheming with Makenna was enticing, he wondered if any kind of prank was necessary. He was tired of hiding this amazing woman he was in love with.

Still, he knew he would go along with it. Be a sexy accomplice.

"We should make them think something went wrong with us. Play with them a little bit," Makenna said.

Dan thought for a second, then his face lit up. "I got it. Piper and Holden."

Makenna's face scrunched. "What? Holden hates her. *Hates* her."

"You said they need to get together so sparks can fly, right?"

"Maybe?" Makenna said.

Dan sat up, spreading his hands. "Picture it. Lillyvale, 2021. Piper and Holden, together at last. Boning like the world is ending. All because of little old us. A challenge built into a scheme. My forte."

Makenna laughed, getting his *Golden Girls* reference. "I'm listening."

"We can talk them into being our fake dates to throw our friends off, but really we're trying to get them together. Then we can formally announce we've decided to take our friendship to the next level because our 'relationships' crumbled under holiday pressure."

Makenna shook her head. "I like where your head's at, I really do. However, Holden would *never* go for it."

"What if we don't tell him at first?" Dan asked. "Piper

will do it. I'll offer her first pick of new members to my dating pool," Dan said.

Makenna pondered it. "I don't know if it'll work. Holden's love language is food so I'm going to have to buy him *a lot* of food."

"I feel a wager coming on," Dan said, kissing Makenna's neck.

"What do you want to wager?" Makenna asked.

"If I win, they get together by the end of the year, you come to Vegas with me for my birthday."

"I would do that anyway. And if I win?" Makenna asked, rolling on top of him. The blanket around her fell away, revealing her naked body. He traced the flower tattoos under her breasts, the ivy that snaked down her side. The lipstick print on her ass.

"Woman, I'm tired. My dick is tired too."

"Lies," Makenna said. "If I win, I'll go to Vegas with you. How's that?"

"Done," he said, rolling to the coffee table. The other lube was nowhere to be found so he pulled out his coffee table stash.

"How many bottles of lube are in this house, Dan?"

"I am *baby* to you," Dan said indignantly. "Seven in this room alone."

He coated his cock and his fingers in lube, pushing two fingers into her, rubbing her clit with his thumb. She moaned loudly as she settled onto his cock and began riding him. His hands cupped her breasts as she rolled against him.

Her fingernails sank into his chest.

How the fuck did he get so lucky?

19

CAROLINE'S CHRISTMAS PARTY

"Thank you so much for doing this," Makenna said. "Again."

"Not a big deal at all," Holden replied. "The amount of followers I've gotten and the women who have been sliding into my DMs? It's been solid."

Makenna had posted a couple pictures to Instagram with Holden in them. Her thirty thousand followers immediately started asking if he was her new boyfriend, and the comments would fuel Holden's ego for the next two years. The pictures didn't suggest anything more than a friendship, but everyone assumed more, including her circle of friends in Lillyvale.

"Is Dan going to sing again tonight? I wouldn't put it past him," Holden said. He started laughing at the memory. "He is so extra. He knew all the moves to that song too. I can't believe *that's* the guy you fell in love with."

Makenna laughed, but then paused. Besides Sierra, Holden was the only person in her life who knew that she and Dan were together. Being on the Internet, having a somewhat popular Instagram, she usually let negative comments roll off of her.

But that comment from Holden hurt.

Dan was extra and silly and sexy, and she didn't want to be with anyone else. He had perfected his "Cry Me a River" number, including the slinking JT did in the music video.

"Wow, baby," she had said after he performed it for her, in his gray sweatpants with no underwear, his cock flopping everywhere. "You really committed."

"I thought I would give you a private show," he said. "Since I'm your private dancer."

"Whatever, Tina Turner," she said.

Dan had pulled down his pants, so he was completely naked and picked her up from her perch on the couch back and laid her out on the cushions to bury his cock inside her.

He then sang a few bars of "The Best" as he thrust into her.

Dan had planned the karaoke night for Kirk, who had moved back to New York, and then planned to move back to Lillyvale to be with Addison. Dan suggested karaoke as Kirk's grand gesture, and it was an excuse for him to sing "Cry Me a River" and act sad and dejected when Makenna showed up with her "boyfriend" Holden. They decided not to invite Piper that night, so Holden wouldn't be suspicious of their real plan.

Kirk's performance was the cutest thing Makenna had ever seen, and in some weird way, Dan singing Justin Timberlake to cover their secret relationship made her love Dan even more.

Their friends had eaten it up. Caroline had stopped asking about Dan, and all was well in the world.

Now, the ruse would continue at Caroline's annual

Christmas party. Today, Piper was attending. And Holden had no idea.

Holden looked up at the house, festooned with tasteful white lights lining the border of the home, and green wreaths with buffalo plaid bows hanging on the porch lights. "Caroline Rhodes has done okay for herself," Holden said.

"Just wait until you get inside. It's intense."

She zeroed in on a parked car down the street with two dark figures inside, like they were on a stakeout.

"That's Dan and his fake date," Makenna said, pointing to the car down the street.

"Showtime," Holden said. "Who did he bring?"

"Just a client of his from Happily Lillyvale After," Makenna said. *Don't smirk. Don't evil-grin.*

"I know that look, Makenna," Holden said. His goofy grin disappeared when he caught sight of Dan's "date." "Not Piper..."

"Yes, Piper Harding."

"Why her? She is literally the devil," Holden said. "I love you, Makenna, but you're like the shittiest friend ever for this."

"I'm sorry," Makenna said, lifting her hands. "But don't you think it's time to settle your beef with her?"

"I don't just have beef with her, I have the whole cow," Holden said.

"Hey, look. I know what she did to you was shitty. But it was ten years ago. What is in the past is in the past."

"So, are you and Piper cool now? Since I remember you hating her too."

Makenna quieted and Holden pointed a finger. "I knew it. Why do I always have to be the bigger person? You should try too, Makenna."

"Okay, fine," Makenna said. "I will squash my beef with Piper if you do as well."

Holden nodded once. "I can live with that."

They walked up the pathway and Holden touched her arm. "Real talk, why don't you and Dan come clean? You're in a committed relationship. You love each other. This is just weird."

"Because, because of my brother and my parents said I shouldn't date anyone…"

And we've been lying forever and people will be mad. People will tell Dan this is just another one of my faults and he should run while he can.

Makenna clamped her hands on his arms. "Oh, shut up. Just look pretty and act like you're obsessed with me."

"Fine." Holden wrapped his meaty arm around her shoulders and walked up to Caroline's aggressively wreathed front door.

The door opened into Caroline's home. It looked like Pottery Barn's entire Christmas catalog had thrown up on it.

"What's up, everyone? I brought my own drink," Makenna said, holding up the large bottle of vodka her parents had gotten her for Christmas. Everyone shook hands with Holden, except Addison, who hugged him, like the kindhearted person she was.

"Where's Dan?" Addison asked.

"He's coming with his new girlfriend, *Piper.*"

Eyes stared her down. *Did that sound I like know too much? Was it my tone? Why is everyone looking at me?*

"What? Piper and I went to high school together, and she is not my favorite. She's fake and not a good person…"

Where are you, baby? I'm dying in here.

Then Dan walked in, his arm slung around Piper as she chewed gum.

She knew that this was all pretend, but seeing her man with his arm around Piper made her want to grab her by her pink hair.

We're being nice. We're being cordial.

"Oh hey," Makenna said, her voice hitting an octave only dogs could hear. Piper waved to her and followed Dan in. Their hands casually linked, like they were dating.

Whose idea was this anyway?

Holden wrapped his arms around Makenna in a friendly hug, kissing her cheek. Her flinch reflex went unnoticed.

He leaned in and lowered his voice. "You have to pretend to be into me, Makenna."

"Sorry," she muttered.

"God, this is high school all over again," Holden said under his breath.

Dan's gaze flicked to hers for a nanosecond before he took Addison and Kirk into a bear hug. "What did I miss? I'm sorry I'm late."

As Caroline cycled through the group and reveled in all the happy pairings—Jonathan and Zoey happily married in Phoenix, Taylor and Malcolm together and probably on the fast track to marriage and kids and happily ever after, and now Addison and Kirk, a small longing burrowed in her chest.

A small part of her wished Caroline would include her and Dan in the happily ever afters.

Still, too soon.

Addison and Caroline paired off, running upstairs. Brady approached Holden, shaking his hand.

"So you're dating my little sister again."

Holden stiffened. "Don't shoot."

Brady laughed to mask an incoming threat. "I only shoot if you hurt her."

"I promise I won't. We're for real this time." He pulled Makenna close.

Oh my God.

"To be honest, man, you're my favorite she's dated."

Shoot me *now.*

"That means a lot, thank you," Holden said, taking Brady in for a full hug, not just a one-armed bro hug. Her brother awkwardly embraced him back but dropped his arms.

What is happening?

"Someone is touching the piano, and Caroline will kill me if I don't stop it. Merry Christmas," Brady said, touching Makenna on the shoulder as he scampered off.

Makenna smacked Holden on the arm. "Why did you do that?"

"Seemed like he needed a hug," Holden said. "He said I was his favorite."

"Don't get a big head."

"I need a drink if I have to be in the same room as *her.*" Piper was twirling her hair as Dan talked to an older couple in front of the tree. As Makenna walked into the kitchen, he looked at her.

Why were they doing this?

"Stop checking out other men, dearest," Holden said, pulling out the dopey pet name he had given her in high school, knowing it pissed her off. Makenna rolled her eyes.

Makenna said hi to a few mild acquaintances and located her parents on the couch, discussing something with Caroline's parents, complete with lots of hand movements.

"You know Holden," Makenna said. Makenna's dad, Mike, stood up, and Holden also took him in for a hug, although Holden had maybe met Mike twice over the years.

"So you're the boy my daughter is seeing," Makenna's mom said.

"Guilty. Don't shoot," Holden said, holding up his arms.

Makenna made a mental note to talk about *don't shoot.*

"I'm so glad our Makenna is with a nice boy like you," Angela said, patting Holden on the chest. Thankfully, he didn't hug her.

"I'm glad to have Makenna. She's the perfect woman." He pulled her in for a side hug without warning, so she jerked, colliding with his meaty frame like a rag doll.

"It's wonderful you think that," Angela said with a fake smile.

This was a terrible idea. The lie was getting deeper, more complicated. She was going to look like the bad guy for dumping Holden and getting with Dan immediately after.

Why the fuck was this a good idea?

"Well, let's get a drink. Put my birthday present to good use," Makenna said, holding up a bottle of vodka.

"Be safe," Angela Brady said. "We don't want you dancing on the lawn again like three Christmases ago."

Makenna bit her tongue as she turned around.

The ice was easy to locate, thank God. She needed some vodka in her system as soon as possible.

"Do you want some?" Makenna asked Holden after she poured a hearty serving of vodka over ice.

"Let me find something to mix it with, you booze-hound," Holden said, opening the fridge like he lived there. Makenna poured the vodka, and he finished the drink with some cranberry juice. After a few stirs with his finger, they clinked their glasses together.

"To me being hopelessly devoted to you," Holden said. "When do I get my Tuscan Grove again?"

"After this party," Makenna said.

"Can I order anything off the menu?"

"Within reason. I don't want you to bankrupt me."

"I like their chicken alfredo. I'm a cheap date," Holden said. He took a sip of his drink.

"So, Piper," Makenna said. "She's totally changed, you know."

"Did she grow a heart?"

"Do you still think about her?"

"Of course not. I haven't thought about her since high school. Now I have to pretend to be dating a girl I've never slept with while the first person I slept with is in this house," Holden said. "Exactly what I wanted for Christmas. I'm goddamn Mariah Carey."

"Keep your voice down," Makenna warned.

Holden smirked. "I feel like I have a lot of power right now. I can blast your secret to everyone."

"You wouldn't."

"I'm thinking about it. Oh, it's so fun watching you squirm."

"I hate you."

Holden pursed his lips into a kiss with a wink before taking a sip of his drink.

Piper wandered into the kitchen and stopped when she saw Makenna and Holden.

"Piper," Makenna greeted.

"Makenna," she said, immediately clearing her throat afterward. She peered around Makenna. "Hi Holden."

"Hello Piper." Holden's demeanor changed, the smile wiped from his face. "I see you got roped into this too."

"Keep your voice down," Makenna said.

"I got to say, Makenna, this is weird," Piper said, riffling through the bucket of drinks, finding the white wine.

"That's what I said," Holden agreed.

"He would not shut up in the car about you. It made me want to barf."

"Makenna talked about him in the car too," Holden said. He broke his hand to his head. "Am I agreeing with Piper Harding? Who am I? Is this my hand?" He held out his hand like they were foreign.

"I know. It's shocking me too."

Holden and Piper looked at each other and burst into laughter.

"Look, you're laughing," Makenna said. "You're getting along!"

"No, we still hate each other," Holden said.

Through laughs, Piper said with a finger point, "He's still the worst."

"You should just tell everyone. No time like the present," Holden said.

"I agree with Holden," Piper said. "Ugh, gross. What is happening?"

Makenna poured herself another vodka over ice. She pulled out her phone.

Dan: People are buying it. I can't find Piper.

Makenna: She's in here with me and Holden.

"She's talking to him," Piper said, standing next to Holden. "So cute."

"Shut up, Piper," Makenna said. She couldn't keep a straight face.

"Will we ever find love like this, Piper?" Holden asked.

"I doubt it. Across all barriers, across a substantial height difference, Makenna and Dan, together forever."

Makenna's eyes darted to the areas around the kitchen, looking for witnesses or people who might hear the conversation. Part of her wanted to say something, tell someone, even as another part of her froze in fear.

But this lie had gone too far, too long.

Dan stood along the edge of the living room with Taylor and Malcolm, his phone in his hand. Makenna just texted him, saying Piper and Holden were together in the kitchen.

Perfect.

"Piper seems...nice," Taylor said.

"Yeah," Malcolm agreed with his girlfriend. His arm settled on Taylor's shoulders, and Dan wished he could be like that with his own lady love.

"When did you start dating?"

Oh, they're talking about Piper.

"October," Dan said, his arms crossed.

"Makenna looks really good tonight," Taylor commented.

"So good," Malcolm added. Taylor smacked him on the arm. His voice immediately went to grovel. "No one looks as good as you, baby. You're the love of my life."

He leaned down and kissed her teasing smile.

He wanted Makenna to lean down and kiss him. Call him *baby* like they did at his house. Why wasn't he with Makenna right now?

"Doesn't Makenna look good, Dan?" Taylor asked.

Makenna was wearing tights that he wanted to tear off with his teeth and a sweater dress he wanted to push all the way up so he could feast on her tits.

"She looks okay."

"Holden seems like a nice guy. I'm happy for her. She

finally has a good one. Are you happy for Makenna, Dan?" Taylor asked.

Dan shot a death stare at her. She jutted her bottom lip and shrugged one shoulder. She looked like she just farted in an elevator and it got blamed on someone else.

"So happy," Dan said, although his jaw clenched.

"You don't look happy."

"Leave Dan alone, Taylor," Malcolm said.

Dan's phone vibrated and he pulled it out.

Makenna: Meet me in the in-laws' quarters.

"I have to go," Dan said. He wiggled his phone. "Girlfriend."

They both nodded, watching Dan walk to the sliding glass door. He breathed out a sigh of relief.

Caroline and Brady had a garage set back from the house that they had converted into an extra living space. The door was unlocked.

"Hello?" he asked, walking in. He felt a hand on his back, and he jumped three feet off the floor.

"Sorry, baby," Makenna said.

"I almost had a heart attack," he said, grabbing his chest. Makenna turned on a lamp to illuminate a small corner. The room held a bare mattress with a small table and smelled like bleach.

"Piper and Holden still hate each other," Makenna said.

"Oh well. At least we tried."

Makenna bit her lip. "Listen, baby. What are we doing?"

"Doing? I'm in this very private room with my secret girl-friend," he said, kissing her neck.

"No, baby, focus," Makenna said. "I mean we don't tell people for months, and then we rope two people in to be our fake dates in the hope they get together. What is wrong with us? This was a mistake."

Dan shrugged.

Makenna ran her fingers through her hair. "Everyone is going to be so pissed. My mother is going to think I haven't changed at all."

Dan paused. Brady would be furious too, after he told him repeatedly not to pursue Makenna. To find out he had been dating his sister for months behind everyone's back might ruin the friendship. He had gotten mad at people asking about Makenna to mask what was going on. At first, they'd kept it a secret in case it didn't last. Now they kept it a secret because it had lasted so long.

"We're in too deep. The lie has gotten too big," Dan said.

"Exactly," Makenna said. "My mom is going to kick me out. This is exactly the kind of shit I pulled in high school."

"If she kicks you out, you could come live with me," Dan said.

Makenna didn't respond, chewing a hangnail on her finger, something she did when she was nervous. "I have no idea what to do."

He put his hands on her arms. "This is what we do. We go back in there, pretend like everything is fine. We 'break' up with Piper and Holden over the holidays, and after our Vegas trip, we announce we're together. Say we decided we have feelings for each other and we're together now."

Her face relaxed into a smile. "That could work. Won't we look like the bad guys?"

"Everyone will be so happy that we're together, they'll forget about Piper and Holden. No one is thrilled with them for us anyway. Taylor was trying to bait me about you."

Dan looked at the bare mattress in the room, and back at Makenna.

"You want to fuck in here, real quick?"

"Sure, why not?"

"I come prepared," Dan said, pulling a tiny bottle of lube out from his jacket pocket.

He picked her up and kissed her, taking off only what was necessary to gain access.

"I love you," Dan whispered as he took her from behind, thrusting like he might get caught at any moment.

"I love you too. And is that all you got?"

MAKENNA LEFT FIRST, rearranging her tights as she walked back into the party. The warm air hit her when she opened the sliding glass door. Caroline's co-workers stood by the door, and Makenna's shoulders relaxed.

She walked into the kitchen, the last place she left Holden and Piper. Nowhere to be found. Makenna found Addison and Kirk, chatting and flirting in the dining room.

"Have you seen Holden? I lost him," Makenna said.

Addison's brow scrunched. "He was just here, talking with Dan's girlfriend. What's her name again?" She looked around, lifting onto the balls of her feet to look around. "I don't see them."

"Thanks," Makenna said. She walked into the family room, her parents still talking to Caroline's parents on the couch.

"I've seemed to have lost Holden," Makenna said. Her mother shrugged but leaned forward.

"Honey, you look flushed," Angela said, standing up, moving closer to Makenna. Makenna froze as her mother wiped something from her face.

When she pulled her hand away, her eyebrows knitted. Her fingers rubbed together as she examined the substance.

Oh my God, my mom is touching lube that was on Dan's dick.

"What's on your face? It's slippery," she said, examining her fingers.

"It's spit!" Makenna said, a little too loud. "You should go wash your hands. Right now."

"I've had a lot worse bodily fluids of yours on me," Angela said with a laugh.

You haven't had my pussy juices mixed with my boyfriend's juices on you, I bet.

"I have an infection," Makenna lied. If she was already lying tonight, what was one more?

"Not again, Makenna. Fine, I'll go wash my hands. I need more wine anyway," Angela said, walking to the kitchen. Makenna breathed in and out, walking away from the couch to the hall mirror. The lube had taken off a chunk of makeup, creating a streak of normal skin.

Just fucking great.

She heard light moaning from down the hall. A soft female cry floated out.

Makenna inched closer to the source of the sounds of pleasure.

"Oh Pipes, I've missed you," she heard, the gruff voice familiar.

Is that—?

She pushed the unlocked door open. There was Holden's bare ass, thrusting into someone on the bed. He looked back with an outstretched mouth.

"Oh shit," he said, scrambling to quickly pull up his pants. The woman under him sat up, her shirt pushed past her bra. Makenna covered her eyes with her hand.

She heard clothes rustling.

"I'm so sorry, Makenna," Piper said.

Makenna dropped her hand and crossed her arms. "So, Holden, you gave her a holly jolly Christmas?"

"It's not what it looks like," Piper said.

"It looked like you were fucking Holden." Makenna tried to look mad, but inside, she was smirking.

"Don't hate me, Makenna," Holden said.

"No, you should get off. I'm glad," Makenna said, crossing her arms. She looked back as she closed the door. "Just make sure you lock the door. Merry Christmas."

She closed the door, heard a click, and the moaning began again. She shook her head with a smile.

It was perfect. They could tell everyone that Holden and Piper decided to date, leaving Makenna and Dan free of any wrongdoing. They would tell everyone after a little time had passed, pretending like they just got together.

It would all work out. No one would get mad, no one would call her a liar.

No one would think, *oh, it's just Makenna again, being reckless.*

Makenna pulled her phone out.

Makenna: I just caught Holden and Piper fucking. You win.

Dan: YAAAAAASSSSSSS. Veeegggggggaaaaaasssss.

Dan: Want to come home with me right now?

Makenna: Absolutely.

20

NEW YEAR'S EVE

"Vegas, baby!" Dan said, snaking an arm around Makenna's waist as they walked into the Venetian. A large marble fountain stood in the middle of the grand lobby. Makenna looked up to the ceiling and marveled at the intricate paintings and the architectural features.

The hotel buzzed with tourists and excitement for the new year.

"This hotel is so beautiful," Makenna said.

"Only the best for you, my love. And for me since I only turn thirty-five once."

"You sure you didn't want a huge party? We could've gotten everyone together," Makenna said.

"No, this is perfect. All I need is you, Vegas, and Coors Light," Dan said, pulling her toward reception.

After the Venetian employee confirmed all the information and looked through the records, she said, "So, a Grand King Suite."

"Yes, ma'am." Dan handed over his credit card without flinching. Makenna's cheeks warmed as Dan signed the paperwork and slipped his credit card back into his wallet. When Makenna came to Vegas, she always stayed at a cheaper hotel like the Flamingo or a motel off the strip. Staying at the Venetian had always been a bucket list item for her, and Dan knew it. Other people might pick the Bellagio or Caesar's, but the Venetian always called to her.

"Come on, M," he said, taking her waist in his arm. "Let's finish this year off in style. The best year of my life, because of you."

When they took the elevator up to their floor and located the room, Makenna gasped.

"This is huge," she said, walking in.

"I think you said the same thing when you saw my dick for the first time."

Makenna laughed and slung an arm around his neck.

The room was open and bright, full of golds, whites, and maroons. There was a half-bath by the entryway, a full dining room table, and a closed-off bedroom.

This must've cost a fortune.

"Dan, are you sure you don't want me to chip in? This is *your* birthday. This is expensive, especially during New Year's."

"Don't worry about it," he said, with a wink. He hung up their suit bag in the closet and dragged their luggage to the sitting area.

Makenna approached the window overlooking the strip. The sky was clear with a random puffy cloud floating above all the sparkle.

"This is gorgeous," Makenna said. "I love Vegas."

"Gah, I love it too," Dan said. "Thank you for coming with me. This is so special."

"Awww," Makenna said, nuzzling into him.

"So, do you want to start having sex on every surface

now, or do you want to wait until we've eaten a steak and drank some?"

"Now sounds great," Makenna said.

"Now is the right answer," Dan replied, pulling her sweater off of her bare shoulder and kissing her as she laughed from the tickles.

After they christened the bedroom, Makenna freshened her curls and makeup, pulling back on her ripped black jeans and oversized sweater she pushed to her elbows.

"What do you want to do first?" Dan asked.

"Let's go explore."

They walked to the Grand Canal Shoppes, and Makenna's shopping sense perked up. Every now and then since she'd moved home and sold most of her high-end pieces, a familiar urge to shop, to spend money she didn't have, overcame her.

"You look so happy," Dan said, their hands swinging between them.

"I just love malls. Is that bad?"

"Not at all. Sometimes after I visit you at work, I just walk around and people-watch."

"I agree, people-watching is great," Makenna said, looking around. They watched a bride and groom in traditional attire walk by, enjoying their afternoon like Makenna and Dan were.

"So casual," Dan commented on the couple. "Do you want to look in any stores?"

Makenna shook her head. Looking led to wanting, which led to temptation and to a spiral into bad habits. She had a five-figure reminder on her credit card statements of what "just looking" did. "I have, like, two hundred dollars in my bank account right now."

Dan shrugged. "It would be my treat. Anything you want."

"No," she said. "All of these stores are really expensive and it's *your* birthday."

"If you haven't learned, I'm a giver," Dan whispered. "I want you to have something pretty to remember this weekend by. Besides me, of course."

Like an angel descending from the shopping heavens, the Jimmy Choo storefront appeared.

Makenna bit her lip and pointed.

"Let's go," Dan said, pulling her into the store.

It smelled like luxury in there.

As she looked around the store, she deliberately picked up the simplest pairs, probably retailing around seven hundred dollars, but put them back. Dan, however, found the most audacious and orgasmic shoes.

"What about these? They're similar to the pair you were wearing when I first met you."

It was trivial to be devastated by shoes, but she had parted with those sparkly Louboutins months ago. She negotiated heavily with a mom from Granite Bay just to recoup a quarter of what she paid for them.

"I sold them. I loved those shoes."

"Try these on, then. To replace the other ones," he said, handing her the shoe.

"They're too expensive," Makenna said. Those shoes were killer, but way out of anyone's price range.

"What size are you?" Dan asked. Makenna told him, and he approached the employee. The employee disappeared in the back and returned with a box holding possibly the most beautiful shoes in the world.

"I can't try them on, or I will fall in love with them."

"Like me?" Dan asked. Dan shooed the employee away

and knelt down. Makenna removed a flip-flop to sink her foot into the delicious suede as Dan maneuvered the shoe on.

"There. A shoe fit for a queen."

They were comfortable immediately, no need to break them in. She looked down on them on her feet. Sparkly with a pearl and crystal-crusted strap. The most decadent and gorgeous shoes she had ever had on her feet.

She looked down at Dan, his eyes wide as he watched her. "You lit up when you put these on. I have to buy them for you."

"Dan, they're so expensive."

"But you, my love, are priceless."

After a smidge of arm-twisting, Dan handed over a credit card, and she was the proud owner of the heels.

After Jimmy Choo, they walked back to the room to get ready for dinner. One of her dresses, a one-shoulder cream number with a slit up her thigh, matched her new shoes perfectly. She felt like herself again, a version she was in L.A.. Money didn't matter, the future didn't matter. Live for *this* moment.

It was fun to play again.

Dan emerged in a slim-fit sports coat over slacks, his hair gelled back and his face clean-shaven.

"Those shoes were definitely the right choice."

"Is this too much?" Makenna asked, towering over him.

"Absolutely not. I have the hottest woman in Vegas," he said, reaching onto the balls of his feet to kiss her.

Dan wanted to play Blackjack, so Makenna followed him to a five-dollar table. He had just dropped thousands on the shoes on her feet, and he was bidding five dollars a hand.

It was still fun to watch.

"Oh my God, baby," Makenna said as Dan turned

another hand over, beating the dealer and spreading his arms out. "You are on fire."

"You're my lucky charm. I always knew it," Dan said, taking her hand in his and kissing it. She massaged his shoulders, watching Dan throw a five-dollar chip down like it was a thousand.

Makenna always knew Dan had money, but never really asked how much. They usually ate takeout from mid-price restaurants. He didn't own expensive cars or furniture. He drank Coors Light.

Now in Vegas, he was extravagant, dropping thousands on a single pair of shoes and hundreds on dinner at the steak house. The steak had melted in her mouth, and Dan didn't blink at ordering a red wine recommendation that glided over her tongue. If she had seen the bill, she probably would've fainted. She was currently holding a forty-dollar cocktail in her hand, and Dan didn't even flinch.

"What do you want to do after this?" Dan asked. "We could do the gondola, or we could do more shopping."

"You've already spent enough money on me."

"Darling, when I say it's not a problem, trust me." Dan leaned the back of his head into her stomach. She draped her arms over his front, getting a handful of his pecs in her grip and let them go.

"You two are so cute," a woman sitting at the same table as them said.

"Thank you. She's the cute one," Dan said.

A man walked over to the woman and set down a drink. "There you are, *wifey*."

The woman beamed at her husband. "Thank you, *hubby*. Oh, that's so exciting to say."

Was she still talking to them? Her eyes looked at Dan and Makenna like they were in on the conversation.

The woman leaned forward. "We just got married. A total-spur-of-the-moment thing!" the woman said, showing a simple gold band. The man circled his bride in his arms. "We thought, why the hell not. It's Vegas. We've been together for ten years, and it just felt right."

The couple just kept talking. "We went to the Grace and Roll Little Chapel just off the strip. We got married by *Elvis*."

"It was the only way I could get this one to marry me," the woman said, nudging her new husband.

"It was affordable too. We don't have that much money. We just walked in, and they took us right away. We were surprised, it being New Year's and all. Gave us this picture."

They pulled out a single eight by ten glossy of him and bride in a lip-lock while Elvis outstretched his arms over the couple with a lip snarl. Makenna giggled. It looked ridiculous.

Still, deciding to get married on a whim sounded terribly romantic.

"Congratulations," Makenna said.

"Yes, congratulations," Dan said, picking up a chip and handing it to them. "Here, my wedding present."

Makenna's eyes bulged when she saw the figure on the chip.

"Dan, that's a five-hundred-dollar chip," she whispered to him frantically.

"I know," he said.

"Thank you, mister," the man said in awe, shaking Dan's hand. He pinched the chip in his fingers and looked at his new bride. "We can have a fine night tonight to celebrate."

A single black tear trailed down the woman's cheek from the eyeliner that surrounded her eyes. She took a small bouquet of flowers, wrapped with a simple ribbon, and handed them to Makenna.

"Here, for you, as a thank you. They gave them to us at the chapel, but I want you to have them."

"I can't accept these. These are your wedding flowers. Don't people save these?"

"It's fine. Your generosity is more than those flowers are worth," she said.

"I spent ten years with this woman, and I should've done it sooner," the man said. "Just don't wait too long to lock that one down."

It wasn't clear who he was talking to, Dan or Makenna.

"As soon as she lets me, I will marry her," Dan said, squeezing her forearm. "She just has to say yes."

Her heart squeezed at that comment. Makenna was convinced that any moment it could end and dissolve, that he would realize how flawed she was or that she would do or say something that would ruin everything—but Dan's confidence that they would end up together never wavered, never faltered, and it buoyed hers.

Makenna watched the newlyweds leave the table, giddy with their wedding present from Dan. She rubbed his shoulders as he collected his chips to take to the cashier. After they handed him some fresh bills, Dan grabbed her hand.

"That was a really nice thing you did for them."

"They deserve to have a night out on the town. It's their wedding night. And it's New Year's."

Makenna's gaze narrowed. "How much money do you really have?"

"It's not polite to talk about finances," Dan said with a smirk. "Considering marrying me for money?"

"That chapel looked insane."

"Insanely fun," Dan said. "I've always wanted to get married by Elvis. He's the King."

"That would be fun." Makenna's cheeks warmed. Getting married. She had never thought she was the marrying type, after running away from two entirely decent marriage proposals and ghosting people the minute they said the L-word.

Now she saw a future with someone, and it...didn't feel scary.

She knew in her bones that Dan would love her forever.

They flitted among the various casino floors of the Vegas strip. Dan plunked down his credit card every time they wanted a drink and put three hundred dollars on black at the roulette table...and won. The chips and money kept piling up.

The shoes were finally catching up to her, so she suggested they rest at a bar.

"You must be up a lot," Makenna said, sipping another outrageously priced cocktail.

He shrugged. "I think maybe a thousand. Two? I lost count."

Her face relaxed as she rested in the small back on the stool at the bar, stirring her drink with the garnish on a toothpick. When she looked at him, his eyes stared at her.

"What?" she asked.

"You are so beautiful," he said. "I feel like the luckiest man in the world."

"You are," she joked. He kissed her cheek.

"I'm ready to tell everyone. I'm ready to tell my family, and my colleagues, and our friends how happy you make me."

Coming clean had been a long time coming. Makenna had had time to get to know Dan and fall in love with him without the outside world telling him to get away, that she was bad news. The alcohol's haze had drifted away, and Makenna felt stone-cold sober.

"I'm ready too. Let's tell everyone when we get back," Makenna said. Dan's shoulders relaxed, and a huge grin spread across his face. "So, is the story that we declared our love over Christmas?"

"Or we could come clean. About everything. Piper and Holden and what happened at the wedding."

A thought stumbled into her mind. The man earlier, who waited ten years just to do it one night in Vegas.

Don't wait too long to lock that one down.

Everyone would take them seriously if they were married. Would realize their relationship was real, not a joke. That she was done running from men.

That she loved Dan more than any man she had ever known.

That other people's opinions couldn't sway Dan away from loving her.

"You know what would be hilarious?" Makenna said as Dan massaged her neck.

"What?"

"If we came back married."

Dan's face fell.

"Sorry, that's a terrible idea." Her cheeks warmed. "Never mind."

"I don't joke about marriage," Dan said.

She smiled to appease the situation. "Forget I said anything."

Dan's face was serious. "If you married me, that would be it. Happily ever after. We would grow old together and have a family. You couldn't run away."

"I don't want to run away," she said fiercely.

His serious expression softened, and the corner of his lip

quirked. He took her face in his hands. "You're not drunk, are you?"

"No," she said with a laugh. "I'm shockingly sober. Maybe the clearest I've ever been."

"What are you saying?"

She closed her eyes and took a deep breath. "If we're telling everyone, if we're proclaiming to the world we're together, I want to do it with you as my husband."

"Are you serious, M? Marriage is forever for me. No matter how bad it is, we're in this together. We stay together. Always."

"Always," she repeated. "Let's go visit the King."

Dan stood up and did a back flip on the casino floor. The security guards looked alarmed.

"This woman said she wants to marry me. ME!" Dan yelled, touching his chest. A lone old lady with an oxygen machine smoking a cigarette clapped. He wrapped his arms around Makenna's waist. "I *love* this woman."

"You're my hero, man," a random guy called out. A slow clap started by the Walking Dead slot machines and slowly escalated. Dan ate it up, dipping her into a kiss.

"I'm getting ahead of myself," Dan said, shaking out his hands. He took Makenna's hands in his. "I need to do this right."

Then he lowered to one knee. Although a cluster of people had formed, two separate gasps happened from the crowd.

Nothing had felt more right in her life.

"Makenna Rose Brady, I loved you from the first moment you dismissed me at your brother's engagement party. I *knew* you were the one for me then. I don't have a ring since I had no idea this would happen, but I love you. Will you marry me? Tonight?"

She nodded, her eyes squinted she smiled so hard.

"She formally said yes. To *me*," Dan shouted to the crowd. He received two fist bumps from people on the outskirts, and he high-fived the lady with the oxygen machine.

"Let's go get hitched!" Dan said, pulling out his phone.

21

It was eleven-thirty when they arrived at the Grace and Roll Little Chapel's empty parking lot off the strip. The driver looked nervous as he dropped them off, speeding off without a word or a farewell.

"Either we're going to get married or murdered," Dan said, looking around.

"Let's go inside before we find out. These shoes are expensive," Makenna said, reaching for the door.

A bell announced their entrance, and a plump middle-aged white lady came out from the back, with her arms outstretched.

"Good evening. Happy New Year. I called a little bit ago. Dan Price?"

"Oh yes," she said, shaking his hand. "My name is Doris. And this is your beautiful fiancée?"

She blushed at the term. He pulled her close.

"Yes, Makenna." She held out her hand, and Doris, the woman who'd greeted them, had a surprisingly gripping, squeezing handshake.

Dan took a deep breath, looked at Makenna and then

back at Doris. "We would like to get married by Elvis, if the King is available."

"Of course!" she said, pulling out a large baby blue binder, placing it on the glass counter with a thunk. She flipped through the packages, going over the prices, letting her fingernails settle on the pages as they were flipped.

"We want the best package you have," Dan said, looking up from the binder.

"Aw, the Hunka Burning Love package is our deluxe package," Doris said. "What outfit do you want Elvis to wear?"

Without missing a beat, Dan said, "Obviously the gold lamé."

Doris closed the binder with a closed-lip smile. "A fine choice."

"We don't have any rings or anything," Dan said.

"We have some you can purchase. They're not much, but they get the job done. I'll be right back." She disappeared to the back, and Dan took Makenna's hands in his.

"Are you sure? You can still back out."

"I'm sure. Don't worry. This is *so* fun," she said, leaning down to give him a kiss. She pulled him in for a hug as he settled against her breasts. He kissed her cleavage before he pulled away when they heard Doris close to reemerging.

"These are all 14K gold-plated. I have the certificates proving so, if you need them."

She opened a black velvet flat block, with rows of rings arranged by size. Dan had seen nicer jewelry at swap meets. Still, he scanned the sizes and pulled one out, trying it on his ring finger.

"That looks so sexy on your hand," Makenna whispered.

Dan's cock hardened against the zipper of his pants, and he stepped one foot out so he could readjust. Sex with

Makenna was always great, but sex with Makenna as his wife sounded even hotter.

"I will be your hubby," Dan whispered into her ear.

Makenna pulled back with a lip snarl. "Ew, that word."

"Any man can be a husband. Only the best men are called hubby."

"I call my husband 'hubby' all the time," Doris interjected.

"See," Dan said, with pursed lips that made Makenna roll her eyes.

After they took care of some paperwork and payment, Doris straightened the stack of papers and looked up. They were led into the gaudy chapel, decorated in red and gold with a neon "Welcome to Las Vegas" sign. The colors were so strong, they hurt Dan's eyes.

"Will there be any other guests arriving for your big day?"

Makenna and Dan shook their heads. "Just us."

"Perfect," Doris said. "If you are ready, I will get the King. He can walk you down the aisle if you would like."

"No need to walk down the aisle," Makenna said, swinging their joined hands between them.

"Whatever you'd like, dear." Doris walked down the red carpet and disappeared into the lobby.

Dan turned back toward Makenna, looking up at her with her hands gripped in his.

"You can back out now," he said. "It's a big step so I would completely understand."

Makenna shook her head. "This is perfect. I'm so excited."

An Elvis impersonator walked in like he just got off a ten-hour horse ride. He wore the gold lamé suit with the black pompadour wig and dark sunglasses. There was a lot of pointing and swaggering.

"Are you the lovebirds?"

Dan looked up and said, "Yes, my King."

"Uh-huh uh-huh," he grunted, walking to the raised platform in front of them.

The sound system bellowed the opening notes of "Can't Help Falling in Love" as the impersonator sang surprisingly well into a rhinestone-encrusted microphone. Dan and Makenna stood frozen.

"This is so awkward," Makenna whispered.

"Dance with me. It's romantic and somehow *less* awkward."

Dan pulled her to him in a slow dance, his hand pressed against her back, her scent surrounding him.

When Elvis finished, he asked them to look at each other.

"My assistant told me that you have been in a love affair for some time. A *secret* one, at that."

"Yes, my King," Dan said. Doris had asked a few questions about their relationship as they filled out paperwork.

"And now you're in the wonderful, enchanting Las Vegas, pronouncing and declaring your love for one another, sealing it in the sacred institution of matrimony."

"Yes, my King," Dan said again. He winked at Makenna, and he noticed a glimmer at the corner of her eye. Her face broke into a wide grin.

With the love of his life in front of him, holding his hands, a tear slipping down her cheek, Dan knew without a doubt this was the most romantic wedding he had ever been to.

His heart could explode out of his chest at any moment with the joy he felt.

"Makenna Rose, please repeat after me."

As Makenna repeated the vows, her eyes held Dan's. This had to be a dream, an alternative version of reality where he got everything he wanted. As he said his vows, Dan couldn't believe that this woman had agreed to be his wife on a whim and they were sealing the deal in this completely audacious and ridiculous chapel.

He watched her for the tiniest sign of remorse, but there was none.

She was done running.

His cheeks hurt from smiling so hard.

He said his vows with all that he was, staring into her eyes, repeating after Elvis.

When the vows were said and the rings were exchanged, they both let out a collective breath. Dan wanted to get on top of the Bellagio and scream that he was finally a married man, and it was all because of his wife, the sexy, smart, and funny Makenna Brady.

"By the power vested in me by the state of Nevada, I pronounce you hubby and wife."

Makenna smirked and play-slapped Dan on the shoulder. Dan had snuck in that request when Makenna was in the bathroom to put on her veil.

"You may kiss your bride," Elvis said. The sound system played "Viva Las Vegas," and Elvis sang with committed hip gyrations.

Dan dipped Makenna and held her gaze and lowered his mouth to hers.

This was a kiss of passion and promise, a sign of new beginnings.

They would finally tell all their friends and family their secrets.

They would do that as hubby and wife.

22

NEW YEAR'S DAY

"Oh my fuck," Makenna said, rubbing her eyes. She sat up with a wave of nausea, coupled with a splitting headache and the spins.

Leaning against the headboard did nothing to anchor her.

Their room's frigid air tightened her nipples, making her look down in confusion. She wore only a pair of men's boxer briefs and a layer of goosebumps.

Did they...?

She held up her left hand and scream-laughed, falling over with her arms across her chest.

"One day in, and I just find out now that you laugh like that," Dan said. He sat up, rubbing his eyes with the palms of his hands. Makenna saw the identical piece of jewelry on his left ring finger.

"No fucking way." She laughed harder, flopping onto her side, kicking the comforter with her feet in excitement. "That was real?"

"I have the paperwork to prove it," he said. "It's around here somewhere."

He stood up, almost stumbling. Makenna bit her lip as she watched his cute ass and powerful thighs carry him around the room.

"Here," he said, plucking it from a folder and handing it to her.

"Oh my God," Makenna said. "You're my husband."

"You're my wife, Mrs. Price," Dan said, winking and kissing her on the head.

Just like Celine Dion, it was all coming back to her now.

Elvis.

Slow dancing to "Can't Help Falling in Love."

Signing the marriage certificate.

Saying vows.

Proceeding to get absolutely shit-faced and staying up way too late and having sloppy, drunk sex to consummate a legally binding marriage.

"My parents are going to shit their gallbladder," Makenna said, still laughing.

"Can I call them Mom and Dad?" he joked, looping his arms around her waist.

"They should probably know about you first," Makenna said. "Our friends are going to lose their shit. Oh my God. Oh my God." Dan trailed kisses down her shoulder, along the ridge of her collarbone. "Stop kissing me so I can think. I can't think. I'm *freaking* out."

Dan sat back, his hands clasped at his stomach, his cock tenting the comforter.

"How are you so calm right now?"

Dan shrugged. "Weirdly, I feel like this was destiny."

Makenna held out her hand, examining the cheap, gold-plated wedding band the chapel sold them. She never thought she'd see a ring on her finger, ever. That she would actually go through with it.

This made the lying worse. That their relationship had gone so far, that she had fallen in love and gotten married. Everyone would think this was just some cry for help.

Makenna, Lillyvale fuck-up, marries local hero in quickie marriage in Vegas. What a mismatch they are! There's no way she's with him for the right reasons. He should run away as fast as he can.

"I don't remember if I said it when the clock struck midnight, but happy birthday."

"Thank you," Dan said, rising to his knees to tackle her to the bed. "This is the best birthday of my life."

"I'm kind of freaking out right now," Makenna said, lying on her back. "I also think I'm going to throw up."

Dan pulled back his hands so she could rush the bathroom. Nothing came up.

She stared at her dark circles in the mirror as Dan joined her at the sinks, grabbing his toothbrush.

"What do you want to do today?" Dan asked. His hair stuck out in every direction.

"Not die."

"Oh baby," he said, snuggling into her. "You partied so hard."

"I haven't been this hung over in a while," she replied, leaning over.

"You earned that hangover. Hennessy and vodka. Girl."

"That wasn't my best moment," she said. "I can't believe we got married. I *was not* drunk for that."

"Thank God," Dan said, through mouth suds. He spat into the sink and cupped some water to rinse.

"We need some coffee, some grease, and plan of attack."

"We can always call everyone right now," Dan said.

That *definitely* made her want to vomit. "I can't. We need

to do it all at once, in public. So no one can get angry and make a scene."

"Oh, they still might," Dan said, examining his face.

"Who?" Makenna asked, turning. She caught a glint of the wedding ring on his hand, which somehow sent desire straight between her legs.

"My mother."

His mother? Oh God, what if she doesn't like me?

Dan sensed her thoughts, like he always did. "She'll like you. Don't worry. It's just—my mom told me explicitly not to elope. Sam, my older brother, ran off to Reno with his son's mom, and she kind of sobbed." Dan turned on the faucet to wash the suds down the sink.

"And..."

"She might cry when I tell her we got married. Nothing personal, though."

Dan tilted his head to the side, as if he'd suddenly remembered something. He tapped his pointer finger against his lips.

"What? Who else?"

"My attorney might be *slightly* mad. Just a little bit." Dan held up his thumb and pointer finger an inch apart.

"What? Why?" The nerves bumbled in her stomach, and a wave of nervous nausea took over. Having an attorney mad at her couldn't be a good thing.

"He'll be mad I didn't get a pre-nup. Also nothing personal."

Makenna leaned on the counter.

"He also might want us to get it annulled. But I will tell him no, M, don't worry."

"Okay," she said, but inside she was freaking out. *A prenup? The fuck?*

"Everything will be fine. Promise," he said, kissing her cheek. "Let's get brunch. Brunch will help us think straight."

Thoughts of food made her stomach lurch. She hunched over on the counter. "I don't know if I can eat anything without it immediately coming back up again."

"You're not the first person to be hung over in this town," Dan said. "And accidentally married."

"You were just so charming and cute..."

"Hey, whatever works. I snagged you."

Makenna turned to look at her husband. *Her husband.* "You don't regret doing it, do you?"

"Absolutely not," he said firmly. "You're it for me." Dan brought his hands down her sides, letting his thumbs skim her breasts and settle on her hips, the tips of his fingers flirting with the top of her ass. "I will never stop believing in us. It's always been us against the world. If people are mad, they'll get over it. We're stronger than that."

He pulled her head down to his, capturing her lips in a kiss so scorching that a few brief moments sent her skin ablaze. Even hungover, she still wanted him, wanted his caress, him inside of her. Her hand went to his cock and squeezed, a laugh escaping her lips.

"Don't keep doing that unless you want me to bend you over this counter," Dan said.

"At least my face will be over the sink," she replied. She pulled down Dan's boxer briefs, and turned around, rubbing her ass against his hard cock. She bent over, her elbows anchored on the marble.

"Good God, you are so hot, even though you look green," he said, brushing her hair over her shoulder and gripping her neck.

"So we'll tell people when we get back," Makenna said as Dan slipped inside of her.

"Immediately," Dan said, bracing his hand on the counter.

23

MALCOLM'S SURPRISE PARTY FOR TAYLOR

"Okay, we tell our friends today," Dan said, breathing out rapidly over the steering wheel.

"Today is the day," Makenna agreed, holding her purse in her lap. The fear in her eyes matched Dan's.

Dan and Makenna had every intention of telling people as soon as they got home.

And then...they didn't. Almost two months had gone by and nothing changed.

Her parents left around the first of the year for an impromptu trip to Hawaii and had been there for three weeks. Makenna had lived with him for that time, going home to collect the mail every few days and water the plants. It didn't seem fair to tell one set of parents over the other.

Then, Dan's mother had surgery to remove her gall-bladder and was recovering. Dan knew his mother would have a hard time with their elopement, since his older brother Sam's elopement caused her to lose her mind for a good couple months, as Sam and his then wife, Kylie, dealt with an unexpected pregnancy to top it off.

Dan got super busy at work and all their friends had been busy, so it was tough to wrangle everyone. Until today.

It made sense to delay breaking the news.

However, there was one thing that irked Dan.

Makenna didn't wear her ring. At all.

He asked her once in mid-January why.

"Because no one knows yet. I'll wear it when we tell people," she had told him.

It made perfect sense, he supposed. It made no sense why it bothered him so much.

Maybe she needed a better one. That had to be it. His wife deserved more than a cheap "gold" ring. His had turned his finger green, but he still wore it.

"So this is a surprise party for Taylor? Does Taylor have any idea?" Makenna stayed glued to the passenger seat.

Dan shook his head. "I saw her this morning at yoga. She has no clue."

"Oh, her birthday party. That's when we got together."

"So it's fitting that we tell everyone today."

"Yes," Makenna said. "It's perfect."

The look of nausea on her face did not match her words.

"Let's go," Dan said. "The plan of attack is for Taylor to be surprised, settled, and then we lower the boom."

"Sounds perfect," Makenna said. She stepped out, establishing her heels against the gravel before standing up. She wore her tailored black jacket over a wide-leg slacks. Her new Jimmy Choos looked so good on her feet, a signal to him that everything was amazing, even if they hadn't told anyone yet.

Dan grabbed for her hand, and Makenna's awkwardly fumbled in his. She pulled her hand away when they reached the pathway to the restaurant. He felt a small tear in his heart when Makenna ripped her hand away.

"Do you want to stagger our entrances?" Makenna asked.

Dan shook his head. "We're going to tell everyone, so it doesn't matter at this point."

Makenna's face drained of color, although she wore layers of blush and contour, something Dan had learned about as she explained all the products she used, naked.

A little part of him wished they could stay in their secret love bubble forever.

Makenna didn't say anything as she opened the restaurant door, going in first while Dan held it open. They walked to the rear of the restaurant, to the patio where the party was to be held. Heat lamps dotted the space, and Taylor's and Malcolm's friends milled around, holding cocktails or water.

Makenna went one direction, and Dan went to another.

He saw Makenna chatting with Kelsey, the manager of Taylor's studio, Cycle Yoga Love.

Come on, baby, look at me.

Her head turned toward him, and they locked eyes. She winked, and the corners of her lips turned up.

Calm flowed through him. *It's just us. We'll tell everyone today. Then we'll tell our parents, and she'll move in with me permanently and we can finally start our lives together.*

"Dan," Zoey said, walking up to him, her husband Jonathan falling shortly behind. He had been the officiant of their wedding back in October, and his heart no longer twinged when he saw her. Still, Zoey hugs were some of his favorite things in the world.

Jonathan shook Dan's hand and pulled him in for a bro hug.

"How's married life?" Dan asked, crossing his arms. His

gold ring laid on his hand, resting on his bicep. He always tempted fate, but no one noticed.

"Oh, it's wonderful," Zoey said, hugging Jonathan's waist, while Jonathan put his arm around her, rubbing her shoulder.

"Couldn't be happier," Jonathan added.

"I'm so excited for Taylor and Malcolm! This is so fun to do it this way," Zoey said.

"Yeah, it's so nice he could do this for Taylor. I'm sure he's excited to see her reaction."

Zoey's eyes narrowed with a slight nod of her head. "It's more than nice."

"Stupendous, romantic, pure orgasmic joy then," Dan said.

"That's more like it," Zoey replied. She play-punched him in the chest. "What about you? When are you going to meet a lucky lady and get married?"

Funny you should ask.

"Well," Dan said. "I may have met someone."

"Ooh," Zoey said. "Anyone we know?"

Dan rubbed his hands together, sure Zoey would notice the ring. Instead her eyes stayed on his face. "I'll tell you later."

"Oh, mystery. Gossip. I can't wait," Zoey said. "I'm going to go say hi to Taylor's parents. I haven't seen them in a few years."

Zoey hugged him again and trailed off, Jonathan following behind her. Taylor's parents lived in Texas, and rarely came back to Lillyvale.

That's strange. Come all this way for a surprise birthday party. On a Wednesday. Huh.

Taylor's sister Ellie ran in, wearing a dress and out of breath. Connor, Malcolm's little brother, followed, being yanked in by Ellie.

"They're close!"

Ellie rarely wears dresses. Something is up.

The crowd organized, facing the doors that led to the restaurant. Dan was on the opposite side of the room from his wife, and he wished that her hand was in his. Or his hand was squeezing her butt.

They heard footsteps outside the double doors and Taylor's voice.

"They're coming. SSSHH," Ellie scream-whispered, loud enough to give away the surprise.

When they opened the door, Taylor and Malcolm held up their left hands, *both* with rings, and shouted, "Surprise!"

What.

Dan looked across the room at Makenna, and her shocked face matched his.

What do we do? Makenna mouthed, her eyes wide with terror.

Caroline burst into tears with a loud wail. Dan rubbed his face.

Well, telling everyone tonight was out of the question. Stealing Taylor and Malcolm's surprise marriage thunder wasn't going to happen.

"Oh my goodness, they fooled us!" Addison said nearby, covering her mouth with her hands. "They are so silly."

"The silliest," Kirk said. He kissed Addison's hair.

Dan crinkled his forehead and pulled his phone out to check the invite again.

Help surprise Taylor after I propose to her!

Shit.

Dan hadn't read the entire email. He had just assumed since it was around her birthday that this was a surprise party for her thirtieth. It was actually to surprise her after he *proposed* to her. And instead, they had eloped, just like Makenna and Dan had done, and told people immediately.

They didn't wait two fucking months to say anything.

His phone buzzed in his hand.

Makenna: WTF do we do?

Dan typed back, *I don't know* and slipped his phone back into his pocket.

It was time to do what he always did: fake it until you make it. He had to pretend he knew about this the entire time.

"I *knew* it," Dan lied, taking Taylor and Malcolm in for a tandem hug. "My first success story of Happily Lillyvale After Matchmaking."

His little matchmaking and dating coach service had taken off, making the nights Makenna had to work bearable. Taylor and Malcolm hadn't formally hired him; he just did a lot of greasing the wheels between them so they could realize they were meant to be.

They chatted a little bit more until Taylor looked behind him in the direction of his wife.

"I see Makenna is here. What's going on there?"

You could say something. That was the plan.

Dan's heart raced. Makenna's eyes were wide underneath all the eyeliner.

"Nothing," Dan said, walking away.

When he looked back, Taylor's parents had already swarmed her and her new husband, distracting her from his terrible performance.

His phone vibrated against his thigh.

Makenna: Meet me in the bathroom. Now.

He looked around. No witnesses. The bathroom was at the far corner of the restaurant, and once he slipped down the hall, fingernails cut into his flesh and he was pulled into one of the single-room bathrooms.

Makenna's hands went to her head. "What do we do?"

"We can't say anything today. It would be tacky," Dan said.

Makenna shook out her hands, her bracelets jingling. "I feel like I want to jump out of my skin."

"Same," Dan said. He gripped her waist, pulling her in for a hug. "It'll be okay. We'll just tell them later."

"I psyched myself up for today being the day. I drank two Red Bulls. I want to claw up this wall."

Dan kissed her before he let her go. "We could tell one person. It could be a way to dip our toe in. Complete our mission. Well, kind of."

"Who should we tell?" Makenna asked, her lips parted.

"ADDISON," Makenna said, finding her seated next to her boyfriend, Kirk. Dan had walked out first and was currently joking around with Jonathan. His eyes flicked over to see any reaction from Addison. There would definitely be something.

They decided Addison would be the best "dipping your toe in" person. She was incredibly forgiving, kind, and a steel trap. She wouldn't tell anyone.

"Hi Makenna. You look so gorgeous today," Addison said, her face a bright smile. "I love the shoes."

"Thanks. Hi Kirk."

"Hi Makenna. I think your shoes are nice too," Kirk said, his arm around his girlfriend.

"Thanks," Makenna said. "Addison, I have to talk to you."

"Sure," she said. She kissed Kirk before she stood up, letting her hands linger on his shoulders for as long as possible. A smile stayed on Addison's lips like a dream as she followed Makenna out into the restaurant.

Makenna longed for the day she could kiss Dan freely, after everyone got mad and then over it.

Addison walked in first to the bathroom, and Makenna locked the door behind them.

"What's up?" she asked, turning around, her eyes bright and happy.

"I have something to tell you," Makenna said. Her hands shook and grew clammy as she paced the small room.

"Okay." There was some nervousness in her voice.

"I don't want you to freak out or tell anyone. Please."

"Your secret is safe with me. Promise," Addison said. She pantomimed zipping her lips, locking it and throwing away the key.

Makenna breathed in and out. "Dan and I have been seeing each other."

Addison stood there, her mouth parting. A curl fell in her face, and she tucked it behind her ear. "Are you joking? You're serious."

Makenna nodded. Addison said nothing and took Makenna in for a crushing hug. Makenna sunk into her arms and wrapped her arms around her upper back. She heard whimpering in her ear.

"I secretly hoped this would happen after Piper and Holden were caught, you know," Addison said.

Makenna could've mentioned they were seeing each other sooner. Or that she was married. Admitting she was seeing Dan was enough of a step. She could tell everyone the full story later, all at once.

"You're the only one who knows," Makenna said. "My parents don't know. His don't. None of the gang knows."

When Addison let Makenna go from her death grip, she wiped her eyes with her hands. She pulled down a paper towel. "I'm honored you told me first. Oh my goodness, Makenna."

"What do you think?" Makenna asked.

"I think it's *wonderful*," Addison said. Her face morphed into the prettiest ugly cry face she had ever witnessed. Through sobs, she asked, "Are you in love?"

"Yes," Makenna said. Addison grabbed another paper towel and dabbed her eyes.

"I've been hoping and praying that you two would find your way to each other. I'm just thrilled it happened. I'm so happy for you."

"You are?" Makenna asked.

Addison looked at her. "You're such a special person, Makenna. You deserve a man like Dan. He is the best." Addison's face broke out with more sobs. "I'm so glad you got together."

Addison crushed her in another hug, swaying her side-by-side.

Guilt wrecked Makenna. She wanted to say there was more to the story, but the inertia consumed her. How would they admit Piper and Holden were fake? That she'd been lying for over a year every time someone questioned her? That she married him, since they were in a committed, loving relationship, not just some random thing?

Addison had been such a good friend, and Makenna couldn't admit it, couldn't lose her right now.

Addison looked in the mirror and fixed any smudges near her eyes. When she turned around, it seemed like she hadn't been sobbing five seconds prior.

"Let's go back to the party," Addison said, turning back to the bathroom door and unlocking it. The skirt of her dress swooshed as she stepped out of the bathroom, and Makenna followed.

When they reached the patio, Addison zeroed in on Dan. Addison beelined toward him and took him in for a crushing hug.

"I assume you told Addison," Dan said, his voice straining since Addison was hugging him so hard. Addison let him out of her grip and took both Dan and Makenna under her arms.

"I told Makenna, but I wanted to let you know your secret is safe with me. I'm so glad you came to your senses, after Piper and Holden."

Dan tilted his head, looking at Makenna. "Yeah, we just realized we were made for each other."

"When are you going to tell everyone?" Addison asked, setting her hands on her hips.

"Soon," Makenna said. "We don't want to rain on Taylor and Malcolm's day."

"I'm sure everyone would be thrilled. You two together, boyfriend and girlfriend. It's so perfect." She took them in a hug and told them she needed to get back to Kirk.

Dan's jaw clenched. "Bathroom. Now."

After the door was closed, Dan put his hands on his hips.

"Does Addison know we're married?"

"No," Makenna said.

"What does Addison think we are, Makenna?" No *baby*, no *M*. Dan saying her full name twisted her insides.

"That we got together after Piper and Holden were caught together."

"Why doesn't she know about the wedding?"

"Because," Makenna hedged. "I froze. I'm sorry. She'll understand. She's Addison."

"I thought we were done lying," Dan said. His face had zero joy to it, a face she had only seen once, after a contractor let him down and he chewed him out over the phone.

"We are. After today," Makenna said.

Dan wouldn't look at her. Over a year of seeing each other, and they had never fought. Now they were two months into marriage, and it was already tense.

"Is everything okay?" Makenna asked.

"It's fine," Dan said. He smiled, and it made her feel slightly better. "Please sit with me by the meal. I want my wife next to me."

"Sure," Makenna said.

The tension melted away after that, thank God.

They ate, laughing and talking, sitting next to each other at a long table. When Taylor and Malcolm gave their wedding speeches to the crowd, Dan rested his arm on the back of Makenna's chair. His fingers brushed her skin slightly, sending shivers up her arm.

Everything would be okay. Once everyone was told, life would return to normal. They would be happy.

As Taylor held the microphone, looking around the room, Makenna felt liquid warmth through her torso. Everyone was so forgiving of Malcolm and Taylor eloping. Maybe she could hope for the same for her and Dan. Still, Dan flinched when she tried to put her hand on his knee.

24

FOUR DAYS LATER

"I'm excited to meet her. What's her name again?" Dan's mom asked, perching on the couch's armrest.

"Makenna," Dan said. He checked his phone. No messages. His knee bobbed nervously.

"There must be traffic since your brother is late as well," she said. "I'll be in the kitchen. Call me when she gets here."

Nick walked in the great room, his nose buried in his phone. "Is the girlfriend here yet?"

"Not yet," Dan said.

A knock came at the door, and Dan bolted to open it.

"Hi," Makenna said, her smile tinged with stiffness. She wore a long-sleeved dress that barely scooped in the front and reached her knees. Her thigh tattoo peeked out from the hem, but most of the other ones were covered. She wore flats, and he wasn't used to how short she was without her usual heels.

He hugged her and whispered, "Don't be nervous. They'll love you."

Makenna pulled away, her smile still showing the same level of nerves. It was finally time to start telling everyone.

Dan had also been waiting for this moment for his baby brother to encounter the Instagram model he had been whacking off to in the flesh.

Nick's mouth fell open when they rounded the corner and he saw Makenna.

"You're, you're…"

"Makenna," she said, holding out a hand. "Pleasure to meet you."

"I have to go to the bathroom," Nick said, run-walking down the hall.

"What was that?" Makenna asked.

"I'll tell you later," Dan said with a wink.

"Is she here?" Dan's mom asked, appearing from the kitchen. Her smile froze. "Makenna," she said, holding out her hand. "It's so nice to meet you. I've heard so much about you." Dan's mom took her hand like it was a gift she didn't want. "I'm Joyce. Can I get you something to drink? A glass of wine, a beer, water?"

"Wine would be lovely, thank you."

Dan's mom walked to the kitchen as the door opened and Dan's nephew barreled in the front door in an astronaut helmet, his hands on the plastic to keep it from wobbling.

"I'm sorry we're late. We couldn't find the helmet, and we just had to have it," Sam said, closing the door. Dan waited for Sam to put down the duffel bag he carried at all times as Elijah's pack mule and snack bitch.

"Sam, I would like you to meet my lady, Makenna."

"Makenna, it's very nice to meet you," Sam said, shaking her hand. "Elijah, come here and say hello to your uncle and his friend."

Elijah reappeared from his trajectory down the hall.

Dan crouched down in front of the four-year-old, tapping on the face shield. Elijah pushed it up to show two mischievous green eyes and a slight dusting of freckles over a nose.

"I want you to meet a very special lady," Dan said, standing up. Makenna leaned down in front of the little boy.

"Hi Elijah, my name is Makenna."

The little boy looked to his father, and then to Dan. Out of nowhere, a large wail slash scream echoed out of the space helmet.

"I scared a child. Oh my God," Makenna said, standing up.

"She looks like a *witch*," Elijah said through tears.

"Let's take this helmet off so you don't waterboard yourself," Sam said. Another ear-piercing scream rang out. Sam twitched. "I'm sorry. We didn't have a nap this afternoon so we have *this*."

"Do I look like a witch?" Makenna asked softly.

"If you do, cast a sexy spell on me, Broomhilda." Dan squeezed her butt covertly.

"Baby."

"What? That was a great joke," Dan said.

Sam walked down the hall with an exhausted child in his arms.

Dan wrapped his arm around Makenna as they sat on the couch. Makenna shivered under his arm so he pulled an afghan off the back of the couch and arranged it around her shoulders.

"Thank you," Makenna whispered. Dan gave her a wink. "I'm so uncomfortable."

"It'll be fine," Dan said. He smiled as his mom approached them, presenting a glass of wine to Makenna and a Coors Light to Dan.

"So," Joyce said, sitting down and tucking her feet under her. "Tell me about yourself, Makenna."

Nick had wandered in and sat down in the recliner, still shell-shocked that his Instagram feed had manifested itself in their living room.

"I'm a makeup artist. I work at the Eloise Winston counter at the Nordstrom at the Galleria. I also do some freelance work, for weddings and prom. Stuff like that."

"Oh, interesting," Dan's mom said, pointing to her eyes. "Your eye makeup is very... dramatic."

Dan looked at Makenna, who was wearing her standard smoky eye. He rubbed her shoulders. "Makenna is very talented."

"I'm sure she is," she said. "How did you meet my son?"

"At my brother's wedding. Almost two years ago."

"Is that the wedding where Addison's old boyfriend fought the grandpa?"

Makenna nodded. "The very one."

"Oh," she said. She took a sip of wine and remained quiet, as Makenna's wine teetered on her own knee.

What is happening?

He didn't know what to expect from his mother. It was his hope that she would open her arms and home to Makenna, since she was the most amazing woman ever. She hadn't cared for Zoey either, but she'd slapped on a smile and gabbed with her all through dinner and after.

This reaction was tough to read.

Dan turned to his younger brother, whose mouth still hung open like a broken ventriloquist dummy. "Can I help you?"

"She's on my Instagram feed. Now she's here," Nick said in awe. "My teacher was right. All I have to do is put it out into the universe, and it will come true."

"I saw her first," Dan said. Makenna's body stiffened more, her shoulders hunched under his arm.

Nick leaned forward, eyes locked on Makenna. "I'm eighteen, if you want to trade in for a younger model."

"Nick!"

Dan had hoped Sam would materialize, so he could do this all at once but he couldn't hold it in anymore.

"Well, she's now your sister," Dan blurted out.

"What?" Dan's mom and brother said in unison.

Dan shifted on the couch to reach into his pocket to pull his ring out. "She's not only my lady friend, she's also my wife."

The shock hung over them like a cloud of smoke.

"Dan. Daniel. What?" Dan's mom said. He could see the puddles of tears forming. Nick sat there, dumbfounded.

"We've been seeing each other for a year, and when I went to Vegas for my birthday, she came with me. And we got married."

Makenna shot him a look. There were so many versions of the story of them, but Dan wanted to tell one version. The truth.

Dan's mom covered her face with her hands. "It's Sam and Kylie all over again."

"Is she really my sister?" Nick asked, distressed. "I think I need to wash my eyes out with bleach. Mom, I need to go see the priest. ASAP."

"Sister-in-*law*," Dan's mom corrected. "Are you pregnant? Is that it? Oh my God. Oh my God," she said, leaning over, putting her head between her legs.

"I'm not pregnant," Makenna said.

"I love her," Dan said, looking at Makenna. A tentative smile crossed her face. "I married her because I love her."

"Why didn't you tell us before you got married?" Dan's mom said, still in tears. "Do you think so little of us that you couldn't introduce this...special woman to us? You just sprung this on us?"

"It would save me a lot of angst if you would've told me." Nick leaned back in the recliner. "You're paying for my therapy. Mom, does this mean Dan is no longer the favorite?"

"I'm always the favorite," Dan shot back.

"I'm going to go finish dinner," Dan's mom said, standing up and walking to the kitchen. "Makenna, will you join me?"

Makenna's nervous expression worried Dan. "It'll be fine, baby. Promise," he said.

She stood up tentatively and followed his mother into the kitchen, looking back like a calf about to go to slaughter.

"I'm going to go talk to Sam," Dan said.

"I'll just be here, considering all my life choices," Nick said, his face lit by the screen.

Well, that couldn't have gone worse.

Dan walked to the room Sam used when he visited and nudged the door open. His nephew sat with his hands in his lap as Sam knelt by him.

"Hey you little stinker," Dan said, approaching Elijah.

"We just had a good long talk about meeting strangers introduced by me or Uncle Dan," Sam said. Sam stood up and moved close to Dan. "We just watched one of those effed-up 'Stranger Danger' specials from the nineties Mom showed us, and he's still a little raw."

"How dare you. You had nightmares for weeks when we watched that."

"The music really dials it up a notch. It's the sole reason I don't date," Sam said. They both studied the dejected little boy sitting on the bed.

"So, I have something to tell you," Dan said. "Makenna isn't just my girlfriend, she's my wife."

"What?" Sam croaked, his hand wiping down his face. "Seriously?"

Dan nodded.

"Does she love you? Does she need a green card? Did you knock her up?"

"No! She loves me and I love her. She was born in Lilly-vale, you jackass," Dan said.

Sam put a finger to his lips and they looked at Elijah, entranced by a large picture book.

"I just worry about you. Some of the girls you've brought home haven't been the best for you."

Dan breathed in and out. Sam had called Zoey's uneven affection for him from the beginning, but Dan ignored it. "It's different with Makenna. She loves me as much as I love her."

"Are you sure it's not just..." Sam said, punching his fist.

"What, Sam?"

I want to hear you say it in front of your son.

"Playing volleyball?" he said, his voice an uptick at the end of the sentence. Dan laughed, since Sam actually played volleyball in high school and definitely hadn't got laid.

"Trust me, we do a lot more than play volleyball."

"I want to play volleyball!" Elijah yelled.

"If we've learned anything from Britney Spears and Kevin Federline, good volleyball playing does not mean you are compatible in other areas," Sam said.

"That is true. However, Federline never deserved our queen Britney."

"Who is Britney?" the little boy asked.

"We're going to need a whole afternoon to discuss that," Dan said. "However, all you need to know is 'Free Britney.'"

"Free Britney," the little boy repeated, giggling.

"What is your attorney doing about this?"

"He doesn't know yet."

"He's going to *freak*." Sam knew how extra Andrew could be. He thought for a moment, then nodded. "But I trust you. If you say you're happy, I'm happy for you. Just be careful."

"Makenna is *not* Kylie," Dan said, referencing Sam's ex-wife. Sam and Kylie had eloped to Reno when Kylie was three months pregnant with Elijah. She left them right after the baby was born, saying she wasn't ready to be a wife and mother.

Dan didn't plan to rush into parenthood with Makenna. It was something he definitely wanted, but there were so many steps.

Tell everyone.

Move in together.

Get Makenna out of debt.

"Don't get her pregnant right away," Sam said. "For the love of God, please."

"I promise I won't."

"You're a great guy, baby brother. You have so much to offer, and I just don't want to see you taken advantage of. You should tell Andrew as soon as possible to protect yourself."

Dan nodded, knowing he would have to tell his attorney. His attorney who might suggest annulling the marriage or, at the very least, drafting an iron-clad document to protect his assets. He didn't care about all of the risks. He had Makenna. She was worth more than all of his money.

"Does Dad know?" Sam asked.

Dan shook his head. "I haven't heard from him in a while."

"I wouldn't tell him unless he calls you," Sam said.

"That was the plan," Dan said.

"Just look out for you. I don't want you to get hurt," Sam said, clamping him on the shoulder.

"I appreciate your concern, but Makenna would never hurt me," he replied.

They looked over to see Elijah splayed across the bed, out cold.

Sam walked out of the room and Dan followed. Once they had told everyone, they could start the rest of their lives. Once that happened, everything would be perfect.

ONCE MAKENNA CLOSED the bathroom door, she stumbled to the closed toilet to sit down. Her hands went into her hair, and she clamped her hands together.

Joyce had been perfectly polite, smiling with tight lips as Makenna tossed the salad and set the table. At one point, she had to leave the room, clearly near tears again, and Makenna stood in the empty kitchen with the salad tongs and bubbling glaze for the pork chops. Right before dinner was announced, Makenna excused herself to wash her hands.

It was an excuse to have a moment alone and text Sierra.

Her best friend would know the right thing to say. Sierra had been surprised about the quickie wedding, but nowhere near the devastation Dan's mom had experienced.

Makenna: We just told Dan's family. Dan's mom cried. Not in a good way.

Sierra's blinking three dots appeared immediately.

Sierra: It's probably a shock. Give it time. Show her your sparkling personality LOL

Sierra: Remember you love him. And he loves you.

Makenna breathed in and out. "She just has to see your

love for him. She will come around," she said out loud to herself in the mirror.

When Makenna left the bathroom, Dan caught her and pulled her into a different room and closed the door. She looked around at all the photos on the wall-- toothless smiles of Dan as a kid holding a baseball bat. Pictures of Joyce holding a baby next to Dan's older brother Sam. She wondered if a photo of her and Dan would make it to the wall.

"How are you doing? Everything okay?" Dan asked.

"I don't think your mom likes me," Makenna said, crossing her arms.

"It'll be okay," he said, taking her in a hug. "My mother is very loving. She will love you. I'm her favorite and she told me explicitly not to elope, and I did. It's just a shock."

His arms felt reassuring around her, and his back rubs were her favorite.

"Let everyone see the Makenna I know," Dan said, kissing her and pulling her by the hand.

Makenna felt better as she walked out to dinner. She sat down and placed the napkin in her lap. Sam sat across from her, holding his hands over his plate.

"I'm sorry my kid scared you," Sam said. "He can be a little a-hole sometimes."

"Where is he now?"

"Sleeping, thankfully," Sam said. "He's been fighting naps, and it's been tough."

They stayed quiet as Joyce and Dan came in and out with dishes, placing them on the table. Nick wandered in, a video playing from his phone. He dropped like a ton of bricks on his dining room chair, never looking up from his screen.

"Nick, get off your phone," Sam said, swatting at it. "We need to get to know Makenna."

"Fine," Nick said, the human equivalent of a passive aggressive sigh. "What kind of music are you into?"

Makenna smiled wide. Music was something she was passionate and *very* opinionated about.

"My favorite is Metallica. I also really like this band called Ghost. Their stage shows are like art. Tool is also a favorite. I also like the Rolling Stones and blues, jazz. I like it all, really."

"Except Taylor Swift," Dan said, walking in with the salad. "I found that out, and I still married her."

If she was anywhere else, she would go into a long rant about Taylor Swift. Instead she said, "I'm not really into pop music."

"Lame," Dan said, kissing her on the top of her head. "I still love you."

"Oh, don't make me vomit all over this clean floor," Nick said.

Dan settled his hands on her shoulders, standing behind her. She brought her hands to his.

"I still can't get over it," Sam said. "We didn't even know you were seeing anyone. Now you're married."

"You're one to talk," Dan said, from behind Makenna.

"The family at least knew about Kylie, Dan," Sam countered. His jaw looked tight, like he was swallowing back his comments.

Joyce and Dan sat down, and they all linked hands. Makenna's family only went to church on the major Christian holidays, so praying before a meal was foreign to her. Makenna surveyed the table while everyone's head was bowed.

"We also want to thank you for Makenna, the newest

member of our family. May she...may she be a welcome addition to our family." Joyce's voice rattled into a sob.

"Mom, are you okay?" Dan asked.

Joyce stood up and escaped through the kitchen.

"I'll be back," Dan said. He kissed Makenna on the cheek and followed his mom outside.

"The last time she cried like that was when you told her that you married Kylie," Nick said to Sam.

"Be quiet," Sam replied. He smiled at Makenna and began passing the dishes around. Makenna took the rice pilaf but felt an undeniable brick in her stomach.

"Mom, what's wrong?" Dan asked, closing the sliding door behind him. Dusk had fallen, and the luminescent lights that surrounded the grass area by the pool glowed.

He couldn't see his mother clearly but knew she was a mess.

"I just worry about you honey. You have such a big heart, and you love so hard. Are you sure she's worth it? That she's in it for the right reasons? I would support you one hundred percent if you decided all of this was a mistake."

Heated anger pounded through him.

"She is one thousand percent worth it," Dan said. He could feel a dramatic monologue coming on. "She understands me in a way that no one does. I know her, and she knows me. We are made for each other. I love her with my whole heart."

"She doesn't know how lucky she is to have you," his mom said tearily.

"I'm the lucky one," Dan said. "This is real. I promise. I wouldn't marry just anyone."

Even though Makenna had been acting funny, even if she was overwhelmed by all the next steps, he loved her. He remembered how it was before they got married. How easy it was. Now, there were just some growing pains, some adjustments that needed to be made. Everything would be fine.

Dan's mom dropped her glasses with a tink on the patio table. She rubbed the bridge of her nose. "I don't know, Danny. I just have a bad feeling."

"I promise I know what I'm doing," he said. His mother opened her arms, and Dan walked into them, like he was a five-year-old who had a bad dream. She was slightly shorter than him, so she always fit, and her hug felt like a warm afghan on a chilly night.

"I just want you to be happy. You deserve everything. My sweet baby angel."

"I know I'm still your favorite."

She smiled and swatted him. They both knew it was true.

"Does Andrew know about your marriage?"

"No," Dan said. "I'm going to tell him soon."

Dan's mom gave the signature "Joyce Look," a tilt of the head and raised eyebrows, a look of judgment.

"Don't look at me like that. I don't need it from you and eventually from Andrew."

"I trust you. And I love you. I just don't want you to get hurt."

"Makenna wouldn't do that. We have a great relationship," he said, holding his mom. "Please give her a chance."

"I will," she said, patting him on the chest before going back inside.

Dan loved like his mom, unconditionally and unyieldingly. But he knew she had her own issues related to his dad leaving and that she was probably putting them on Makenna. Makenna wasn't like his dad at all. She whispered "I love yous" in the dark and kissed him with all the heart-soaring feelings that melted him into a puddle and hardened his dick to granite. He knew it was right when she looked into his eyes in front of the King in Vegas, saying her vows without pausing or fumbling.

He decided that all she needed was a better ring to wear with pride and to get through this awkward period of transition, and then they would live happily ever after. And as they endured, they would prove everyone wrong.

Everyone just needed time.

The dinner improved after that. He watched his wife relax, laughing at jokes and stories of Dan as a child. His mom told the story of how Dan carried an old-man handkerchief for a full year and finally got his moment to shine when he happened upon a crying woman at the food court at the mall. Dan, at six years old, approached the woman and dabbed away her tears.

"It was the first time I charmed a woman, and I got a thirst for chivalry," Dan said, taking a sip of his beer.

Elijah had woken up from his nap and rubbed his eyes in his booster seat.

"What do we say to Makenna for being rude and yelling in her face?" Sam asked.

"Sorry," he said.

"Thank you," Makenna replied.

After that, Elijah quickly warmed up to Makenna. At one point, he even gave her a high-five. Watching his wife interact with children made him so hot and bothered, he couldn't wait to cover her with kisses when they got back to his place.

It'll all be okay, Dan thought. *It's just awkward right now.*

He caught Makenna looking off, chewing. His hand on her knee didn't turn her head for moments. When she looked at him, she smiled, but shifted her eyes away for a moment.

Dan shook it off, but it bothered him all the way home.

25

"I can't wait to meet this new boyfriend. It was so terrible what happened with Holden," Caroline mused, taking a sip of her water and rubbing her belly.

Her brother and Caroline were finally pregnant. Makenna knew about her miscarriage in October, but Caroline had quickly become pregnant again. Now, she looked like she had a basketball under her shirt. They had just found out it was a boy.

It was nice to talk about anything else but that.

"I can't wait for you to meet him either," Makenna said. She stuck her finger in her mouth to bite off a hangnail.

"Makenna, you're acting really, really weird," Brady said.

I don't know if you're going to punch Dan or hug him.

The doorbell rang, and Makenna shot up from her seat and adjusted her shirt. She walked over to the door and opened it to find her husband holding two bouquets of roses.

Dan wore a gray suit with a black tie, his hair combed back and his three-day-old scruff gone.

"Baby," Makenna said, closing the door behind her. "You look so nice."

She hugged Dan, smelling the cologne she'd purchased for him. It smelled like teakwood and campfire, whiskey and leather.

"I wanted to look good to meet my in-laws," he said, clearing his throat with a cough. "I brought roses. I wasn't sure what your mother would like. I know Caroline likes roses."

"They're perfect," she said. She turned back, catching a glimpse of a face in the window. When Makenna reopened the door, Caroline was wiggling on the couch, readjusting her skirt over her knees. Makenna deliberately blocked Dan from view, so when she stepped to the side, Caroline brought her hands to her mouth and Brady's jaw dropped.

"Hole-lee shit," Brady said.

Makenna's mom rounded the corner, holding a charcuterie tray. "Makenna, why is Dan Price in a suit in my foyer?"

"Dan, you know my mom, Angela."

"It's a pleasure to see you again," Dan said, approaching her mom with trepidation. Her mother looked frozen in shock as Dan took her hand and kissed it and then presented her with one of the bouquets of roses.

She looked down at the roses and back up.

"Makenna, what is going on?" Angela asked, looking at the roses and back up at her.

"Well, that's a funny story actually," Makenna said. "I went to Vegas for New Year's. With Dan."

Her mother nodded.

"And...we kind of got married," Makenna said.

"What the *fuck*, Dan?" Brady said from the couch.

"I'm sorry. I'm sorry," Dan said. He walked over to Caroline. "Here, have some flowers. I know they're your fave."

Makenna couldn't look at Caroline or Brady.

"Are you pregnant?" Caroline asked.

Makenna sighed. "No, I'm not," she said. Why was that everyone's first question?

"Was this an impulsive thing or...?" Caroline asked.

Makenna looked to Dan, who took over. "Yes and no."

"I thought you were just friends," Brady said. Brady rarely got mad, but his eyes looked black as coal and zeroed in on Dan. Makenna and Dan looked at each other, standing there for their punishment. "You've been more than friends." Brady's neck vein popped, his pale skin growing pink.

Makenna opened her mouth, but Dan answered. "We've been seeing each other almost a year now. Consistently."

"Makenna, you have done some wild things. But to get married out of nowhere, without a good reason, is just crazy," Angela said.

"It's not out of nowhere. We've been together for over a year. I'm in love with him." Makenna grabbed for Dan's hand, and he lifted her hand to his heart. "We have a great relationship. I promise this is real. It isn't fake."

"Wait. You were lying to us the *whole* time?" Brady asked.

Caroline was looking down. "So, all those times we got in fights and you told me I was crazy, you were seeing him?"

Makenna nodded, Caroline's face fell, and she stared at something nondescript in front of her, her mouth slightly agape. Was she...hurt by this? Their fights always stung, leaving Makenna bruised and broken on the inside. She didn't take the time to think the fights could've hurt Caroline too.

Caroline wasn't her favorite person, but seeing her look down, upset, hit Makenna in the gut.

"What about Piper and Holden? You were dating them

at the end of last year." Makenna's face fell and Caroline's did too.

"We pretended to date them. To throw everyone off our scent," Dan said with a laugh. "Funny joke, right?"

No one laughed.

"I need to go outside before I say something I'm going to regret. Excuse me," Brady said, walking out.

"I'm going with him," Caroline said, following him to the backyard.

Makenna knew it would be bad. She knew her brother and Caroline might be upset. The look in their eyes echoed looks she had been getting her entire life—disappointment mixed with disgust.

Mike Brady walked down the hall and looked around. "Oh, hi honey. Hi Dan. Is our Makenna with Dan now?"

"They're married," Makenna's mom said quietly, her eyes flicking to Makenna.

"They're *what*?"

Dan walked to Mike and stood in front of him.

"Sir," Dan said, clasping his hands behind his back. "I know it's archaic and Makenna is a grown woman. Still, I'm a traditional guy. I regret very much that I did not ask for your blessing in marrying Makenna."

"Makenna, what have you done?" he said, looking around Dan to her.

Even when a good man wanted to marry her and did, she still felt like a fuck-up.

"Sir, your daughter is the best woman I have ever met. I am so in love with her. We got married in Vegas because we are in love."

"Makenna, what the hell?" her dad asked.

Makenna's spirit crumpled.

"Angela, what do you have to say about this?"

Her mother's look ruined her.

Like a flash, Makenna was sixteen again, having lied about damage to her dad's car. Saying "that's not mine" to weed in her sock drawer. Getting so wasted at a party she walked home and fell asleep on the lawn.

Any progress she had made in her parents' eyes, the consistent work, the freelance gigs, the saving and paying off debt, evaporated.

"Dan, can you excuse us for a moment?"

He looked each direction, unsure where to go. He held up his keys. "I'll be waiting in the car."

He kissed her and left.

Once the front door closed, her parents looked at her with a look that almost made her pee herself.

"Makenna, out of all the things you could do…" her dad started.

"How could you? How could you entrap that nice, kind man?" her mom said.

"I didn't *entrap* him," Makenna said. "He proposed to *me*. And it was a joint decision. I love him. Why don't you believe me?"

"You've said you love men before and then you leave them."

"Do you understand that marriage is a commitment? It's not just something fun you do on a whim?" her dad asked.

Don't cry. Don't cry, she told herself.

"Can you get it annulled?" her mom asked.

"I don't want to," Makenna said.

"You have to," her dad said. "You are not ready to be married."

Her throat froze and tears stung her eyes. She looked to her mother and then her dad, but red with fury. She had bit her tongue for almost a year of being home, but *this* was too important.

Her marriage was too important.

"You might be right," she said through gritted teeth. "I'm bad with money and I've fucked up more times than I can count. I've hurt people and I've lied. I don't know a lot about life, but all I know is I love him. This is real. I married him because I feel it *in my soul* that it was the right thing to do."

"If this is so real, why didn't you tell us?" her mom said.

"Because you would tell me it's fake, just like you're telling me right now. Make me feel like I'm not fucking good enough. I don't need anyone's reminders. Dan is too good for me. Somehow, that man loves me..." Makenna pointed toward the front door. "And I don't need anyone telling me I'm going to mess it up because I already worry about it all the time. That someone will tell Dan I'm not good enough or he'll realize it and he'll leave me."

Her parents stood, looking at the ground with crossed arms.

Makenna stormed to the door.

"Where are you going?" her dad asked.

"I'm going to stay with Dan," Makenna said. "My husband."

"We're not done with you, young lady," her mom said.

"Yeah, you are," she said, slamming the door.

Hot tears covered her cheeks as she walked down the path to Dan's car. She heard muffled Taylor Swift the closer she got.

"Baby, what's going on?" Dan asked.

"Can I stay with you?" Makenna asked.

"Of course you can. You don't have any of your stuff."

"Just go," Makenna said.

Dan grabbed for her hand like he always did, and it made her cry harder.

It felt like the only person who truly loved her was Dan. She had never felt more alone.

She dragged herself into Dan's house and dropped down on the bed in his room. She was so tired. Dan sat down next to her, his arm going around her shoulders.

"Do you want to talk about it?" Dan asked.

She shook her head. When she turned her head to look at Dan, there were tears in her eyes. "Why do you love me?"

"Oh, baby, where do I start?" Dan asked. He scooted up the bed to lay down and Makenna did as well, curling into him.

"I can't explain it or rationalize it. It's been there since the day on the beach. You make me calm and grounded and I can't imagine going through life without you by my side. You're my favorite person, thorns and all. I've thought I was in love before, but I wasn't. You are the only woman I'll ever love."

Makenna looked up. "You were right at the wedding."

He chuckled and pushed her hair back from her face. "About what?"

"I hadn't been in love before you. Not even close."

"I love you," Dan said. "Everything will be fine."

"I love you. And I hope so."

26

"Why are we at this restaurant?" Makenna asked.

"Since it will soften the blow," Dan said. "I know it's terrible, but this is a strategic move. Zoey's gotten a warning once, and she doesn't want to be banned forever."

Although they both hated Tuscan Grove with all of their being, they had scheduled a group dinner at the restaurant. They were the first ones there, sitting next to the mural, already drinking. Dan had one Coors Light in front of him and another on the way, and Makenna had ordered the nicest bottle of wine they had to butter up the crowd.

When Dan had called Caroline to invite them, his call went to voicemail after two rings.

He received a text an hour later stating they wouldn't come.

"I'm shaking," Makenna said, holding out a hand to notice the tremors. She still hadn't been back to pick up anything else from her parents' house. Dan had volunteered to go there to get some items for her, but she refused. She had some clothes at Dan's, but needed to do laundry every three days, all to avoid going back over there.

Dan knew her voicemail had piled up with messages as people found out. Her phone had lit up when she was in the shower, and he knew her parents were trying to reach her. Makenna just went to work and hung out on the bed or the couch.

Remarkably, none of the crew had heard. Caroline was nosy, but she knew this secret wasn't hers to tell.

"Don't be nervous. Trust me. This will be the easy part," Dan said.

"You're right," Makenna replied. The first to arrive were Addison and Kirk.

"Hello," Addison greeted.

Kirk stood behind her, his hands on her shoulders. "I know about you two now. I tickled it out of her," Kirk said. Once the words slipped from his mouth, he blushed and slid in next to his girlfriend. He reached across the table and shook Dan's hand.

"I'm sorry. I told Kirk because it's Kirk," Addison said. She pulled out her phone and flicked away notifications. "Taylor is on her way. Class ran late."

"What's up?" Zoey said from across the restaurant, her husband Jonathan following. Addison turned around and clapped at Zoey's appearance. Zoey held up the bottle of wine on the table and said, "We're celebrating something, aren't we?"

"Yes," Dan said, standing up to give Zoey a hug and to shake Jonathan's hand. "I'm so glad you were in town."

"Of course. I don't miss out on drama that doesn't include me. I'm dying to know what the big reveal is," Zoey said, looking around the table. "Where's Caroline?"

"She couldn't make it," Makenna said.

"Either someone else is pregnant or engaged," Zoey said. She looked at Addison, who was under Kirk's arm.

Or married. Dan sipped his draft Coors Light, avoiding Zoey's truth-finding gaze.

Addison held up a bare left hand and smiled, looking at her boyfriend. Kirk kissed her, a sign that it wasn't a matter of if, but when.

Zoey looked at Dan and then at Makenna. "Maybe you two finally hooked up for real."

Makenna and Dan let out matching cackles at her prediction. Zoey's eyes narrowed on them, her glare only broken by the cyclone of Taylor and Malcolm arriving. Taylor's hair was wet, up in a high ponytail.

"I'm so sorry we're late." Taylor slid in next to Kirk and hugged him, Kirk rapidly patting her on the back. She looked around the table. "So, what's up? Whose news is it?"

"I thought it was you guys," Zoey said.

"Nope," Taylor said. "Still married. Not pregnant."

Dan looked at Makenna. She nodded once to him, and he rose to his feet. All the faces of people he loved, whose happily ever afters he'd had a hand in.

Now, it was time to tell them about his.

"Makenna and I are together," Dan announced.

His eardrums immediately hurt. Taylor began profusely cursing. Malcolm lit up like the Griswold house and stood up to give him a big hug. Addison clapped in excitement, and Zoey laid against the table in a fake swoon, then popped back up.

"No fucking way," Zoey said. "You little sneaks. I can't believe..."

Dan took a deep breath. "And we got married over New Year's."

The table went silent.

"What?" Taylor asked, loud enough to startle a nearby table.

Dan held up his left hand, showing a ring on his left finger. "We got married."

Makenna held up her hand as well. The same gold sat on her ring finger. She rarely wore it, so seeing it on her hand made his heart burst with glitter.

"Is this a joke?" Zoey asked, looking confused. She looked around the table. "Am I being punked right now?"

"It's the truth," Makenna said.

"I'm going to pass out. Literally pass out," Taylor said, fanning her face.

"Give me a minute. I'm *shook*. You have to prepare me for shit like this. I almost had a heart attack," Zoey said. She held up a finger. "I have many, many questions."

"Me too," Taylor interjected.

"Me three," Addison added.

"First question, when did this start?" Zoey asked. "I need to know everything. Leave not a single detail out."

Makenna opened her mouth, but Dan interjected. "It started at Caroline and Brady's wedding."

"I knew it," Zoey said, pointing. "I *knew* it."

"But I thought..." Addison said. "You didn't first get together at Christmas?"

"No, we got together at her birthday," Makenna said, pointing to Taylor.

"And the country concert?" Addison asked.

"We were totally together," Dan said. "We were never just friends."

The entire table went silent. The server appeared, taking everyone's drink order.

"Booze all around," Zoey said. "And keep it coming."

"Order whatever you want. I'll get the bill," Dan said.

"Oh, you're gonna," Zoey agreed, crossing her arms.

"Don't let her order pie," Jonathan said with a laugh. The table looked at him like he joked about dying babies.

"So, what about Holden and Piper?" Taylor asked.

Dan and Makenna grimaced and looked at each other. Dan held up both hands. "Don't hate us."

"Oh my God," Taylor said, covering her mouth.

"We kind of talked Holden and Piper to pose as fake dates. It was mostly to get them together. And it worked! They're actually moving in together," Dan said.

The table grew even more quiet. The occupants looked at each other for responses. Kirk started laughing. The women all looked deadly serious.

"This is hilarious," Kirk said. He looked around the table. "Isn't it?"

"Dan, that is fucked up," Zoey said, crossing her arms. "Fucked up."

"So weird," Taylor added.

"I just wish you would've told us," Addison said quietly. "I don't understand why you wouldn't."

"Well, I'm happy for you," Jonathan said.

Zoey's eyes narrowed. "Maybe I should order pie."

"I'm still shocked about all of this," Taylor said, turning to Malcolm. "Are you shocked?"

Malcolm tilted his head. "Not really."

"I'm not shocked either," Kirk said, raising his hand. "Dan is not really sly on the phone at work."

"Don't make me fire you," Dan said.

"Any wedding deserves a toast," Addison said. She held up her glass of wine. "To happily ever afters."

"To happily ever afters," the crowd grumbled.

"Let's order," Zoey said. "I've barely eaten all day since I wanted to test the all-you-can-eat cheesy bread."

The server reappeared, and Dan noticed everyone ordering lavish dishes, a second or third cocktail. Dan had always felt like part of the group, although he was older by five or so years and his initial connection to the group was his former relationship to Zoey.

This was the first time he had felt tension toward him. Makenna pushed food around her plate, smiling like she was on the brink of tears. His fingernails against her back didn't relax her hunched shoulders.

The group chatted, they all wished them well, but it felt different. Weirder. Distant.

When the bill came, he dropped his card down for a five-hundred-dollar bill, a feat he was impressed by. Everyone was still pissed.

Makenna barely spoke.

With time, everyone would forgive them.

They all just needed to be angry, feel their feelings, and then everything would be fine.

Even with all his optimism, he knew something wasn't right. He just didn't know what it was.

27

"You did *what?*" Andrew shouted, his glasses immediately fogging up. "Dan, are you an idiot? Truly."

"Remember, I sign your paycheck," he said. "And yes, I'm an idiot. An idiot in love."

"How could you get married without consulting me? Do you know how many assets you have?" Andrew asked. "I'm going to need a Tums. Or five."

"Calm down, Andy."

"You know I don't like it when you call me that," Andrew said, his coat flying out with his finger point. Dan held up his hands, seated at his desk.

"Can you get it annulled? Oh my God, I don't know the laws of Clark County. I'll have to research. This was *not* how I wanted my Tuesday to go. I'll need to stay until nine tonight."

"I'm not getting it annulled. Take your lawyer hat off and put your friend hat *on*," Dan said, pantomiming taking a hat off and putting another one on.

"How well do you know this woman?" Andrew asked sitting in a seat opposite Dan's desk. "Is she trustworthy?"

"Absolutely," Dan asked, checking his watch. "I'm expecting her in about ten minutes. You can meet her and do your attorney laser scan."

"How many times have I told you I am not a robot."

"I haven't seen you *bleed*," Dan said, leaning forward.

Andrew spun around and sat down, resting his lips on his hand. "I worry about you. You trust people too much. We'll have to draw up a post-nuptial agreement for you two to sign. I know you trust her, but people change. Does she know how much money you have?"

Dan shook his head.

"She must've figured it out. I don't know how, but she did," Andrew said. He began pacing Dan's office.

"She didn't marry me for my money," Dan said. "She honestly doesn't even know how much money I have. You really need to get laid."

Andrew fiddled with his glasses. "This is *not* about me."

"Don't blow a microchip. Sit down," Dan said.

Andrew huffed out a breath and said down. A piece of his gelled hair fell in his face.

"You're more than my boss, you are one of my best friends. I just don't want you or your bank account to get hurt."

"It won't. Promise."

Tiana appeared in the doorway. "She's here."

Dan stood up, buttoning his jacket. He usually wore his company's polo shirt and jeans to work, sometimes a baseball hat with his company's logo on it. Today, he picked a full suit to look good for his lady. So she thought he was professional and shit.

"Thank you, Tiana. I'll go get her."

"I just hope you know what you're doing. I'm saying that as a friend," Andrew said.

"I appreciate it." Dan slapped him on the bicep and walked out of his office to his love. Andrew would meet her and see what he saw. At least the fact he signed Andrew's paychecks would mean he wouldn't act like Dan's mom or Makenna's parents. Andrew would turn on the professionalism and look for the positive.

He rubbed his hands together. He couldn't wait for what he had planned today.

Today would be straight out of a fairy-tale. It would make everything better and make things feel like they did in their secret days.

MAKENNA SHOOK her foot as she sat in her husband's waiting area. She looked around, seeing "Price" in shiny letters on the wall and an office full of people who worked for him. It made her break into a sweat.

Tiana, Dan's executive assistant, typed, her long fingernails clacking on the keyboard, stealing glimpses at her here and there. She wondered how much Dan had told Tiana about her, if she knew. Her dark brown eyes narrowed in her glances.

Dan walked through his office in a full suit, tailored to perfection. He kissed her on the cheek.

"Have you met Tiana, the best assistant in the world?" he asked.

"We did," Tiana said, then went right back to her work. Her dismissal of Makenna clawed at her.

"It was nice to meet you," Makenna said as she followed Dan.

Tiana didn't look up from her computer. "It was nice to meet you too. Say hi to my mother."

They walked away. Makenna leaned into Dan. "Why did she say that?"

"You'll see," Dan said with a wink.

Dan grabbed her hand and pulled her through a few cubicles. She met a couple project managers from his development company and some agents from Dan's real estate brokerage.

"My attorney wants to meet you. He's in my office," Dan said.

Dan's office was spacious, kind of messy, but the light filtering through the trees cast an optimistic glow. A tall wiry man wearing brown-rimmed glasses stood in the middle, already outstretching his hand.

"Makenna, so lovely to meet you. I'm Andrew, Dan's attorney," Andrew said. He studied her like he was assessing risk in his head.

"Pleasure," she said, detaching her hand from Dan's to shake Andrew's. Andrew covered her hand with his, and Dan scoffed.

"I would love to know a little bit about you," Andrew said. Andrew sat down in Dan's chair, facing them like it was his office. This felt like a job interview, and Makenna's confidence was nowhere to be found.

Makenna sat down in one of Dan's visitor chairs, and Dan sat down next to her.

"Isn't this your office?" Makenna whispered.

"Yeah, but I let Andrew do this once in a while. So he feels like he has power." Andrew rolled his eyes at that.

Makenna took a deep breath. Andrew motioned so she began speaking.

"I'm twenty-seven, I grew up in Lillyvale. Went to

Hudson High School. I went to Sac State for a couple years, and then moved down to L. A. to be a makeup artist. That didn't work out so I'm back up here."

"Oh, I see," Andrew said, folding his hands and resting his lips on his outstretched fingers.

"I love Dan, very much," Makenna blurted.

"I'm glad you love him. Dan is an amazing man."

Dan blushed. "Oh."

Andrew leaned forward, resting his elbows on the desk. "I will be transparent with you, Makenna. I wish Dan would've told me you were planning to marry before you did. As his attorney, I worry about him and his assets. While you seem completely trustworthy, I want to protect my employer as much as possible."

"Understood," Makenna said.

"I highly suggest we draft up a post-nuptial agreement as soon as possible," Andrew said. "Makenna, do you have an attorney?"

Makenna shook her head. Should she have gotten one?

"Okay," Andrew said. "We can schedule another appointment once I've had the opportunity to draft the agreement, and then we can go over the terms and see if there needs to be any changes or amendments."

"Thank you, Captain Buzzkill," Dan said.

"I fully anticipate you will love each other forever and stay married," Andrew said. "I think this will give my client —and me—peace of mind, just in case. It'll also give you realistic expectations, should you ever separate."

Realistic expectations? What?

Andrew's tone was businesslike and unfeeling. Makenna felt uncomfortable in her chair. He stood up, and Dan popped up as well. Makenna stood up, outstretching her hand to shake.

"Thank you," Makenna said. "I'm glad I could finally meet you."

"The pleasure is all mine," Andrew replied. "If you'll excuse me."

Andrew walked out, leaving them alone in his office.

"I have a very fun afternoon planned for us," Dan said, smiling.

"Okay," she said. "Let me say hi to Kirk. Is he in the office?"

"He never leaves, although I tell him all the time to go for a walk. His office is across the hall," Dan said. He sat down at his computer and tapped the space bar. "I have a few emails I need to answer really quickly, and then we can go on our adventure."

He winked at her, and she pressed her lips to her fingers and blew an imaginary kiss. He pretended to catch it like an invisible feather and slapped it on his cheek.

When Kirk had moved back temporarily to visit with his grandmother, Dan had given him a part-time gig to help him get his finances in order. An offer of a permanent position got Kirk home permanently to Lillyvale and Addison's arms.

Makenna found Kirk holding papers, entranced by numbers and figures.

He looked up and smiled.

"Hi. I heard you were coming into the office," Kirk said, standing up and opening his arms. Makenna walked into them, and Kirk pat her back rapidly, something he did with every female who wasn't Addison.

"I'm sorry. About, you know, the lies," Makenna said.

"It's okay," Kirk replied. "It's not a big deal to me. I wasn't there for most of it, and it's none of my business."

"How is Addison taking it?"

"She'll get over it," Kirk said. "You should call her."

"I will," Makenna agreed. "I just met Andrew."

"Oh, Andrew. He comes off as uptight, but he's really good guy. Don't base any assumptions off of your first time meeting him."

The knots in her stomach settled a bit at that. "Thanks. I'll keep that in mind."

"I heard Dan has something special planned for you this afternoon."

Dread washed over her, and she couldn't pinpoint why.

"Listen," Kirk said, standing up and walking behind Makenna to close the door. Kirk perched on the lip of his desk.

"What's up?"

"I'm planning to propose to Addison soon," Kirk admitted.

Makenna covered her mouth with her hands. "Oh Kirk."

"I know we've only been together since October, but she's the one for me. You know that line from *When Harry Met Sally*? I want my life with her to start as soon as possible."

"I know that line. It's perfect," she said. Dan and Makenna had watched it on one of their quiet, secret nights at the Price Palace. Makenna attacked Kirk with a hug, and he rapidly patted her back again. She felt a little twinge of jealousy. Addison was ready to get married, and she and Kirk had had some hardships before they got engaged. Now, they were perfect.

It seemed like all the hard stuff was coming after Makenna married Dan, making her question everything.

"I'd like your help. The ring is being designed, but I'm hoping you could help with surprising her," Kirk said. "I already asked Caroline, and she said she would help too."

There were those knots in her stomach again.

"Why that face?" Kirk asked.

"Oh, it's nothing," she said.

"Addison does that shit to me all the time," Kirk said. "Something is wrong."

"Caroline and I aren't exactly on speaking terms right now."

"I know Addison would love you to help. You've become such good friends. Can you do it for her?"

Makenna thought back to all the friend dates she had with Addison. All the times they laughed and bared their souls. She could overcome some awkwardness with her sister-in-law for her. Makenna nodded. "Of course. I would love to."

"Great," Kirk said. "I'm almost done perfecting the plan and the PowerPoint."

She tilted her head. "You have a PowerPoint?"

"I think best using Microsoft products, okay?"

Dan knocked on the door and opened it, peeking his head through. "I'm ready if you are, baby. We have an appointment to make."

Kirk pointed at Makenna. "I'll text you. Probably in three weeks or so."

"Definitely."

It was a short drive to the same shopping center as Cycle Yoga Love and MG Fitness. From her parking spot, she could see a bootcamp class led by Malcolm's business partner, Anna.

Dan parked, and Makenna looked through the windshield at the storefront directly in front of them.

Robinson Jewelers.

Makenna looked at Dan with an open mouth.

"What are we doing here?" Makenna asked.

"We're getting you a ring you'll actually wear," Dan said, opening the car door. Makenna followed him in.

A ring you'll actually wear.

The gold ring they bought at the chapel still lived in the bottom of her purse. When she put it on her finger, it looked foreign among her other rings. She loved seeing Dan's on his finger, but something about hers didn't feel right.

Maybe a new ring was just what she needed.

A smiling middle-aged Black woman approached them with folded hands.

"Patricia," Dan said, opening his arms. The woman squeezed him and swayed back and forth. Makenna loved to see the affection everyone had for Dan. She wished she could inspire that same fondness.

"Patricia, I would like you to meet my bride, Makenna."

The woman offered Makenna her hand and she shook it. "Pleasure to meet you. Dan is so funny and has taken such great care of my baby and taught her so much that I'm over the moon happy for you two."

"You're Tiana's mom."

"Yes ma'am. She wasn't rude to you when she met you, was she?"

"No, not at all."

"Tiana is an angel," Dan said. "I hope she never wises up and leaves me."

"Nonsense," Patricia said. Her laugh warmed Makenna like her favorite bourbon. She walked into the store and Dan and Makenna followed. "So, Dan tells me you would like to get a ring. Would you like something to drink? Champagne? Wine? Beer? Coffee, tea?"

Why the hell not. "Champagne would be great."

"I'll be right back with that. Please take a look around."

The woman disappeared, leaving Dan and Makenna

alone in the bright white store, with glimmering stones and shiny gold, all demanding Makenna's gaze and interest.

She had always liked looking at pretty things, so she peered into the various glass cases. The prices made her heart flutter.

"Whatever you want, baby. Any Price is right." Dan giggled at his own pun. "Get it?"

"Yes," she said, pulling him in for a quick side hug.

"Here we are," the woman said, handing her a glass flute of champagne. She handed a tall beer glass full of golden liquid to Dan, who took it happily. Makenna took a sip and examined it. This was *not* cheap.

"Is that Coors Light?"

Dan nodded. "Patricia takes good care of me."

"My sweet boy," Patricia said, caressing his cheek. "Should we start looking at some diamonds?"

Dan rubbed his hands together. "Definitely."

"Have a seat," she said, as Makenna sat down at a desk, topped with cases and cases. Dan sat down next to her, his hand glued to her leg.

"Is there a shape you like? Do you want to compare and contrast any?"

"I don't know," Makenna said. "I've never really thought about it."

"The bigger the better," Dan added.

Patricia winked at him. "Let me get a few different options, and we can go from there."

Patricia disappeared again, and Makenna turned to Dan. "This is too much."

"Nonsense," Dan said. "I want the space shuttle to be able to see the ring I got you."

"The ring we got at the chapel is just fine."

"Oh, the one you never wear?" Dan asked, his lips pressed together.

Words jumbled within her, and she didn't have the right words to say when Patricia reappeared, multiple paper packages in her hands.

"I brought out a few diamonds around two carats. We can still go up in carat weight, but you can get an idea of the shapes."

She unfolded the packets, and Makenna got nervous that one would spring out, falling into the carpet, never to be seen again.

"So, this is the cushion cut, very popular style right now." Patricia handed Dan the pair of forceps holding the stone, taking the magnifying tool to inspect the quality.

He handed it back to her. "I will need bigger. Everyone needs to know that she's mine."

"It's okay, Dan. Really," she said, taking the forceps and the tool. When she looked through it, the diamond sparkled and shined. A lump appeared in her throat as she handed it back.

"Are you having fun?" Dan asked.

"Yes, this is so fun," Makenna said, trying to sound excited. Inside, she wasn't sure what she felt.

It felt so romantic and spontaneous to get married on the spur of the moment. But getting a ring, moving in with Dan, everyone knowing, felt like really being married. It felt final and inescapable.

Her life was a hundred times more chaotic now that they were married and the truth was out.

Patricia's face lit up suddenly, and she stood from her seat. "Maybe white diamonds aren't for you. We got some exciting new hues I want to show you."

Patricia disappeared again.

"She's just letting us sit here with all these diamonds," Makenna said.

"This place has security like the military," Dan replied, picking up the forceps again to examine the diamond. "We wouldn't make it to the parking lot."

"True," she said.

"We don't need to get you a ring. I just always thought I would get whomever I married a really nice ring. You don't wear your band, and I thought..."

Makenna shoved her hand into her purse, finding the loose piece of jewelry. She put it on. "There. I promise, this is fun. Thank you."

She leaned in to kiss him.

Patricia reappeared with more packets. "I picked out some different diamonds for you to see. This is a salt-and-pepper diamond. Very unique."

She unwrapped the tissue and presented a stone, gray and clear. Makenna was intrigued.

"Can I look at that?" Makenna asked.

"Of course." Patricia secured it in the forceps and handed them to Makenna along with the magnifier.

Makenna looked at it and felt a tug at her heart strings. The oval shape and the color of the diamond were unique, different; some might call it odd or unconventional. Just like her tattoos and the streak in her hair, this diamond suited her.

"This is beautiful," she said. "I really like it."

Her husband's face glowed with excitement.

"We can do a lot with an oval. We can do it straight up and down, or turn it on its side for an east-west ring."

Makenna scrunched her forehead in confusion, but Patricia held up a finger. She rushed out then reappeared with a rose gold setting, flanked by two round white stones.

She nestled the diamond in the prongs and handed it to Makenna. The diamond wiggled in its setting, but it was the prettiest ring she had ever seen.

Dan watched as she slipped it on, next to her band from the chapel.

Putting that ring on felt like the moment Dan proposed to her. That it was meant to be.

"I love it," Makenna said softly.

"You do?" Dan looked just as happy as Makenna felt.

"This isn't as big as you wanted," Patricia said, looking at Dan.

"If my wife is in love with it, I'm in love with it. Just like I'm in love with her," Dan said, kissing her.

Wife. It was still odd to hear Dan call her that. The first time it happened, the word felt foreign. Now it settled on her like a cozy sweater. A sweater that felt itchy and comforting, all at once.

Makenna nodded. "This is the one."

"Great," Patricia said with a clap of her hands. They measured Makenna's ring finger, and Dan signed the paper-work, handing over his credit card without flinching. She couldn't wait to see the ring. Maybe it was just what she needed to settle the unease—a gorgeous, unique ring to symbolize their love.

Patricia held out her hand. "Thank you so much for your business. I'll call you when the ring is ready in a couple weeks."

"I can't wait to see it," Dan said. He wrapped his arm around Makenna's shoulders.

Her smile lasted into the car.

"Do you love it?" Dan asked, turning his car on and backing out of the parking space.

"I'm so in love with it," Makenna said. "Like I am with you."

"I have one last surprise," Dan told her, turning onto the freeway. They headed up the hill and pulled off in Auburn. The route to the restaurant was familiar, and she let her head drop back in memories of the night they had over a year ago.

There it was. La Scarola. A fixture in the history of Dan and Makenna.

So many things happened that one night at that restaurant. They were almost found out. It was the start of their relationship. Then-Makenna wouldn't believe the Now-Makenna could ever exist. In love. Married. Soon the owner of an exquisite wedding ring she *never* thought she would get to wear.

She still felt like the old Makenna. Something gnawed at her. This felt a smidge off, not completely perfect.

The restaurant was empty when they walked in, officially closed to everyone but them. A woman wearing black and white greeted them, leading them to a table in the back. It was covered with its typical white tablecloth, but in the center were white roses, red petals scattered across it. An envelope with *Makenna* in thick black ink was lying on the table.

Dan pulled out her chair, and Makenna sat down. The server took their drink orders. She picked up the envelope.

"What's in here?" Makenna asked, holding it up.

"Open it," he said.

She turned it over, slipping her finger under the sealed flap. Once opened, she pulled out a card. It said *I'm so glad I'm your hubby* under a picture of Dan's smiling face.

When she opened the card, her eyes bulged.

"What is this?" she asked.

"A check. That's enough, right? To clear your credit card and student loans?"

Her eyes deceived her. Had to be. A check for fifty thousand dollars made out to Makenna Brady.

Makenna looked up. "More than enough."

"You don't have to worry about debt anymore," Dan said. "I will take care of you."

"This is too much," Makenna said in shock. "This is too much money."

"It's fine."

Makenna shook the check. "I don't make this in a year. And somehow it's *fine*?"

"No, really. It's fine," Dan said calmly.

It was the nicest thing anyone had ever done for her. It also churned her stomach. How did this successful, charming, so-good-in-bed-it-wasn't-even-right man love her? Wanted to buy her a ring? Wanted to write checks to pay off her bad decisions?

Makenna didn't get nice things. They always went away.

"I need some air," she said. Her cheeks were hot to the touch and her hands shook.

She closed her eyes and breathed in and out. Her heart still raced.

In her soul, she was in love with Dan. No question in her mind. Just everything else was a whole lot at once, and things were happening around her she couldn't pinpoint. She should be *elated* that her debt was gone. But something about it felt weird.

"Are you crying?" he asked. He had followed her out. His hands were shoved in his pockets. "I thought you would be happy."

"I am," she said.

She bit her lip. Was it rude to bring it up? They were married, so it wasn't a bad question to ask, right?

"Dan, how much money do you have?"

"Um...a lot?"

"Define 'a lot.'"

"Let's go back inside," Dan said, steering her back into the restaurant.

When they sat back down in the middle of the restaurant, Dan punched some numbers into his phone and turned it toward Makenna. She took the phone to get a better look.

That couldn't be right.

There were so many numbers...and commas.

"Is that...is that a million dollars?"

"One point seven, to be exact. In this account. I own a few commercial properties, and I have money in other investments that aren't reflected in what you see here."

"How much is your net worth, Dan?"

Dan looked around the empty restaurant and lowered his voice.

"Last time I checked, it was almost eleven million dollars."

"Oh my God," Makenna said, lowering her head to the table.

"I know it's a lot of money," Dan said. "But we're a team now. My money is your money."

"No millionaire talks like this!" she said, running her fingers through her hair.

"I can tell you're freaking out," Dan said. He waved the server over. "Whiskey neat. Double."

"How the hell did you get that much money?"

"Would you believe me when I say it was an accident?" Dan asked.

"Not for a second."

Dan shrugged. "I've never cared that much about money. I like challenges and building businesses. It's fun for me. There's not this huge end goal or number I'm trying to achieve. It just *happened.*"

"How do millions of dollars just *happen*?" Makenna asked.

Dan shrugged.

"You drink Coors Light, for fuck's sake!"

"I drink Coors Light because it's delicious," Dan said. "My tastes didn't change because I have money."

"You wear T-shirts with holes in them to bed."

"They're comfy," Dan said.

"Oh my God," she said, leaning against her elbow. "That's why your mom acted all weird around me. Here comes this tramp with fake tits and tattoos trying to steal my son's fortune. College dropout who lives with her parents, just looking for a sugar daddy."

Dan shook his head violently. "She wasn't thinking that."

"That's why Andrew looked at me that way. Does everyone in your office know I'm broke?"

"No, they don't know anything. Most of my employees honestly have no idea how much money I have. I am, however, very generous."

After a few moments of Makenna staring off, Dan asked, "What is going on? You've been acting really strange."

Makenna swallowed. "The ring, the money. It's a lot."

"That's what people do when they get married. Sometimes before. Why is it different now?"

"Everything is different!" Makenna cried. "It's just not *us* anymore. It's your family, my family. Our friends. The world. Everyone hates us."

"Everything will be fine!" Dan said. "They don't hate us.

They're just adjusting. They'll forgive us. They'll just have to see how we are with one another, and some time needs to pass. I might need to buy some very expensive apology gifts. It will all work out."

"What if it doesn't?" Makenna asked. "Everything I touch turns to shit."

"No, it doesn't. It won't," Dan said firmly. "You have to believe me."

Makenna squirmed in her seat. She wanted to believe him. However, everything in her past had told her it would never work out. It couldn't. She wasn't lucky or worthy. Marrying Dan had felt right at the time, but it had fucked everything up. People were mad at them. Their relationship had now shifted into some weird money exchange.

"Let's just eat," Makenna said, feeling a wave of exhaustion flow over her. "Thank you for the money."

"You're welcome," Dan said. "Do you know what you want?"

"Yes," she answered. He called over the server to take their order.

28

TWO WEEKS LATER

"Thanks for meeting me," Dan said as he slid off a barstool and shook Brady's hand. Brady took off his coat and laid it across the bar.

"I haven't been here before," Brady said, looking around. "It's nice."

Dan asked Brady to meet him at the Craft Beer Vault in Rocklin, a few miles away from Lillyvale. It was out of the way enough that people wouldn't recognize Dan or bother them. It was time to have a bro-to-bro talk. Clear the air.

Brady studied the menu on a screen affixed to the wall without a word. After they tasted a couple and settled on their choices, Brady and Dan looked down at their beers.

"Brady, I'm really sorry," Dan said. "You're one of my best friends, and I know you told me not to touch your sister."

"I didn't tell you not to touch her, I told you to be cautious," Brady said. "You were the one who said you wouldn't touch her."

"From the bottom of my heart, I am sorry," Dan said. He stood up, in front of Brady. "You can punch me if you want."

Brady shook his head. "I'm not going to punch you."

"Okay, I just wanted to offer," Dan said.

"How did it happen? I'm still flummoxed on the whole thing."

"Flummoxed. What a great word."

"Shut up and tell me," Brady said, taking a swig of his beer.

Dan huffed out a breath. "We just really connected. I can't say it was one thing or another. At first, it was just sex..."

Brady plugged his ears. "Please leave sex with my baby sister out of this."

"Fine," Dan said. "As we got to know each other, we just noticed that the other person was what was missing in our lives. She makes me feel calm, which you know is something I'm not."

"Absolutely not. You're unlike any person I know," Brady said. He looked out of the window to the parking lot. "I think I'm the angriest about the lying. You should've just come to me right away if you wanted to pursue something. I wouldn't have been that mad. So why didn't you?"

Makenna. The secret relationship had been fun and it was what she wanted, so Dan had gone along with it. It was fun for a few months, but then it stopped being that way. He wanted to say something a lot sooner than she did. Dan had the sneaking suspicion that their friends and family wouldn't have been so mad if they had come clean when they first started seeing each other.

Makenna still hadn't even moved all of her stuff from her parents' house to his.

She still wasn't wearing her wedding band.

There was no mention of him on her Instagram.

"It was my sister's idea, wasn't it?" Brady asked.

Dan nodded and took a sip of his beer. Not Coors Light, but pretty good.

"I've never understood Makenna. No one in our family does. She doesn't make much sense sometimes. If you ever figure her out, please let me know."

Dan laughed and nodded. He thought he had her figured out, then they got married and started telling everyone, and everything changed.

They sat side-by-side in silence, just drinking their beers.

"My parents want to talk to her. But she's pushing them away, like she always does. Can you tell her for me?"

"Of course," Dan said. "I want everyone to get along."

"Good," Brady said.

"Do you forgive me?"

Brady swallowed his beer and looked at Dan. He noticed the same hazel eyes the love of his life had, the same cheeks and chin. When Brady opened his mouth, he paused just like Makenna did before he spoke.

"Of course," Brady said. "You're one of the best friends I have. I can't think of a better spouse for my sister. You two did a shitty thing, but we'll get over it. Caroline will get over it, eventually."

"I'm so relieved."

"And we are *never, ever* talking about your sex life with my sister again."

"Noted," Dan said. He stood up and opened his arms. "I need a hug."

Brady rolled his eyes and stood up, taking each other in a two-armed, all-in bro hug.

Their conversation eventually moved to sports, discussing March Madness, but he couldn't stop thinking about Makenna.

Makenna had stood in front of him, in front of God and Elvis and promised to love him for the rest of their lives. She had signed the marriage certificate, and when they were alone together, she still showed her love to him in all sorts of ways—when she threw back her head in throes of ecstasy, or their quiet nights on the couch watching *Golden Girls.*

But *after* they announced their marriage, things had shifted. He saw her pulling away from everyone. Looking off into space instead of at him. Her hesitation at looking at rings and accepting his gift to pay off her loans.

It would all be okay. He just needed to talk to her about it.

His monkey thoughts settled as he and Brady ordered another round and laughed like they did, the pressure of the secret gone. But now the secret was out in the open, and just like Makenna predicted, it created the one problem they both feared.

It has shifted their relationship into something he didn't quite recognize.

His phone rang, and Brady motioned it was okay to answer it.

"Hi Dan, it's Patricia."

"Hi, how are you on this fine day?"

"Wonderful. I just wanted to let you know your wife's ring is ready."

"Excellent," Dan said. He said goodbye and turned his phone over. Everything would be okay once the ring was on her finger. He turned back to Brady. "I bought your sister an engagement ring, and it's ready."

"That's great, Dan," Brady said. "It looks like you make my sister happy too. I'm glad you're both happy."

Dan smiled. He couldn't wait to get the ring and slip it on Makenna's finger.

29

"How was my brother? Is he still mad?" Makenna asked when Dan walked in from the garage. Dan sat down next to her on the couch, his hand landing on her knee.

"It went well. He's still a little angry, but he forgave me," Dan said. "He said your parents want to talk to you."

Makenna bit her lip. Her voicemail finally became full the other day from her parents leaving multiple messages a day, trying to reach her. "I'll call them."

"Good. I have a surprise for you."

Dan shifted on his left leg to pull out a black box. Her heart stopped. It had been a few weeks since they had picked out the diamond and the setting. Panic took over as he opened the hinged top. "Patricia called me while I was out so I swung by and grabbed it. Isn't it magnificent?"

It was a ring deserving of a queen. Makenna looked at it sadly as Dan held it out to her. It sparkled and shined, but she couldn't pick it up and put it on her finger.

Dan's smile dropped. "What's wrong?"

"It's beautiful," she said.

"Put it on then," he encouraged.

Makenna stood up and faced the fireplace. A picture of them at their wedding rested on the mantel. She wished she could go back to that moment. Do everything over.

"I love you. So much," Makenna started.

"I love you too," he said, confusion in his voice. "Please put on the ring. Please. It's exactly what you wanted."

Makenna heard a small sound. When she turned around, she saw the ring box, open, on the coffee table.

"Why won't you put on the ring, Makenna?" Dan asked quietly.

"This feels like a lot," Makenna said, a sob escaping her lips. "Everything is happening so fast. I can't get my head around it."

"Everyone will forgive us. Brady said that Caroline is coming around."

"It's not that," Makenna said. "The minute we got married, everything was ruined."

Makenna looked up to see Dan's jaw clench. Dan had never gotten angry with Makenna, so seeing flames in his eyes, his skin grow red, his cheeks tighten, was a new experience.

"Everyone is mad because we didn't tell them, Makenna." His voice had deepened to a tone Makenna had never heard before. "They were bound to be mad at us because we hid it. We hid it because you didn't want to come out publicly and say you were dating me."

"You went along with it," Makenna said.

"I went along with it because I was in love with you."

"Does that mean you're not in love with me now?"

Dan's face crumpled. That exact look is what she had been avoiding. It's why she wanted to keep it a secret for so long. Now that it wasn't a secret, everything was ruined.

"I'm so in love with you," Dan said. "Are you in love with me still?"

"Yes," she cried. Her eyes filled up with tears.

"What do you want, Makenna?" Dan asked. "I want to be married to you. I want you to wear that ring and move in with me for real. I want you to make peace with your parents because I want to have a good relationship with them one day. I want you to use my money to pay off your debt. I want to buy you a better car than that beater you're driving. I want you to find something that makes you happy instead of that terrible job at the makeup counter. I want to have children with you one day. Do you want that? With me?"

Makenna ran her fingers through her hair. Dan was angry at her. This wouldn't have happened if they'd stayed secret, hadn't gotten married, hadn't told anyone. Everything felt like too much. It scared her to her core.

"Why can you love me only when it's a secret?" Dan asked. "Why can't you love me out in the open?"

Makenna's mouth gaped open. Dan's words were like a sledgehammer to the kidneys. One tear ran down her cheek. Finally, she found the words. "I don't know." Something that had been nagging her came out of her mouth. "Why did *you* keep your money a secret?"

Dan dragged his hand down his face. "I tell literally no one how much money I have. My family only knows because I paid off the mortgage to my mom's house and my brother's college education is taken care of. People get weird about money."

"People like me. *I* get weird about money," Makenna said. "The broke girl who can't handle a credit card without maxing it out. The girl who defaulted on her student loans."

"You're not that person anymore," Dan said. "You've

changed. You were working so hard, working all those hours, and taking all those gigs. I would've offered the money to you even if we weren't married. I just thought..."

"People are going to think I'm a gold digger. They might already think it."

"No," Dan said. "They don't."

"People think I'm not good enough for you." Makenna's voice cracked. "I'm not good enough for you."

"Why are you doing this?" Dan's face was a mix of hurt of confusion. "Don't destroy this."

"I don't know if we should've built this to begin with," Makenna said, turning away from him. She couldn't see his hurt.

"I can't believe we're having this conversation."

"I think I need some space."

"Fine," Dan said tonelessly.

Everything that happened after that was a blur. Dan came down with luggage a half hour later while Makenna sat dumbfounded on the couch, staring at the gold pillow she'd bought when she offered to decorate a little bit.

"I called the Finches, and I'll be staying up there for a little bit. You can stay here. Call me when you're ready to talk. But Makenna? This is not over," Dan said. He paused at the door, waiting for her to hug him or kiss him goodbye.

She just sat on the couch, staring at the gold pillow.

The door to the garage closed, and Makenna collapsed on the couch in tears.

30

THREE DAYS LATER

When Makenna looked out the peephole, she saw a cluster of women waiting, chatting among themselves. She centered herself.

Here we go.

The cover story had quickly shifted to a staged intervention for Makenna and Caroline to mend their friendship so Addison would be surprised with a proposal. Makenna had already taken Addison out to Cork & Barrel, brought her flowers, and bought her wine to apologize for lying to her at Taylor's birthday party. When Addison hugged her with a squeeze that hurt her organs, Makenna knew all was well between them.

She had called Taylor and Zoey to apologize, and they had graciously forgiven her too.

All Makenna had to do was endure at least an hour of being around Caroline, and then it would be over as soon as Kirk dropped to one knee.

She debated telling them that Dan left. She was still flip-flopping as she opened the door.

"Hi," Makenna said, opening the door. "Wow, the gang's all here."

"You know it," Taylor said, walking past Makenna into the house. Zoey and Addison followed, holding five packages of Oreos. Caroline stood on Dan's porch, her hand on her stomach.

"Hi," Makenna said.

"Hi," Caroline replied.

"Do you want to come in?"

Caroline walked through the door, her eyes flicking to Makenna's then darting away.

Addison splayed the five Oreo packages out on Dan's coffee table. "I picked up one for each person, based off of their Oreo varietal favorites."

"I brought wine," Taylor said, pulling out a bottle from the satchel on her shoulder. "Where are the glasses?"

Makenna walked to the kitchen and opened the cupboard. She pulled down four wine glasses and got a glass of water for Caroline.

"You know, I've never been to Dan's house before," Taylor said. "And we've been friends for years."

"Me too," Addison said. "This is nice!"

"He used to have a Coors Light sign right there," Makenna said, pointing at the wall above the fireplace. Remembering that sign brought her back to the first time she visited his house.

It made her heart ache.

They walked the wine glasses over to the coffee table. The Oreo packages had been ripped open, and Zoey had already opened a cookie and was licking the crème from the center.

"I love Oreos. It's a shame no one is breaking up with anyone anymore," Zoey said.

Funny you should mention that...

"We can have Oreos anytime, not just when people are breaking up," Addison said. "Oreos are an every-occasion cookie."

"Agreed," Taylor said, snatching a Carrot Cake Oreo.

"Dan left," Makenna blurted out. She flapped her hands down on her crossed legs. "I'm done lying to you all. We got in a huge fight, and he left. Are you all happy now?"

The women looked confused at each other.

"No, of course we're not," Taylor said. "What made you think we would be happy about that?"

Her cheeks flushed. "You all were mad at Tuscan Grove."

"We were mad because you kept it a secret. We all thought we were the bad ones since we kept pushing you about Dan. We were right all along. I have to admit, I was angry," Zoey said. "It's not because I dated him, or I thought you weren't a good fit."

"Same," Taylor said.

"Makenna already apologized to me, and I accepted her apology," Addison said, taking another Oreo. "I have nothing further to say. The past is the past."

Caroline stayed quiet, crossing her arms over her belly. They all looked at her.

"What?" she asked.

"Get it all out," Zoey said. "I have heard enough of your ranting. You should be talking to her, not me." Zoey pointed to Makenna.

"I'm fine," she said.

"What is with all of you and that word?" Taylor asked. "Yell at her. Let's get this over with since we have a reservation soon at the new Greek fusion restaurant in Central Lillyvale in forty-five minutes, and I'm hungry."

"Fine," Caroline said. Her lips pressed in a thin line.

Here we go.

"I *tried* to be your friend. I wanted you to like me. But every time we're together, you dismiss me or roll your eyes or gaslight me," she said. "I asked you several times about Dan, and you lied to my face, every time."

"Maybe it wasn't any of your business," Makenna said. Her defenses were going up faster than new construction in Lillyvale.

"Maybe it wasn't. But you made me feel like I was going crazy. I was questioning everything." Caroline stared at Makenna, and her voice quivered when she spoke again. "Why do you hate me?"

There were moments she could've sworn she hated Caroline.

Now, she wasn't so sure it was that. Maybe at the end of the day, she was just a jealous bitch.

"I'm not perfect, obviously. I've done some shitty things, like this, and I'm sorry," Makenna said. "Caroline, you have it all together. You fit into my family better than I ever did. I wish my parents liked me the way they like you. I don't hate you. I'm just really jealous."

"Makenna, your parents love you. They worry about you and care about you. So much," Caroline said. "I'm jealous of *you*."

Makenna let out a guffaw. "How?"

"You don't take any shit. You are so firm in who you are. I wouldn't be brave enough to do half the things you've done. You're so fearless. All the travel and adventures you had…I'd be lucky to go to Hawaii once a year once this kid is born."

"I feel the same way," Zoey said. "Jonathan makes fun of me since I'm obsessed with your Instagram."

"I'm right there too," Taylor added with a pointed finger to the sky.

"Whatever makes you happy," Addison said. The group looked at her and she shrugged her shoulders. "I'm not the biggest fan of traveling, but if Makenna likes it, then good for her."

"You don't have to be alone anymore, Makenna," Caroline said. "Let us in. We love you."

Makenna's mind was blown. This whole time she felt alienated, but it was her own doing. "You're so sweet, Makenna," Addison said, taking her in for a hug. "It's been an honor to be your friend."

"I get so excited when you're in class. I look forward to it. You're the coolest person I've ever met."

"I can't think of a better person for Dan than you," Zoey said. "I'm honored you listened to me."

"I'm not good enough for him," Makenna said. "That's the long and short of it. I'm a mess, I'm a fuck-up."

"No," all the women said in unison.

"We got married and everything was hard, right away, and everything had been so easy before. We were so happy when it was just us, alone. I was terrified it would change the minute we went public, and then my worst fears came true."

"I hate to break it to you, but marriage is hard," Zoey said. "It doesn't stop being hard the minute you have a ring on your finger."

"Amen," Taylor said.

Zoey continued, "Marriage isn't some fairy-tale. It's hard work. It's getting up every day and saying, 'I will fight for you. I will fight for us.' Jonathan and I are still learning, but we made a commitment to each other to never stop working. Never stop giving a shit. Marriage isn't the end of all the hard stuff. In a way, it's just the beginning."

"That is the goddamn truth," Caroline said.

"I agree one hundred percent. My marriage isn't perfect. I shouted at Malcolm yesterday because he was chewing almonds too loud," Taylor said.

"Oh, the first month Brady and I were married, I almost moved out," Caroline said. "He was being ridiculous about drapes for our front room. We were arguing in Bed Bath & Beyond like lunatics. We worked it out, of course, but the first year of marriage was *bumpy*. I love Brady more than anyone else I have ever met, but sometimes, I straight-up want to kill him. Then I love him again."

"Same," Zoey said. "I love the shit out of Jonathan, but at the end of the day, we're two different people trying to figure out how to be together long-term."

Makenna had assumed everyone was blissfully happy, with no cares or problems. She knew the basic outlines of how their relationships started, full of bumps, false starts, and sudden stops. She assumed once they got married that everything was figured out, but alas, it appeared it hadn't.

"Addison is being really quiet," Makenna said.

She sighed. "I'm just maybe a tiny envious. I'm the only one unmarried here. I wish..."

Everyone looked at each other with goofy grins.

Caroline moved closer to Makenna. She could smell Caroline's perfume on her skin and mint on her breath.

"I always thought you and Dan would be so cute together. You both have this carefree side I wish I had," Caroline said. "I think you're perfect for each other."

"We've all thought that," Addison said. "That's why we always asked. We saw it. At least I saw it."

Taylor and Zoey nodded.

"Ladies, do you forgive me?" Makenna asked.

"We forgive you," Zoey said, hugging her. It became a

group hug, all of the women circling her to embrace her. Caroline sat on the outskirts.

It was fine she didn't forgive her right away. She knew she deserved it.

"Come on, loser, get dressed. We have a reservation in thirty minutes," Taylor said to Makenna. "We'll activate a plan to get Dan back in the car ride over."

"And eat Oreos!" Addison said, a package falling from her full arms. "I can't have all of these in my house."

Makenna smiled to herself as she climbed the stairs. She threw on a pair of ripped knee black skinnies, and an oversized gray shirt that fell off her shoulders and showed the top of her tattoo sleeve. Her face was bare, which somehow wasn't a big deal for her. All her hair went to the top of her head, and she slipped on some flip-flops.

"Let's go. We're taking Caroline's new combat vehicle," Taylor said when Makenna stepped off the landing.

Parked in the driveway was a fucking minivan.

"What is this monstrosity?" Makenna blurted out, not able to stop herself, pointing to the gleaming, new Chrysler Pacifica.

"It's actually really nice inside," Taylor said. "But I will not have a minivan. I will be a baseball or softball mom, and baseball moms drive SUVs."

Zoey shrugged and leaned into Makenna. "I don't like it. At all. However, Caroline volunteered to drive, and I can't turn down a chauffeur or a DD."

"Same," Makenna said. Out of the group, Zoey and Makenna were the worst drivers. Makenna had been in four major accidents, and Zoey got into fender benders in parking lots.

"Okay," Caroline said, sitting down in the front. "I'm still not completely used to this car yet, fair warning."

She pressed some buttons, and the car roared to life.

"Do you love Dan?" Addison asked, looking in the rearview. The packages of Oreos were stacked in Addison's lap. "I think you need a cookie."

"Not right now, in this brand-new car, thank you," Caroline said.

"I do," Makenna whispered. "I don't think I've loved anyone more than I love him. It's just overwhelming. It's a lot."

"There's no one right way to be married. If you need time to transition, take the time," Zoey said. "I promise you, Dan is utterly devoted to you. If he could keep you by letting you move at your own pace, well, he would do it. I have zero doubt."

"Okay, we're here," Caroline said, pulling into a parking spot in the parking garage adjacent to Central Lillyvale. The women piled out, and Caroline looked back at her car. "I never thought I would drive a minivan, but I'm kind of obsessed with it."

"I really like it," Addison said. She pulled a cookie out and handed it to Makenna. "So you can get started."

"Thanks, Addison." She bit in the classic flavor, letting the crunch and the softness of the cream fill her mouth.

Life was much better with Oreos.

"We need to swing by Turn the Page first," Taylor said. Her eyes signaled to everyone the next step on the plan Kirk had briefed them on the day before. The group had a plan to get Addison to the meadow by Turn the Page, where Kirk was waiting to propose.

"You don't read, Taylor."

"Well, I'm getting into it!" she said. "I ordered that book you recommended to me."

Addison's eyes lit up. "Oh, which one?"

"Uh," Taylor said. "It's the one with...um...the illustrated cover."

"That's a lot of them nowadays," Addison said, turning around. "Well, I'm never going to turn down an opportunity to go to a bookstore."

Makenna looked at Taylor, who rubbed her hands together as Addison charged ahead.

The women hung back in a pack, like they were following and planning to kidnap Addison.

Turn the Page Independent Bookstore sat at the far end of Central Lillyvale's main strip, with a meadow and benches bordering the trees. Remarkably, there were no people hanging out, eating, or chatting on the benches, and the women breathed out a sigh of relief. If there were people, it was their job to clear the area in any way possible.

Thoughts turned over and over in Makenna's head. Being unsettled had been such a fixture of her life for so long, she didn't know how to undo it. How to be *settled*. Being married to Dan felt foreign and uncharted.

She watched Addison, practically skipping straight into a proposal, so sure about Kirk, so ready to make a home with Kirk and have a baby with him. Makenna simply was not.

"Come on, guys," Addison said, almost to the bookstore. Taylor had been fiddling so much with her phone, trying to pull up the camera, that she had done a terrible job herding Addison to the meadow and the perfect bench in question.

They got in the vicinity, and Kirk busted out of bushes like the Kool-Aid man in a slim cut dark suit with a skinny tie, his curly hair gelled and styled. His beard was neatly trimmed and cleaned up since Makenna had last seen him.

"What is going on?" Addison asked, an unsure smile on her lips.

Kirk approached her, took her hands, and looked into her eyes.

Makenna slapped her hand over her heart, her emotions squeezed the shit out of it. Caroline had already started crying. Both Taylor and Zoey had their phones out filming the whole thing.

They couldn't hear every word, although Taylor got closer to capture their dialogue on the phone. When Kirk dropped to one knee, Addison covered her mouth in surprise.

"Addison Ann Varick, will you marry me?"

Her head nodded before the sentence ended.

It reminded Makenna of Dan proposing in the middle of a casino, surrounded by strangers cheering them on.

Kirk reached up from his kneeling position to kiss her. Makenna clapped along with the rest of the women, as Addison and Kirk floated into another world.

"This is so cute and so them," Zoey said wistfully. Kirk and Addison held each other, swaying.

Makenna wished for nothing more than to go back to the love cocoon she and Dan had created, so insular and protected. So stress-free.

Hot tears spilled down her cheeks.

"It's weird to see you crying," Caroline said.

"Everything okay, boo boo?" Zoey asked.

"I'm fine," Makenna said, sniffling. Kirk's arm settled around Addison as they walked toward the group.

"Let's see the rock," Taylor said. Addison held out her hand, a lovely round diamond on a gold band sat on her ring finger. Makenna thought about the ring Robinson Jewelers had made for her. How perfect it was. It still sat on the counter, lid closed since their fight a few days prior.

"Thank you so much for helping," Kirk said.

"I'm getting married!" Addison said excitedly.

"We're so happy for you two," Caroline said, taking everyone in a group hug. Makenna hung back, until Caroline waved her in.

"You need a hug more than any of us," she said.

Makenna walked in, feeling the warmth of other arms and squeezes, telling her everything was alright.

Caroline pulled Makenna away from the group. "I've been asked to drive you over to your parents' house. They're worried about you."

"Okay."

"Ladies, I'm going to take Makenna to her parents'," Caroline said, loud enough for the women to hear.

"Go ahead," Taylor said. "I was not kidding about the food."

"I never lie about food," Zoey said.

"We'll take them home," Kirk said. "Let's go get some falafel."

Caroline and Makenna walked back to the parking garage where the Chrysler Pacifica sat, gleaming in a parking spot.

"I was a bitch earlier. This car is really nice."

"Thanks," Caroline said with a laugh. She started the car and looked all directions before backing out of the parking spot.

"Do you forgive me now?" Makenna asked.

"I forgive you," Caroline said. "I want to be friends."

"Let's," Makenna replied. "Tell me a day you're free next week, and I'll take you to Tuscan Grove."

"You hate Tuscan Grove," she said. "How about we go to the restaurant in Auburn that Dan likes? Maybe Emily could meet us."

"Emily is your friend," Makenna said.

"Emily is kind of obsessed with you, too, you know," Caroline said. "She follows you on Instagram."

Emily Finch is obsessed with me?

"Wow, I've never had this many female friends before."

"Get used to it," Caroline said. "This is a really good group of women. You just didn't give us a chance."

"I will now."

They arrived at her parents' house. "Good luck," Caroline said. "I'll let you know about dinner. Give me a hug."

Makenna leaned across the center console. "Truce."

"Truce," Caroline said. "I love you."

Makenna's lips turned into a smile. "I love you too."

They hugged and pulled away from each other. Caroline swiped a tear away from her eye. "I'm sorry, these pregnancy hormones are a bitch."

"It's okay. Call me about dinner. Emily is more than welcome."

Makenna closed the door to the minivan, looking at her childhood home. Taking a deep breath, she opened the unlocked front door.

"Mom, Dad?" she called. She walked into the kitchen to find her mother sitting at the kitchen island. An opened bottle of wine stood next to her, her dad not in sight.

"Makenna. Sit," Makenna's mom said.

Makenna watched her mother and sat down on the stool. Her mom stood up and found another glass, pouring Makenna a hearty serving.

"Mom, I..."

Her mom held up one finger. "No, no. You don't get to speak yet."

Makenna felt like a teenager again.

"Your father and I love you so much. Just because you took a different path than Brady does not mean we love you less than your brother. You and your brother are incredibly different."

"No shit," Makenna said. Her mother gave a death stare. "Sorry."

She continued. "You've always done your own thing. I learned really quickly to let you figure it out. Let you fail and let you pick yourself up again. You've made some mistakes..."

That made Makenna fume. Her mom held out a hand. "You've made some great decisions as well. You moved home once you knew L.A. wasn't going to work out. I know you work hard. You picked a man like Dan."

Makenna always seemed to be on the verge of tears lately, and her eyes welled up. "I may have messed that up."

"Why?" her mother asked.

"We had a big fight," Makenna said. "He went out of town to a business he invested in to get away from me."

Makenna's mom laughed, covering her mouth.

"What's so funny?"

"Your father," Makenna's mom said. "We got in this stupid fight sometime in the early years of marriage. I hadn't lived with him before, and he did something, I don't even remember. He went and stayed with your uncle Kenny for a week while we both fumed."

Makenna smiled. Maybe she wasn't abnormal. Maybe marriage was just hard and they were going through a transition period.

"We worked it out. Whatever you fought about with Dan can be fixed. I think you need to talk to him."

Makenna dropped her head to the tile. "You know I can't go talk to him, because you're my mother and I've done the opposite of what you've told me my entire life."

"Fine, don't talk to him. Live with me forever," she said. "Get all the tattoos you like. I think they're fun."

Makenna lifted her head. "Mom."

"And play that music you like as loud as you want. I quite like it."

Makenna picked up her phone and found Metallica's "Spit out the Bone." She cranked the volume all the way up. Her mother shook her head and closed her eyes.

"So you're okay with me playing this?" Makenna yelled over the music.

"It's fine. It's lovely," she yelled back.

"You hate this," Makenna yelled.

"Okay, you win. Turn it off."

Makenna switched it off with a smirk and flipped her phone screen down.

"Please consider talking to Dan. There has to be some kind of compromise you both can make."

"Okay, Mom."

Her mother stood up from the stool and took the bottle of wine to the pantry. "I don't need any more of this."

"Are you mad?" Makenna asked. "About Dan?"

"I was hurt more than anything. Your brother tells me that he's a great man. That we shouldn't be worried."

Her mom walked to a basket holding all of her mail— the bills and other items to short through and take care of. She pulled out folded slips of paper. "Your husband sent a long letter to us."

She handed it to Makenna. Her heart beat wildly as she unfolded the letter.

It was dated the day after Dan met them as her husband.

Dear Mr. and Mrs. Brady:

First off, thank you for creating and raising such an incredible woman. I am so thankful you decided to conceive her the night you did, at the exact moment you did, or I would never have her.

"Oh my God," Makenna said, covering her face.

"He's quite funny," her mother said. "And sweet. And he loves you."

"I know," Makenna said. "I'm sorry, Mom."

"It's okay, Makenna," she said, taking her in for a hug.

Makenna's dad walked into the kitchen, his hands in his pockets.

"Dad," Makenna said. "I'm sorry for not telling you and Mom about Dan. I really do love him."

"I forgive you," he said, opening his arms. "You'll always be my little girl."

"I love you, Dad," she said, her face pressed against his broad chest. It felt good to be in his arms.

"I love you too sweetie. Your husband is not who I imagined you would end up with, thank God. He's better."

"Thanks a lot, Dad," she said, smacking him playfully.

"What, it was a compliment!" her dad said. "He wrote a great letter."

"He's pretty wonderful," Makenna said. She wanted to get in the car and run to him. This day had started with tears and self-loathing and it turned out to be pretty amazing.

"Mike, they're in a little fight, and Dan ran off like you did. Remember that?"

Makenna's dad laughed, his hearty grumbles coming from the pit of his stomach. "I remember you baked a heart-shaped cookie and presented it as a peace offering."

A peace offering. Makenna wondered what her heart-shaped cookie for Dan would be. He rarely ate sweets anymore except for once a month.

Ding. The perfect idea came to her a complete package, fully realized. She just had to execute it.

"I know what my heart-shaped cookie would be. I have to work on it."

Makenna stood up from the stool and walked to the edge of the kitchen. "Oh, by the way, I'm officially moving out."

"Thank God, I can get my craft room back," her mom said.

"It's never been a craft room," her dad said, confused.

"It will be as soon as Makenna moves out," her mom said, with a twinkle in her eye.

31

"Dan, can you close up?" Cameron Finch asked, approaching Dan's table. The table closest to the bathroom had been Dan's temporary work area for the last four days, ever since he left Lillyvale to give Makenna space. The Finches had graciously let him stay at the cabin on their property, and he slept and then worked all day, alternating between coffee and beer at his designated table at the brewery.

Whatever food truck was there was his food for the day or takeout from the local café. He felt bloated and sad, but work helped distract him.

"Sure, I'll close up," Dan said, rubbing his eyes.

Cameron pulled out a chair at Dan's table. "Actually, do you want a beer?"

"Sure," Dan said, holding up his pint glass with the Woody Finch Brewery logo on it. Cameron took it from his hand and walked behind the bar. He pulled Dan's namesake beer, Dan the Man, and pulled another beer, a stout for himself.

When he came back and dropped it down, Dan took a

sip. Tiredness tugged at his eyes, but sleep barely came when he pulled up the covers on the creaky queen the Finches called a bed.

Really, it was all the thoughts about his wife.

"You don't have a date tonight?" Dan asked. Cameron was Goldheart's most notorious bachelor, vowing never to get married. Women tried, though. Oh, did they try.

Cameron shook his head. "I figured I would hang out with my friend."

"Thanks, man," Dan said, clinking a glass with his. "And thanks again for letting me stay at the cabin."

"No problem," Cameron said, lifting his beer. "You saved our asses so it's the least we can do."

"You guys are really turning this place around."

Cameron nodded. "I have big plans for this brewery next year."

"What about for you? Finally getting married?" Dan asked with a smirk.

"You're funny," he said, his grin highlighting a deep dimple. That bastard was so good-looking, no wonder all the women of Goldheart showed up in trench coats, naked underneath. There was a rumor that Emily had opened the door once to breasts and a full bush when the woman was hoping to surprise Cameron since Emily and Olive lived with Cameron.

Emily rushed in from the back, out of breath.

"Where's Olive?" Cameron asked.

"Mom is watching her," Emily said. "Dan, have you been on Instagram?"

He shook his head. He had deleted the app off of his phone after spending hours looking at Makenna's pictures and crying one too many times.

"You need to look. Now."

Dan pulled out his phone, going to the App Store to redownload the app. When it finally loaded, the Finch siblings watched as he opened Instagram.

His notifications were blowing up, and the first picture in his feed was of him and Makenna, from her account.

It was one of the nights they were being silly on the couch. He ached for that time, since it was the most drama-free their relationship ever was, probably right after when he realized he was in love with her.

The caption made his heart skip.

For a year, I pretended to be single, finding myself as I transitioned from an L.A. lifestyle to moving to my hometown.

I lied to you.

I met a man. He is the best person I've ever known. Our road to happily ever after was not smooth, and it still isn't. But I love him with all that I am. I want to be a better woman for him, and I want to spend the rest of my days showing him how much he means to me.

He will always be the King of my Heart.

There was only one hashtag. #hubby

Dan's face hurt from grinning. He swiped to the next picture, and it was them kissing in front of Elvis, then one of Makenna holding the bouquet from the nice woman at the blackjack table. There were hundreds of comments, some of shock, some of disgust. Lots of congratulations.

He looked up to see Cameron and Emily watching him.

Emily held up a black item and pointed it to the sky.

The brewery dimmed, and the mirrorball began spinning. Emily clicked a button again, and "King of My Heart" by Taylor Swift began playing on the loud speakers.

Dan looked around like a gopher.

There, in front of the bar, stood Makenna.

He looked back and pointed a finger at the Finch siblings.

"It was all her," Cameron said, pointing at Emily. "I just helped a little bit."

They slinked away in the shadows, leaving Makenna and Dan alone in this big room, alone, the disco ball casting sparkles on the floor.

"What are you doing here?" Dan asked.

"I'm getting my man back," Makenna said.

He slid his hand around the back of her neck and took her lips with his. Slowly, methodically.

It reminded him of their early falling-in-love kisses, like time stood still just for them.

They were breathless when Dan pulled away, pressing his forehead to hers.

"I realized I still owe you a dance from the night of Brady and Caroline's rehearsal."

"When you kissed me and then refused to dance with me?"

"I feel like I've matured," Makenna said, sliding her hands around his neck. His hands wrapped around her waist, pulling her body to him. Taylor Swift serenaded them from the speakers. He held her and his body relaxed. All of his worries floated away.

"I saw your post," Dan said. "Thank you. I loved it."

"I'm glad," she said. "I have so much to talk to you about."

When the song ended, the room went silent except for the hum of all the machines within the space.

Makenna's hazel eyes stared into his. She lowered her hands, and he grabbed her hands. Her fingers were free of her usual rings, except for one on her left hand.

The ring he got her from Robinson Jewelers.

"You're wearing it," Dan said, his heart full.

She nodded, looking at it. "It's beautiful."

Dan felt emotion bubble inside of him, and his heart swelled. They sat at his table, and Makenna grabbed his hands.

"Being with you scares the absolute shit out of me," she confessed.

"You scare me too," Dan said.

"But I'm done letting fear rule me," Makenna added. "I've moved out of my parents' house. All of my stuff is at your house now."

"Great."

"I took your money and paid all my debt."

"Perfect."

"You're stuck with me forever," Makenna said. "I hope you're ready for that."

"I was ready last year," Dan admitted.

"I will post about you constantly on social media. I will talk about you so much, it will nauseate you."

"I'm here for it," Dan said.

"I'm messy and dramatic and too much sometimes."

"Me too," Dan said.

"Don't ever give up on me. And I promise I won't give up on you."

"I promise," he said. "I've missed you so much, M."

"I missed you too," she said. His lips pressed against her neck, so delicate. Her words shook him out of his mission. "I started therapy again."

"What?" he asked.

"Therapy. I thought I could get by without it, but I need to work on a lot of things."

"I'm so happy," he told her.

His stare heated the space, and she grabbed the back of

his neck and kissed him. His dick swelled in his pants as his hands went everywhere—her breasts, her backside, into her hair. They pulled apart, their breath raspy and uneven.

"You are my forever," he said. "I hope you're ready for that."

"I am now," she said, and then they were kissing again. Their kissing grew heated until they heard a clearing of a throat. They turned to see Emily and Cameron.

"Caroline and I figured out this plan to get you back with Emily's help," Makenna told Dan.

Emily shyly waved. "Makenna, this is my brother, Cameron."

"Hi Makenna," Cameron said. "It's a pleasure to meet you."

"We should go back to the cabin," Dan said.

"Yeah, that's a good idea. Mom and Dad have a strict 'no hanky-panky in the brewery' policy," Cameron said.

"Because of you," Emily reminded him.

"Because of me," Cameron repeated with a sigh.

Makenna followed Dan to the cabin, and it was a frenzy as soon as the door was closed. She tugged his shirt over his head first, and he removed hers.

When she was completely naked, standing against the door, he buried himself between her legs, and she squirmed and moaned. When he plunged one finger, then two, into her, her hands in his hair told him everything he needed to know. When she shook with her release, he picked her up, legs wrapped around him and sat down in a chair by the front door, her on his lap, facing him.

Pushing her hair from her face, he just looked at her, her eyes half-mast with lust.

"It was always supposed to be us," he said. "Just us. We have to remember that when it gets hard."

"I know something else that is hard." She reached between them, gripping his cock. A sigh left his lips as she sunk onto him with a moan of satisfaction.

"I love you," she said, kissing him, tasting her arousal on his lips.

"I love you," he repeated.

The invisible tether that always linked them, from that first day at the lake, never faltered. It always pulled them back to one another, even when they tried to break it.

It was always meant to end like this. Makenna and Dan together, through the messiness and secrecy.

It was why he waited, why he never doubted them.

He always knew she would find her way back to him.

She always had.

32

NINE MONTHS LATER

"This is intense," Makenna said, holding Dan's hand outside double doors. She wore a hot pink dress that flared out with insane tulle while her husband looked dapper and delectable in a navy suit. Makenna barely wore high heels anymore, so Dan was almost eye-level to her, his hair coiffed to almost her height.

"This is going to be so fun." He kissed the palm in his hand as the music boomed on the other side.

"Happy birthday, baby," Makenna said.

"Thanks, baby," Dan said. "I love you forever."

"I love you forever."

"And happy anniversary to us," he said, kissing the ring he gave her on her finger.

It had been a year to remember. Makenna had started classes at Sacramento State, making up credits she failed the first time and finally being able to take new courses and feeling excited about learning. Therapy had steered her back to school after she talked about her regret with her counselor.

Dan took Makenna on a dream vacation to Bali in June,

their honeymoon, and he left his laptop at home. It was the first time in his professional life that he had taken a real vacation. They talked to locals and ate from street vendors, lounged lazily on beaches, the sun warming their skin.

Caroline gave birth to a perfect baby boy in August, naming him Asher Michael Brady, his middle name Makenna and Brady's dad's name. When Makenna held his tiny warm body, her ovaries did spins like they were on roller skates.

She still told Dan that it was a few years out, but she definitely wanted to make a baby with him. School came first, then travel, then finding a career.

When the new semester started, Makenna sat at the kitchen table, working on homework, tired from a long day of classes and a work shift. Dan came in to grab a beer, and Makenna dropped her forehead to the table.

"I'm so tired," Makenna said. "Working and being a full-time student is no joke."

"So quit your job," Dan said. "Just go to school."

Agreeing to quit, agreeing to let Dan support her, was the easiest decision she had ever made.

Besides their individual therapy, they saw a marriage therapist that solidified Dan and Makenna's commitment to each other, more than any ring or signature in Vegas. After one of the sessions, Makenna left with her hand in his.

"I think I want to be a therapist," Makenna said. "They've helped me so much, I want to help others."

"That sounds amazing, baby," Dan said. "You should pursue it."

Now, they stood in front of closed doors, ready to celebrate so many things.

New Year's, their anniversary, renewed vows after a year

of growing, learning to live with one another, loving each other out in the open instead of in secret.

All that, plus Dan's birthday, once the clock struck midnight.

"Ladies and gentlemen for the first time in a party setting, may I introduce Dan and Makenna Price," the DJ said, as the doors flung open to camera flashes. The opening chords of "Nothing Else Matters" by Metallica, her choice, played as he pulled her into a dance, in the middle of the dance floor.

"I didn't tell him to introduce us like that."

"I did," Makenna said with a smirk.

"Oh baby. That's so romantic, but I understand that it's an outdated tradition..."

"Shh," Makenna said, bringing a finger to his lips.

The song switched halfway to "King of My Heart" by Taylor Swift, and even though the beat picked up, her husband held her close, swaying to the beat of the music, barely moving in a circle.

When Makenna looked up, she saw everyone she loved —Addison and Taylor, Brady and Caroline with their son Asher, Jonathan holding Zoey as they swayed to the music, her mom and dad, Sierra with her new boyfriend. Even Dan's brother Sam was there with Elijah.

Dan always held her like he was so damn thankful he caught her.

She had never felt more loved and cherished.

"You look beautiful tonight," Dan said.

"Thanks, baby," she said. "You look ridiculously handsome yourself."

"I can't wait to get you alone."

"Absolutely the same."

His body pressed against hers.

Once the song ended, a large cake was presented with sparkler candles. A picture of Dan's face with a huge grin adorned the top of three white tiers.

The party sang "Happy Birthday" to Dan as his wife clung to his arm, singing into his ear.

Out of nowhere, a microphone was shoved in his face.

"Say something," someone shouted from the back of the room, and the rest of the crowd joined in.

Dan held the microphone to his lips. "I've lived a blessed life. I have a wonderful mother who believed in me and always pushed me to be great and do great things. I have two brothers who I love. My friends are fucking awesome. Sorry. Parents, cover the kids' ears. I will curse."

The crowd let out a collective chuckle.

"I've been incredibly lucky and fortunate to have some strong team players in my business. Andrew, Kirk—you sometimes cramp my style, but you keep me on the right path. I want to thank the good people of Lillyvale who welcomed me with open arms. I fucking love this town—I'm proud to call it my home.

"I had everything, but there was one piece missing. Love. Then this woman came in, turned my life upside down, and now I can't imagine my life without her."

The crowd let out a collective sigh.

"Baby, I love you so much it hurts to breathe sometimes. I'm still shocked you agreed to marry me a year ago on my birthday eve, and I'm so proud of us for how far we've come. I love you."

He kissed her on the cheek and she looked down with a smile.

"Now, let's eat some food and fucking party!" Dan yelled into the microphone, and the crowd erupted into cheers.

Makenna clamped his cheeks between her hands and pressed a hard smooch onto his lips.

He constantly told her how lucky he was to have her, and she always fought him since she felt like the lucky one. He saw her for all her flaws and made her want to be better, challenged her to be better. It was why she studied so hard. It's why she signed the post-nuptial, after hiring her own attorney to review it, and negotiated some points that Dan happily agreed to.

He always said that one day he would scale back his business, let his protégés take over, and semi-retire. Then he would let her bring home the bacon.

When they had a baby.

Everyone had come around, taking their relationship seriously rather than a big joke. Dan's mother now loved Makenna, and sometimes they arranged to drink wine without Dan. The biggest shock was Makenna's friendship with Caroline—they texted each other frequently about what the baby was doing or to arrange a lunch date out, just to talk.

Makenna had met Dan's dad once, an awkward weekend in the middle of nowhere, Nevada. After that, Dan and Makenna quietly agreed not to pursue a deeper relationship with Matt. Through therapy, Dan made peace with the lack of relationship with his father and vowed to be the best dad he could be to their baby, whenever they decided to make one.

The caterers set two plates of cake slices in front of them, and Dan dug in. Makenna had rolled her eyes when he requested Funfetti, but anything to make her patient and wonderful hubby happy.

"God, I love Funfetti," Dan said, forking another bite in his mouth.

"I got you a birthday present," Makenna said.

"I thought my wake-up call was my birthday present." Dan's eyebrows wiggled.

"That was part one." Makenna had dressed in red lingerie with a bow in front, and the front fell open when he untied it. It had led to a very fun morning.

Makenna slid a cream-colored envelope with *Dan* written in thick, black marker. His brow furrowed as he opened the flap and pulled out the cardstock.

His eyes scanned the item and looked up. "No fucking way."

"Way," she said.

It was a copy of her social security card and driver's license.

Makenna had officially changed her name to Makenna Rose Price.

"Oh my God, baby, this is amazing," he said, leaning over to kiss her. "You didn't have to do this."

"I wanted to," Makenna said. "I'm proud of how far we've come, and I know it's a stupid patriarchal tradition, but it made sense to me."

"You're a Price now," he said. "Just remember a Price is always right."

Makenna laughed and leaned in. "Happy birthday, baby."

"Happy anniversary, Mrs. Price."

"We made it."

"We made it."

"Thank you for being the best, and most patient hubby," she said.

"You're welcome, wifey," Dan said with a wink.

EPILOGUE

"You're going to have to push," the nurse said, holding one of her feet.

"You're going to have to yank this baby out of me, because I'm not doing that," Makenna shouted.

"Come on, baby. You've come this far," Dan said.

"You were the one who talked me into this," Makenna said through tight angry lips to her husband, who stood like a solider even while Makenna crushed his hand.

"It's not very long now, Makenna," the doctor said. His eyes were the only thing visible over the mask. "Just give me two really good pushes."

Makenna hunkered down, pushing this baby out. She no longer cared if she shit with an audience. Her bottom half burned with fiery pain, and she was so damn exhausted.

Dan still looked down there.

"I see the head!" Dan said. His eyes were already misty.

"That's right, Makenna. The baby is coming."

Makenna breathed in and pushed, breathed in and pushed. The pain radiated from her pelvis to her hair, and her body shook from the sensations of agony.

It took three more pushes to bring Presley Rose Price into the world.

Dan lost his shit when the baby let out her first real wail. He did three turns and slid down the wall with huge sobs.

When they placed the baby on Makenna's skin, she burst into tears too. When Dan composed himself enough to stand up, he kissed her and hugged her, looking into the eyes of his new princess.

"You did so well, M. I can't...You're everything to me," he said, kissing her sweaty hair. "And you..." His hand shook as he put his hand to the infant's back. Makenna looked down at the infant, minutes old, and looked at her husband.

"Doctor, nurses. Have you seen a more perfect baby? I'll wait," Dan said, standing up from his bent waist.

"Congratulations," Dr. Reinhardt said, standing up. The nurses worked around them, taking away the doctor's equipment, but the flurry of activity around them didn't break them from the dream.

Makenna had always worried how she would feel once she got pregnant. It was a real fear that she would not connect with the baby, that it would feel like an alien and not hers. However, as the baby grew in her, she felt her kick and they found out she was a girl—she loved the baby so much she could not stand it sometimes.

Now that she was out in the world, perfect, she loved her even more.

The nurses helped Makenna breastfeed, and the baby latched on immediately.

"She's definitely a Price. Loves nipples," Dan said. Makenna laughed at the inappropriateness, and the nurse chuckled under her breath.   —

They sat together as a family, and Dan opened his shirt so Presley could settle on his bare chest.

"I knew there was a reason I was working out so hard—just so I could look sexy doing this," he said.

"Absolutely," Makenna agreed. Her eyelashes fluttered, and drowsiness took over. She had been in labor for a day and a half, the only relief being an epidural that took the edge off and allowed her to sleep for a bit.

"Sleep a little bit," Dan said, kissing her on the forehead. "You did so amazing. We'll be here when you wake up."

After a little nap, Makenna opened her eyes wide. The nurses were gone and all that was left was her family. Dan still held their daughter, smiling at Makenna. She held her arms out. "I want to hold the baby again."

Dan handed the infant to Makenna. She kissed the beanie-covered head, and the baby gurgled.

"I can't believe she's ours," Makenna said.

"She's perfect," Dan said. He beamed, and the sunshine emitting from him brought a tired smile to her face too. "I love you."

"I love you too," Makenna said.

"Everyone is here to see the baby. Should I got get them? I hear someone has food."

Makenna's eyes bulged and she nodded violently. Dan leaned in to kiss her, long and slow before he left.

Makenna was all alone with Presley.

She looked down at her daughter, who stared at her, flexing her little hand.

Tears leaked from her eyes.

"Presley, I did a lot of things wrong in my life, but this feels right," she said, kissing her again. "I'm so glad you're with us now. I love you so much."

Her tears stained the baby's hat, and she breathed in the baby scent.

The first person through the door was Addison, carrying a bag bursting with to-go cartons.

Addison covered her mouth and hugged Makenna, resting her hand on Presley's back.

"What's her name?" Addison asked.

"Presley Rose Price," Dan said. "We figured since the King married us, he deserved to have our daughter named after him."

"That is perfect," Kirk said.

Kirk and Addison had had their own daughter, Hazel, a couple years before. Makenna studied her friend's journey religiously, mentally preparing for her own pregnancy. Addison had helped her pick out a lot of baby items for her registry and told her what she did and did not need.

Caroline had been wonderful too. "She's perfect," Caroline said, walking to the opposite side. "Brady, come meet your niece."

Brady slipped between two visitors and approached Makenna and Presley.

"You really did it. You had a baby with Dan Price."

"I did," she said. "Do you want to hold her?"

Addison helped transfer the baby to Brady's arms. Brady looked down at the baby. "So, I'm your Uncle Brady. I'm your cousin Asher's dad, and it will be fun to see you play together when you get older."

Addison shoved a carton of sushi in front of Makenna and she could cry, she was so hungry. The first piece hit her mouth and her eyes rolled back in pleasure.

"Thank you so much," Makenna said between bites.

"I could've kissed her when Addison showed up with McDonald's," Caroline said.

Caroline had had a long, hard labor with Asher, and she refused to have another kid since the birth was so traumatic.

When Makenna got pregnant, Caroline started getting baby fever. She always warned that if she got pregnant again, it was Makenna's fault.

Makenna's mom and Dan's mom stood next to each other, holding each other by the arms. They had become good friends over the course of Dan and Makenna's marriage. Makenna's mom had even set up Dan's mom with a newly divorced friend, and they had been dating over a year. She was much happier now. Her boyfriend, Edwin, was really a lovely guy.

"Congratulations," Taylor said, clinging to her husband, Malcolm. They had had a daughter named Frances, named after Malcolm's mother who passed away due to breast cancer. She had recently told everyone that she was pregnant again, so she and Makenna had been pregnant at the same time, but only for a few weeks.

"Does anyone know if we won?" Makenna asked after swallowing a piece of fish. She looked at her daughter, now in her mom's arms. "I can't believe she has the same birthday as her daddy."

"There was a boy born at one-thirty this morning," Dan said. "I checked. It doesn't matter that she's not the first baby of the new year. You are perfect, Presley Rose."

"Hey, congratulations on graduating," Taylor said. "You did what you wanted—had a baby after you got your masters."

"Barely," Makenna said, still popping pieces of sushi into her mouth.

She had found out she was pregnant going into her last semester of grad school. She had managed all her clinical hours during the morning sickness that had lasted her whole pregnancy, praying the baby would wait until she was done so she could graduate on time. She waddled across the stage hugely pregnant to receive her degree and sighed with relief that her water hadn't broken on stage.

She intended to spend some time with her family until March and then begin her own marriage and family counseling practice in Lillyvale. Dan had scaled back considerably from his own business and volunteered to be a stay-at-home dad. He still would work from home here and there, but Kirk was running the business now as a partner and Dan could step away, knowing the business was in good hands.

"I'm going to have so many women thirsting after me at the playground," Dan had said. He had already bought many things with "DILF" inscribed on it, and packages kept arriving.

Zoey approached the bed and sat down at the end. "Just one. You're lucky."

"You jinxed yourself when you said you wanted twins."

"I regret it every day. Although I love the shit out of them."

Zoey had given birth to twin boys a year before. When Makenna called her, Zoey was always in some version of sleep deprivation and busyness. She had managed to keep her business as a fitness industry marketing consultant going while she parented so it gave Makenna hope she could be a mom and a professional. Having a partner willing to put in the work and take over the majority of childcare made that possible.

"Who would've thought this would happen?" Zoey asked.

"I totally did," Caroline said. "I knew it would."

"Me too," Addison said, shrugging.

Taylor added, "This is the perfect ending."

"This isn't the ending. I'm not dying," Makenna said. "Although I felt like I was during pushing."

All the women nodded in collective agreement.

She finished her food and Dan took away the carton, kissing her on the head before sitting down next to her on the bed. He wrapped his arm around her. The baby was passed to Caroline, then Zoey, then Taylor, and finally to Addison.

Presley didn't cry once.

Hopefully she got Dan's temperament and not hers. They wouldn't know for sure until she was a teenager.

"I'm glad I'm last so there's no one really left who didn't get a turn," Addison said, bouncing and booping the baby on her nose. "I could hold her all day long."

"I will want my baby back at some point, Addison."

"Well, when I'm off on summers and Dan is busy, I would be more than happy to watch this precious little angel."

"Deal," Makenna said. She looked around. This room was full of people she loved. She had run from everyone, deliberately broken everything, and now it was all whole. Her life was whole.

Dan Price was the best husband a girl could ask for.

When they got married, he always had said, "Any man can be a husband, but I'm a hubby."

"What do you mean?" she had asked.

"Only the best husbands are called hubby," he had said.

She agreed—this Price was definitely right.

THE END

WANT MORE?

Want to read a bonus scene of the whole gang ten years after Caroline and Brady's wedding? Want to be the first to know about the Finch siblings and when they get their happily ever afters? **Subscribe to my newsletter** to access this exclusive bonus content for the whole *Here in Lillyvale* series and receive a free novella! Go to **jennybuntingbooks.com** to subscribe!

Loved *Hubby*? Please consider reviewing on Amazon and Goodreads! Your reviews help other readers find me.

Here, Hustle, and *Home,* the first three books in the *Here in Lillyvale* series, are available on Amazon in ebook and paperback.

I'm active on Facebook (Author Jenny Bunting) and I'm on Instagram at @jennybuntingbooks. Find me there; I always love to connect with my readers!

ACKNOWLEDGMENTS

First off, thank you to my husband, Jeremy, for coming up with the idea that Dan was the raccoon mascot in high school. That was so on brand and I love you for suggesting that. You also named him and it's the perfect name for him. Thanks honey.

My editor, Sarah. Your suggestions on the line edits made the book stronger and I've cherished our time together working on the Here in Lillyvale series. Your friendship means a lot to me and I'm so blessed that I met you.

Kari, thank you for the fantastic cover. I know the range of authors you work with and you never made me feel less than because I was new and small. That means so much to me; you're a class act and a true professional.

Thank you to Horus Proofreading for catching all of my misused pronouns and your quick turnaround time. Your comments were so nice and exactly what I needed.

Thank you to my beta readers—Beth, Amanda, Alicia, and Goddess Divine. Your thoughts and suggestions helped mold the book into what it is today. A special shout-out to

GD who read it on her honeymoon since she's the best Internet friend a girl could have.

Thank you to my friend, Michelle, who guided me on what happens in labor and delivery and having your bachelorette party at the Venetian. Who knew this would come back like this, ten years later (OH GOD). Thank you to my sister-in-law Candice for blessing Presley's birth scene and suggested someone bring Makenna food. Game changer.

Thank you to Youtuber Chad Collins for posting a room tour of a Grand King Suite at the Venetian.

Thank you to all the bookstagrammers and reviewers who took a chance on me as a new author. I've loved getting to know you and I appreciate your kind words and thoughtful criticisms. For all the silent readers, the ones who buy my books, borrow them, tell their friends about them and never reach out, I love you.

Now for people I don't know—

Taylor Swift. Your music weaves through these narratives, since your music has always spoken to me. Thank you for being vocal that artists should own their work, strengthening my position on remaining self-published and owning the rights to my books. Your impact knows no boundaries and I really hope I get to see you in concert before I die. I hope you are secretly married to Joe Alwyn for seven years before anyone finds out.

Rachel Bloom. Around May of 2019, *Crazy Ex-Girlfriend* had ended and SPOILER ALERT the series ends with Rebecca finding her true love, creativity. I was lost when this series finale found me and her songwriting got my gears turning. What if I dusted off that manuscript I abandoned? Maybe creating was what was missing from my life. That show changed many things for me, but most of all, it led me back to writing. I can't thank you enough.

Last but not least, I want to thank me. I wrote the book so I figured I'd give myself a self-high five here. God, this was a bitch to write but we did it. Let's never write a book that overlaps with other books again, k?

ABOUT THE AUTHOR

Jenny Bunting is the author of the completed contemporary romance series *Here in Lillyvale*. She does not have any tattoos, but kinda wants one. Her husband was once in a Metallica music video. She has dated men shorter than her, but it didn't work out. She has been obsessed with east-west engagement ring settings since *The Time Traveler's Wife* (the film, not the book). The inclusion of Coors Light is because Jenny's dad loves it and drinks it often. Jenny always wanted to get married by Elvis but her and her husband disagree on what outfit he should wear. Her husband thinks the white is a better option, but Jenny is trash for the gold number. Jenny lives in a suburb of Sacramento, California that she totally copied for Lillyvale with her husband and dog Woody.